THE ISLANDS AT THE END OF THE WORLD

AUSTIN ASLAN

THE ISLANDS AT THE END OF THE WORLD

WENDY
LAMB
BOOKS

Text copyright © 2014 by Austin Aslan
Jacket art copyright © 2014 by Tom Sanderson
Map illustration copyright © 2014 by Joe LeMonier

All rights reserved. Published in the United States by Wendy Lamb Books, an imprint of Random House Children's Books, a division of Random House LLC, a Penguin Random House Company, New York.

Wendy Lamb Books and the colophon are trademarks of Random House LLC.

The author would like to thank the Tad James Companies for their gracious permission to use the translation of the ho`opuka chant that appears on pages 37, 338, and 351.

Visit us on the Web! randomhouse.com/teens

Educators and librarians, for a variety of teaching tools, visit us at RHTeachersLibrarians.com

Library of Congress Cataloging-in-Publication Data
Aslan, Austin.
The islands at the end of the world / Austin Aslan. — First edition.
pages cm
Summary: Stranded in Honolulu when a strange cloud causes a worldwide electronics failure, sixteen-year-old Leilani and her father must make their way home to Hilo amid escalating perils, including her severe epilepsy.
ISBN 978-0-385-74402-7 (trade) — ISBN 978-0-375-99145-5 (lib. bdg.) —
ISBN 978-0-385-37421-7 (ebook) — ISBN 978-0-385-74403-4 (pbk.) [1. Science fiction.
2. Refugees—Fiction. 3. Epilepsy—Fiction. 4. Fathers and daughters—Fiction.
5. Extraterrestrial beings—Fiction. 6. Hawaii—Fiction.] I. Title.
PZ7.A83744Isl 2014
[Fic]—dc23
2013041281

The text of this book is set in 12.5-point Jenson.
Book design by Trish Parcell

Printed in the United States of America
10 9 8 7 6 5 4 3 2 1
First Edition

To my wife, Clare,
and her dad, Jerry,
the best father-daughter team I have ever known

E iho ana o luna
E pi`i ana o lalo
E hui ana na moku
E ku an aka paia

That which is above will come down
That which is below will rise up
The islands shall unite
The walls shall stand firm.

—*Ancient Hawaiian Prophecy*

THE HAWAIIAN ISLANDS

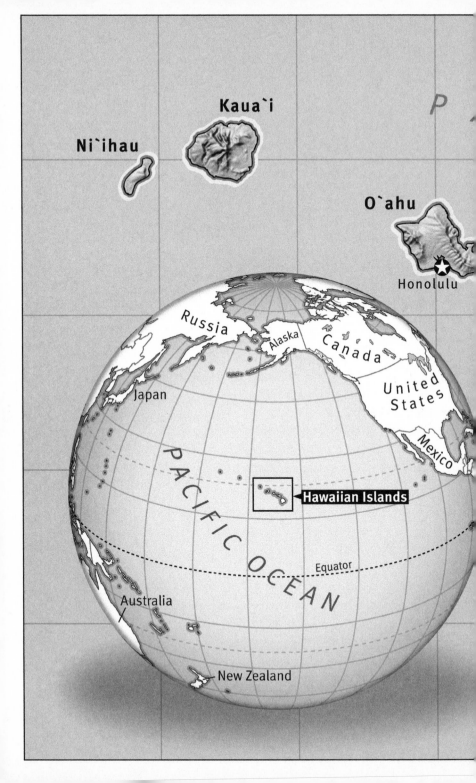

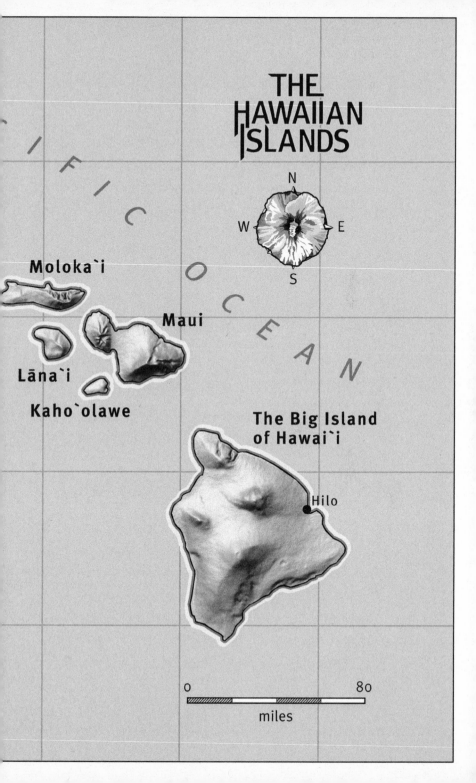

CHAPTER 1

They've been getting bigger all evening. This one might be too big, but I can't be choosy. Dad's waiting on the bluff, arms crossed. I lie down on my board and drive my arms through the water.

No sweat. Just relax.

"Geev'um, Lei!" shouts Tami.

The wave is coming like a train. I paddle fiercely, though the life vest rubs my upper arms raw.

The wave pulls on me, hungry. For once my timing is perfect. The wave surges under me; I catch the break and spring up on the board.

Two seniors on their boards shoot me the stink-eye as I wobble past. One snickers. The life jacket feels like a straitjacket. I nearly tumble backward off the board but catch my balance.

I kick my back leg to the left and angle the board to the right, feeling a rush of speed. I dart between a *keiki* body-boarder and a lazy green sea turtle, finally sinking back into the water as the wave dies. I turn to salute Tami, who's bobbing out past the first breaks. Her honey-blond corkscrews bounce even when wet.

"Next week!" I shout.

"Nice one, girl!" she yells back. "Aloha! Enjoy the north shore!"

All next week I'll be in Honolulu, on the island of O`ahu, with Dad, and he's promised me some time at Banzai Pipeline on the north shore. Just to watch. Only the pros tackle those waves.

I sweep my long, soaked hair out of my face as I clamber over the rocks tumbling in the breaking surf. O`ahu. Anxiety flutters through me. I'm surfing to forget the EKGs and MRIs and OMGs that I'll be facing.

You just nailed one of your biggest waves ever. Focus on that.

I trudge up the steep stairs to the road, using both arms to carry my longboard. Dad takes it from me as I reach the car, offers me a high five. "Way to end the day."

I smile and clap his waiting hand. "Thanks."

He leans against our purple car, a MAY THE FOREST BE WITH YOU bumper sticker broadcasting his dorkiness. We have the only hybrid vehicle in a long row of big trucks at the end of the cliff. Come to think of it, I can't remember the last hybrid car I saw in Hilo—or on the entire Big Island of Hawai`i.

"That was totally gnarly, but I'm still annoyed you made me wait so long." He passes me a towel after he places the board on the car's rack.

"Dad," I groan. A couple of Hawaiian girls from school walk past us on the steep road, giving me a hard look. I turn away as I slip out of my vest. "No one asked you to babysit me. And 'gnarly'? Wrong century."

Dad runs a hand through his Malibu-certified sandy hair. His grin widens. "Whoa. Sorry, dudette." He *intentionally* raised his voice so those girls would hear, didn't he? Drives me nuts.

"You more relaxed?" He ties the board down for me.

No. But I nod. A light drizzle begins to fall. Rain on the Hilo side of the Big Island is as abundant as sun in a desert. It's like background noise. I keep drying off as I sit in the car. I eye the steering wheel. I'm sixteen, finally old enough to drive. The doctor hasn't signed off on me getting my license yet, but I manage to get behind the wheel now and then.

"Can I drive?"

"Haven't you done enough damage to Grandpa's clutch?" *Ha, ha.*

I toss my towel in the back and look in the mirror. Long black hair. Oval face with high cheeks. My eyes are hazel, my complexion is . . . too light. I'm almost as white as Dad. Pretty, I guess, if you listen to my parents. If I ever get a boyfriend, maybe I'll believe it.

Dad performs one of his infamous fifty-point turns to get us facing the right direction on the narrow road. I glance down from the cliff at the strip of rocky beach. The waves are getting big. *Tami better wrap it up.* We pull away and the hard-eyed local girls study our car as we roll past. I know one of them—Aleka. She's always staring me down. I sink into my seat.

"You were good out there," Dad says. "It's coming to you pretty naturally now."

"Dad, being a haole around here pretty much sucks—especially a haole with head issues—"

"You're *hapa*," he corrects me, feigning shock. "You're only half white, hon. *I'm* the only haole here. Your mother and grandparents count for something, don't they?"

Mom and her parents *are* pure Hawaiian. That's beside the point. I was born and raised in the Bay Area of California. Mom always wanted to return to her home. Three years ago she and Dad became professors of ecology at the University of Hawai`i at Hilo, and here we are.

"But . . . I can't go in the water without you spying . . . or without a vest. Goofing off around me in front of this crowd only makes it worse."

"Sorry, hon. I'll stop doing that—on purpose. Howzit, anyway? Looks like you fit in just fine."

I force a smile. "Things are okay."

"Hey, wanna hit Wilson's for some ice shave?" We're at the stop sign leading onto the highway. Our house is to the right, a few miles north of Hilo.

"Sure."

We turn left, toward Hilo.

"Don't let this ruin your appetite for dinner," Dad warns as he turns onto the bay front. The clouds and rain have retreated, the sun is getting ready to set over Mauna Kea, and the sky is full of colors that can only be . . . *Hawaiian*. The "gorgeous colors," Mom calls them.

"No problem. I'm starving."

Wilson's-by-the-Bay is like most Hilo joints—a rundown hole-in-the-wall. We get in line and wait.

I'm reminded of a bumper sticker that I've seen a lot since moving here: RELAX, THIS AIN'T THE MAINLAND. Life moves at its own pace in Hilo. I can't even see an epilepsy specialist without taking a weeklong trip to another island.

I fiddle absently with the medical bracelet shackled to my wrist.

"Wanna talk about it?" Dad asks.

Not really. Or maybe I do. I shrug. "Just nervous."

Wilson's is famous for snow cones—called ice shaves in Hilo. Three bucks gets me one the size of a football, with a vanilla-ice-cream core, drowned in as much flavored syrup as I want, covered in condensed cream, and capped with *li hing mui* powder. Dad gets cherry, piña colada, *liliko`i*, and bubble gum.

"Bubble gum?" I ask.

Like some sort of corn-syrup vampire, Dad's too busy sucking the life force out of his prey to answer.

As we walk back to the car, a siren pierces the calm. Dad and I share a look of confusion. He says, "Tsunami warning?"

I raise my eyebrows. A gigantic wave on the way? I've

done plenty of drills at school, but this would be my first town-wide alert. The ballooning swells at Honoli`i suddenly make sense. "Maybe we're finally in for some real excitement."

"Careful what you wish for," Dad says.

I smile guiltily. Small tsunamis damage the coast every few years. Big ones are rare, but they pack a wallop. An entire class of schoolchildren was once swept out to sea, up near the town of Laupahoehoe, by a wave reported to be fifty feet high. And Hilo's shoreline is full of big parks and grassy fields instead of restaurants and shops and hotels because of a thirty-footer that pulverized the coast in the 1960s.

"Let's go," says Dad. "Don't want to get stuck in town if this is more than a drill."

We zip out of the lot. The coastal belt road is jammed. As we creep along, I finish my ice shave and surf the Web on my phone. "I don't think it's a drill."

"Why's that?"

"There was a meteor strike in the northern Pacific."

"Really?"

"A couple of hours ago. Not very big. It says they usually burn up in the atmosphere before making impact."

"Where?"

"I should warn Tami. Can we stop back at Honoli`i?"

"No," Dad says. "They can hear the sirens from the beach. She'll be fine. Where was the meteor?"

"About eight hundred miles south of Alaska."

"Oh." Dad furrows his brow, booting the calculator in his

brain. "That's far. Should take a couple hours to ripple out to us. Hopefully nothing more than a good surge by then."

The car horns are louder than the distant sirens. Traffic lets up once the northbound highway broadens into two lanes. I text Tami:

Big one on the way. Get outta the water.

She hits me back:

**Thanks for warning. Plenny good if I surfed with my phone.
Wanna hit the swell?**

My thumbs fire back:

I wish. Ur nuts.

The sun has set behind Mauna Kea. The purple silhouettes of the volcano's distant observatories jut above the sacred mountain like a crown. Clouds paint the bruised sky with broad strokes of orange.

We pull up to the house in the shadowy dark of thick rain forest and falling night. Mom and Kai are just getting out of their car.

Dad and I get out and Mom says, "What happened? You were supposed to be home an hour ago. We're starving."

Dad grins. "Yes, we're safe. Thanks for asking. The tsunami—"

"Don't even try that." She plucks a plumeria flower off the tree branch near the lanai steps and guides its stem into her long, velvety black hair, just above the ear. She does this every night. I'm not sure she's aware that she does it. "You were supposed to be back long before the sirens even started."

Dad unties my board from the top of the car. "Uh, Leilani wouldn't get out of the water."

I shoot him a glare.

"You went to Wilson's, didn't you?" Mom sees the crumpled paper cones in the car. Her voice is stern, but when she turns toward me she's holding another plumeria blossom, and she gently tucks it into my hair with a smile. She has beautiful dark eyes and Polynesian features. I wish I looked like her.

"Leilani," she whispers. She always says my name when she puts flowers in my hair. My name means "Flower of Heaven."

"That too." Dad is sheepish. "I bought you one, but it melted."

"My dad's coming tonight," Mom says.

"Grandpa's spending the night?"

"He's going to help me get Kai to school and the gym while you're gone. And he wants to see you off. So, let's eat. Airport at six a.m. tomorrow. And guess what: your son landed his first back handspring tonight, no spot."

"Yeah, Dad." My little brother, Kai, jumps up the steps.

"Nice," I say. "You'll be taking home trophies a solid year before I did." Kai's seven, but he's pretty advanced at everything he tries.

"Yeah, all-around trophies, not just for the girlie uneven bars."

I poke his side; such a tease.

"Keep practicing." Dad runs his fingers through Kai's

12

hair. "And don't make fun—the bars are difficult to nail, and Lei was the best."

Before I was dropped from the gymnastics team for being an epileptic—the chance of my having a stress-related fit during a competition was too great, the insurance company said. Still, I'm happy for Kai.

He gives me a big grin. "I rode my biggest wave yet," I tell him. "And—did you hear about the meteor?"

He nods. "Food!"

"Who are you? King Kamehameha?" Mom unlocks the front door and swings it open. "Lei—are your bags packed? You ready to go?"

"Check," I say.

Dad starts to sing "Leaving on a Jet Plane." He has a pretty good voice. Maybe if he chose to sing somebody other than John Denver, I'd meet him halfway with a compliment.

Kai chimes in, belting the lyrics to compete with the coqui frogs chirping in the darkness. *"Don't know when I'll be back again."*

"Didn't John Denver die in an airplane crash?" I ask as I climb the stairs.

"Leilani!" my parents gasp.

"I'm just sayin', maybe it's not the best song for before a flight."

"Inside," Mom says. "Come on. Mosquitoes."

The living-room walls are draped with volleyball pennants from both UH Hilo and UH Manoa. Posters of Merrie Monarch Festival hula dancers in every pose surround the room. My dusty gymnastics trophies crowd a bookshelf around a photo of a twelve-year-old me twisting on the bars at a Bay Area meet, my black hair in a tight bun and my turquoise leotard shrink-wrapped to my tall, wiry frame.

Now I lean back on the couch, stretching my legs. My Hawaiiana book and a pile of homework lie on the coffee table. It's the last month of my junior year—time to start thinking about finals.

Dad heats up the frozen pizzas in the oven while Mom is on the computer in the corner.

"Good," Mom says. "They're already downgrading the tsunami threat for Hawai`i. The meteorite wasn't very big. No need to worry about them closing the airport."

"How do they even know that?" Kai asks.

"Someone's always looking," Dad says. "Good eyes are all you need. That, and a little bit of math."

"Please, no math," Kai mutters.

"Isn't a small meteorite still pretty powerful?" I ask.

"On land, maybe," Dad says. "The ocean does a better job of absorbing the energy."

"Well, yeah," Mom adds. "Except the energy turns into *waves*."

I absently hear a gecko call out with its strange *kiss kiss kiss* sound; it's walking up the living-room window. I'm texting Tami:

Threat downgraded. No epic wave for you.

Mom stares at the computer. "The president just bailed on the Carbon Credit Conference."

"What?" Dad says.

"He ditched a fund-raiser in Miami, too."

My phone chimes. Tami:

Already out. Chowing down a double teri @ Blanes. You?

I smile. I can just see her freckly face buried in that messy burger. She's a toothpick, but legendary in my family for her ability to eat. Mom says she's like the *amakihi,* the smallest of the Hawaiian birds: always in motion and always foraging.

"What is he thinking?" Dad asks.

I tap back:

Frozen pizza. Ono. You suck.

Mom keeps reading. "I don't get it."

I can see the headline on her laptop:

PREZ SNUBS HIGHLY CHARGED
CARBON TRADING SUMMIT—
NO EXPLANATION
Regional Events Scrapped

"It's two in the morning back east," Mom says. "We'll get the full scoop come morning."

My phone chimes again:

Totally ONO! Yummy. Ha ha! Have a fun week.
Lots of pics from the north shore yeah?
Pics of PROS. Not you. LMAO.

I reply:

Fo real.

15

"Pizza's ready," Dad calls.

Kai cartwheels into the dining room and lands squarely on his chair. "Great. But what are *you all* going to eat?"

Mom comes to the table and glances over at our luggage in the corner. "What's in those bags, you guys? Are you going to O'ahu or running off to the Peace Corps?"

Two big backpacks and a couple of carry-ons lean against each other near the front door, stuffed to the gills with gear. Dad wants to camp at least one night and then climb O'ahu's Stairway to Heaven in the Koolau Range. I saw a stretch of the Stairway once from the highway. It looks like Frodo's climb into Mordor.

My parents have mellowed a little since I was forced to quit gymnastics. They want me to have a normal life—as long as I wear a vest, and Dad is watching, they allow me to surf, even though the doctor doesn't approve. Climbing the Stairway to Heaven is another example of how lax they can be. We'll have gear, of course. Ropes and harnesses.

Now if I can just get the doctor to finally let me drive . . .

"There're duffel bags stuffed in, too," Dad says. "We hardly ever get over there. Might as well do some shopping."

"Kai." Mom is setting the table. "Go into the garden, dear, and pick us a salad?"

The ubiquitous sound of the coqui frogs grows louder when he opens the door. *Ubiquitous* is one of Dad's words. It means "everywhere." Dad actually studies coquis. They're not supposed to be on the Hawaiian Islands at all. They're an invasive species. A few years back, the Hawaiian night sounded completely different. Then a Hilo big-box store garden center accidentally brought them to the island. Because they have no natural predators, you can now find three frogs for every square meter of rain forest. They drown out all other critters. "*Coqui? Coqui?*" Everyone's waiting for the tipping point, wondering when the ecosystem will crash. Well, not everyone, I guess. Maybe just my parents and their geekiest friends.

Kai returns with a bowl of greens. "*Kau kau* time!" We sit at the table and my parents pour themselves wine. We divide up the pizza and practice our traditional moment of silence. Grandpa knocks on the door just as we dig in.

"Tūtū!" Kai shouts, running to the door. He pulls Grandpa to the table.

"Hi, Dad," Mom says. "Trip wen good?"

Mom's pidgin, the local Hawaiian slang, bubbles up whenever Grandpa's around. I understand pidgin pretty well, but I hardly use it. Speak it wrong around a local and you'll get laughed out of town.

Grandpa shrugs. "All good. Construction delays."

"Pizza?" Dad asks.

Grandpa shakes his head. "House calls on the way. Everyone offered food."

"Tending to the flock," Dad says.

Grandpa's become our kahuna, or spiritual counselor. He's big on keeping old ways alive in the new world. Even keeps a blog about it. He's tall and thin with gray hair, and is strong, calm, and thoughtful. He served in the navy, and he remains a great swimmer and paddler. After the navy he was a cop on Maui.

He turns to me. "Evening, Mo`opuna. You set?"

"I suppose."

"Ho! Nervous, ah?"

Grandpa sees everything. There's no point in trying to hide it. "Yeah."

"Well, no worries. You been doing great, yeah?"

"*Been* doing." I had my first big seizure—a grand mal—when I was twelve. We were at a baseball game in San Francisco; I fell out of my seat and my whole body shook for three minutes. I don't remember any of it. We learned that I had also been having little episodes—petits mals—for years. I would often just blank out and stare off into space. My parents wrote it off as "intense daydreaming." The seizures became frequent when I was thirteen. Then, just before we moved, I started taking a new medicine, which cut both kinds of seizure to only a couple a year.

Mom gives me a comforting squeeze. "I know the tests won't be fun, but keep your eye on the prize: one pill a day instead of two, and—maybe—your driver's license."

The clinical trial will go like this: When we get to O`ahu, I'll stop my meds. The next day my trial dosage starts, a stronger medication that's not on the market yet. I won't know if it's the real deal or a placebo. But if I have a grand mal, the trial will stop and I'll resume my current meds. I'm super nervous about the potential of ending up on a placebo—I'd effectively be off meds altogether!—but I'm trying to ignore it and focus on the fact that Dad and I are staying in a nice Waikīkī hotel for free the whole week.

"I know." I try to look excited.

"Well, there's no shame if the new meds aren't for you," Grandpa says. "Pele's your guardian spirit, yeah? Goddess of lightning."

I smile. The goddess of lightning and lava and volcanoes. "Yeah. Goddess of the lightning in my head."

The food disappears. Kai cartwheels away to his room to play video games.

Dad clears the table and settles in at his computer. I help Mom and Grandpa with the dishes, but Mom says, "Lei, you should call it a night. You'll need plenny energy for the week ahead."

"You sure?" I glance from Mom to Grandpa.

Grandpa nods. "It's past my bedtime. I'm going right to sleep."

"Thanks for coming." I give him a little hug and lean against him.

"I had to see you off." He strokes my hair. "I'm very proud of you, Moʻopuna."

"Thanks, Tūtū."

I hug Mom, kiss Dad, and head upstairs. I like to read my Hawaiiana book before bed. But my eyelids grow heavy and I drift off.

CHAPTER 2

Most nights, rain falls long and hard, pelting our metal roof. Tonight it wakes me. All the buildings on the Hilo side have aluminum roofing, and during a good cloudburst the town sounds like a radio set on static.

My heart sighs as I listen to the rain. I'm only half Hawaiian, but I want to belong. I can feel the warmth of their akua—the Hawaiian gods and family guardians. When I'm hiking in the high forest with Dad, Kāne, the creator, is in the ohia trees, watching me. And Grandpa's right: Pele speaks to me—not only when I'm visiting the glowing caldera of Kilauea volcano, but when I'm walking over her ropy black fields of lava, or surfing. I get light-headed and peaceful.

The island itself—it feels like *home*.

Still, I've only lived here for three years, and most Hawaiians around Hilo are slow to accept newcomers. My mind replays the stink-eye I got from Aleka and that other *tita* on the bluff. *Tita*. Mean girl. They think I'm a trespasser.

Tami has it worse than I do. She's full haole, with blond hair and blue eyes. She and her mom moved to the Big Island five years ago. They don't have any roots here at all.

I envy Kai's dark complexion: he can pass for Hawaiian. But it's not the *hapa* thing that gets in the way so much as the fact that I grew up on the mainland. Too many folks come and go from these islands, taking, taking, taking. The locals are right to be wary.

Still, I hate it when people try to take that feeling of *home* away from me.

I only talk to Grandpa and Tami about it. The last time Grandpa and I spoke, he said, "You are *kama`āina*. Child of the land. No one can take that away."

"Try telling the *titas* at my school. They say I don't count, because I grew up in California."

I studied his eyes, the deep wrinkles of his kukui-nut-colored face. So wise, so kind. He returned to the Big Island and discovered his spiritual side when my grandma became sick. Tūtū Lili`u has been gone ten years now. She looked like Mom; I loved to be with her when we flew out for visits, cuddling, cooking, polishing kukui nuts, and making leis with her.

"You can take the child from the `āina," Grandpa told me, "But the `āina from the child? Hawai`i's in your blood. Don't listen to those *titas*. You know, I left the force because of that rubbish. It was big even on Maui. Sovereign Nation people who want pure Hawaiian rule—it's always been a part of our culture. The seizure of Hawaii by the U.S. military was a despicable act. The loss of our lands . . . But should you and your father be kicked out? No! Your dad's just as Hawaiian as I am. `Ohana. Family. `Ohana nui. Place is very strong in us, but `ohana is always stronger."

My dreams often center on the mo`olelo, the stories I read in my Hawaiian class. Sometimes I'm ali`i nui, a great chief. I walk over cooled lava, my attendants beside me. Sometimes I'm the inventor of surfing, catching the world's first wave. The gods always whisper in my ears—from the trees, the `a`a, or the sea. I never catch the words, though; same as trying to read in a dream.

Grandpa says I have a strong spirit, that I'm particularly attuned to the akua around me. It's true that sometimes the dreams seem real, even after I wake. I just think my brain is overactive.

In my dreamscapes, I *am* home.

I'm lulled to sleep by the rain.

* * *

It's still dark when Dad nudges me awake. Mom already has eggs in the skillet. I jump up and dress. Downstairs, Grandpa's eating a Spam *musubi* and a bowl of cornflakes. I wave at him, and he smiles.

"We're a little behind," Mom says.

"What, the airport doesn't keep Hawaiian time?" I ask.

"Eat quick."

"I'm not supposed to eat before the tests."

"Oh. Sorry."

"More for me," Dad says.

He plops a still-sleeping Kai down on his chair. Kai re-settles with his head on the table. Black hair fans out around his head.

"Mike, just let him sleep," Mom says. "Grandpa will watch him while we go."

I rub my hand through Kai's hair. "Take care, kid," I say softly.

He looks up, stretching awake. "Laters," he says. "Good luck."

"I want to see a full backflip by the time I get back."

Dad picks up Kai and carries him back to bed.

We file out to the car, load the packs. I take a deep breath. *Now or never.* I dart into the carport, emerge with my surf-board, place it atop the hybrid with authority. No eye contact with anyone.

"Lei."

I start with the tie-downs, humming.

"Lei, what are you doing?" Dad.

"What does it look like?"

"We've been over this, hon. Please don't—"

"The drug company's paying the baggage fees. Why not?"

"Lei, we're running late." Mom is not amused. I work the straps as fast as I can.

Dad opens his door, gets out. "Enough."

"You get to bring all your climbing gear. Why can't I—"

"Drag your *longboard* everywhere? We surf all the time.

And all of this depends on how the trial goes, Lei. We may not get around to any of it."

Grandpa helps Dad undo my knots.

I get in the car, slam my door, cross my arms, and watch my feet.

Grandpa taps on my window. I hear a muffled *"A hui hou!"* Until we meet again.

I glance up at him and offer a half smile as we pull out. "Bye."

We drive in silence. "See any tsunami damage?" Dad asks once we're along the coast.

"Just terrific surf," I grumble. Unusual five-footers roll in. Surfing was invented in Hawai`i, probably not in Hilo. But on a morning like this, I can imagine my Big Islander ancestors gliding free as spirits over the waters. I want to have what they had. How nice it must have been for them—these small islands surrounded by sea the only world they ever knew, with their gorgeous sunrises and perfect temperatures. *Paradise.*

I sigh.

Mom's driving, which means we go fast and screech up to the airport curb. Cutting it close, a Milton family tradition. Dad and I spring out and retrieve our packs. I can hear the radio through the window.

"The president's whereabouts remain a mystery. Markets are in sharp decline. The press secretary will address reporters any moment; we'll bring you live coverage."

Dad frowns. "What's this about?"

"Huh," Mom says. "I hope he's all right."

"Dad, we're gonna miss our flight," I say.

"Whose fault is that?" Dad leans in through Mom's window to kiss her.

I wave at her from the curb.

"Come here." Mom looks at me.

I drag my feet over. "I'll be fine. It's only a week."

"I know."

Someone on the radio says, "The president may have fallen ill, but let's not jump to conclusions."

"But where's Air Force One?" Another voice. "His plane is missing."

Mom turns the radio off. "Enough. Let's video chat tonight, 'kay?" She pulls me close and kisses my cheek.

"Sure." I jump back to the curb and wave as our car hums quietly away. I follow Dad, who has our bags slung over his shoulders.

Security's a cinch. Twenty minutes later, we're boarding.

"Mind if I take the window?" Dad asks. He loves to gawk at the Big Island from high up.

"Whatevah."

I put my earbuds in, hit shuffle on my favorite surfing playlist on my phone, and close my eyes.

The flight to O'ahu is a forty-minute hop over the stepping-stones of Maui, Lāna'i, and Moloka'i, the tall waves and rough seas nothing but a puddle. And then straight to the clinic.

My playlist keeps resetting. I look down at my hand. I'm clutching the phone, tapping it against my armrest. *Stop*. I tuck the phone under my leg and close my eyes again.

Let the adventures begin.

O`AHU

HONOLULU

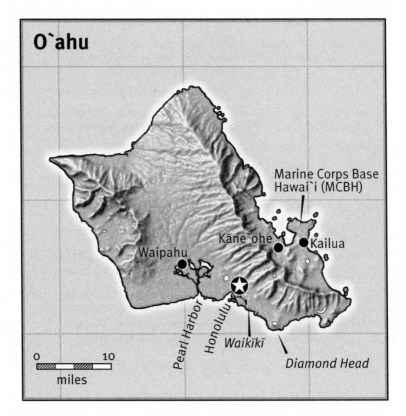

O`ahu

Marine Corps Base
Hawai`i (MCBH)

Kāne`ohe   Kailua

Waipahu

Pearl Harbor

Honolulu

Waikīkī

Diamond Head

0   10
miles

CHAPTER 3

MONDAY, APRIL 27

We rent a car at the Honolulu airport and zip away, shielding our eyes from the rising sun reflecting off the windows of endless skyscrapers. O`ahu is Hawai`i's most populous island. It's about forty miles long and twenty-five miles across. Nearly a million people live here. Fifty thousand tourists scour it for adventure every day. O`ahu is peppered with beaches, hotels, and dramatic emerald slopes.

It's also swarming with military—at least ten percent of the islanders work in the armed forces.

Steep mountain ridges cut the island in two. Honolulu, which contains Waikīkī, is on the southern half. So is Pearl Harbor. The other half is mostly just a big Marine Corps base and white sandy beaches.

On the radio we learn that a press conference happened during our flight. The president is recovering from emergency surgery for appendicitis. Glad he's okay. Hope he recovers well. I know what it's like to wake up and feel like the whole world is watching you.

I just want to be normal. Is that too much to ask? I don't want to be such a burden to my parents. I want more than one friend. I want to surf without constant supervision. I want the grand mal seizures to stop. Forever.

I'm suddenly there again:

August.

It's my third day of ninth grade, and I'm in the cafeteria. We've only lived in Hilo since June. No seizures since moving. I'm excited to be at school, even though I'm eating lunch alone, trying to appear confident. But I had a *musubi* rice sandwich for breakfast and didn't realize the sauce contained aspartame—fake sugar—which can trigger my fits.

And then I feel something rising up, gripping my skull. *No,* I think. Lights flash from the backs of my eyes, but I'm in a cafeteria full of strangers, and there's nothing I can do.

Now, my cheeks are hot. I push the memory away.

Epilepsy can get better as you get older—it can even go away. Mine should, the doctors say.

Hope they're right.

* * *

We arrive at the clinic. Dad collects the intake forms and calls Mom to ask questions as he fills out the paperwork. I shrink into a corner chair, telling myself, *Today is the easy part: a bunch of baseline electrographs. No experiments until tomorrow.*

An older man in a lab coat walks us into his office. "I'm Dr. Makani. Welcome, Leilani, Dr. Milton."

"Call me Mike," Dad says as we sit. "It's a pleasure to meet you in person."

"Thank you so much, Leilani," the doctor says, "for taking part in our study. It's a long way from the Big Island, but you're a perfect match."

We talk about the trial. Control groups, placebos. An adjustment period once I'm back on my regular meds, during which I may continue to have seizures for a while. Dad reveals his plan to scale the Stairway to Heaven, and the doctor says, "Save that for another trip. The Stairway's asking for trouble. Seizures can be induced by stress. Sorry, Leilani, but you need to avoid any adventures for a couple of weeks."

"Should have brought my longboard instead," I mumble.

The doctor's eyes widen. "You surf?"

"Yes."

"Not a good idea for the next several weeks. Promise me you'll give it a break."

I take a deep breath. Dad squeezes my shoulder and then leans over and signs the permission forms.

We follow Dr. Makani down the hall toward the MRI room. I'm not scared, I realize. It's shame. I know it's silly—I didn't do anything to earn my disorder—but as I approach the machines that will pry into my mind and uncover what I desperately want to keep secret, I feel like a criminal being shuffled into solitary confinement.

"Avoid any adventures for a couple of weeks."

I play absently with my medical bracelet.

I'm waiting for Dad to say *I told you so*. But he only takes my hand and squeezes tightly. This brings me more comfort than he can know.

* * *

Later, I fall asleep during the EKG. Go figure. A little nap is good for the baseline, I'm told, but they also need me awake to monitor my brain activity. Dad grades exams by my side and casts me soothing smiles. I'm grateful.

A technician is talking to the nurse clipping electrodes on me. He says, "They just shut down the stock exchange—an hour early. Dow was down over two thousand points and still plummeting when they hit the switch."

Dad stiffens. "Two thousand! *Why?*" he asks the tech.

The guy shrugs. "Serious heebie-jeebies out there. Now the vice president isn't around."

"What?"

"Prime minister of Japan is missing, too."

The nurse stops clipping wires and escorts the tech out of the room. I hear him mumble, "Hey, these folks are supposed to be relaxed. Talk story later."

Dad looks like he was just rear-ended in a car accident. "You should go," I tell him. "Find out what's going on. I'm fine. I'll want you here more tomorrow, but this is no big deal."

He shakes his head. "I'm here for one reason: we do this together."

The tests end, and we bolt from the clinic. We stop for lunch—I inhale a mahi-mahi plate—and head north toward the Banzai Pipeline. On the radio, talk-show hosts freak out about the stock market.

"A twenty percent drop *in one day?* The Canadians halted trading after dropping a *tenth*. And where's the Fed? Nobody's doing anything."

I look at Dad. He continues turning the dial, shaking his head, and then hits the seek button.

An ad urging listeners to buy gold.

Click.

"What if that wasn't a meteor strike off Alaska? What if it was a North Korean nuclear attack? There's a whole series of—"

Click.

A trembling and worn voice. "Then another angel came out of the temple and called in a loud voice to he who was sitting on the cloud, 'Take your sickle and reap, because the time to reap has come. . . .'"

Click.

". . . the Capitol was emptied. All congressional offices closed. Three British banks have already failed. The Euro's in a tailspin—"

Dad smacks the radio off. "Pure speculation, at best. Don't pay attention."

"Dad, come on."

"You know what?" He suddenly turns into the parking lot of a small strip mall. "You're going to kill me, but . . . would you mind if I rented a board?"

"Wait. You want to . . . surf?"

He grins. "Chuns Reef. Whaddya say? You want to watch me?"

"Dad. What?" Chuns has a more forgiving wave than nearby Banzai Pipeline, but it's fierce.

"Come on, why not? I may have lost my 401(k). The sky is falling, Lei. Brought to you by an asinine twenty-four-seven news culture that's finally jumped the shark."

My breathing is a little heavy. I don't know much about the stock market. *401(k)*. That's for retirement, I think. But what does some banking problem six time zones away have to do with us?

People are pouring in and out of the shops here. This stuff on the radio doesn't match up with what I'm seeing. Perfectly normal. Except for Dad. He's upset and trying to hide it.

He needs to surf.

"Fine. Whatevah."

"We never would have used your longboard out here, you know that." He looks at me. "Even without doctor's orders, you wouldn't be trying this wave."

"I said fine."

"Thank you. It'll be fun!"

"Yeah. *You'll* have a blast." We jump out of the car.

Dad rents a quad-fin shortboard at the surf shop. "You can handle that?" I ask.

Just you watch me, his eyes tell me.

Oh, I'll be watching, all right. Taking video.

* * *

34

By the time the sun's low enough on the horizon to light the clouds on fire, Dad is showering off near the restrooms, and I'm speechless.

Dad was a great surfer until he got so busy with work. He came to Hawai`i for the surfing and met Mom on the beach when she was in grad school. He's still got it. The swim out to the larger swells looked brutal, but he's one mean fish. After a few false starts, he nabbed a series of waves with long walls that just kept going and going.

Dad wasn't the only surfer I had my eyes on out there, either; I watched openmouthed as tanned bodies and sun-bleached heads twisted and spun on the waves with the ease of dolphins. One famous pro bulleted flawlessly through barrel after barrel. He's on one of the posters in my room! I tried to sneak a pic of him for Tami (for me, too!) with my phone as he walked up the beach afterward, rubbing his hair with a towel, but he caught my eye and grinned at me. I blushed but got the shot.

I finish sending a vid of his best moment to Mom and Kai and Tami—a quirky little two-step on the board just as he crouched into his barrel attempt. When he reaches me, I look up with awe.

"You like that?"

"Where did you . . . ?"

"I taught you how to surf, didn't I?" he says. "Give your old man some credit."

"I just did!" I say, pocketing my phone. "The vid's on my feed now."

We head for the car, cradling Dad's board. It feels so natural under my arm. Soon I'll graduate to this kind of board.

On the way back into Honolulu, we listen to the radio. Now the French president is missing. Dad and I hunt around the dial for clues, but he finally turns off the radio. "We'll catch some real news back at the room."

The surfing really mellowed him out.

Relax: this ain't the mainland, I remind myself. *Whatever's going on out there won't have much to do with us anyway.*

We stop for dinner at Costco. We're in one of the world's top tourist destinations, and Dad wants a ten-dollar pepperoni pizza from a warehouse food court.

"Pizza two days in a row? Are you having a midlife crisis or something?" I tease.

But this greasy meal feels just right. First we top off our Civic with gas, and then we pile a mountain of snacks into a shopping cart—goodies we can't find in Hilo.

Dad stands in line to fetch our pizza while I grab a table. Tami and I text:

That was ur DAD out there? Some vid.

I know right?

"Moment of silence?" Dad asks as we sit down to our giant pie.

I slip my phone into my pocket. "Dad, you don't thank God for Costco pizza. That dilutes the whole gratitude thing."

Dad gasps. "Don't let Costco the Great hear you say that!" He squeezes my hand. I glance around, then close my eyes.

Every night, I silently recite a traditional Hawaiian chant that Grandpa taught me:

Ai, Ai, Ai.
Ho`opuka e-ka-la ma ka hikina e
Kahua ka`i hele no tumutahi
Ha`a mai na`i wa me Hi`iaka
Tapo Laka ika ulu wehiwehi
Nee mai na`i wa ma ku`u alo
Ho`i no`o e te tapu me na`ali`i e

It's a chant in honor of the dawning of enlightenment. I love how it sounds, and how Grandpa translated it:

Rise up. Make a hole in the sun and find the light hidden inside. May the light of the gods dawn on me like the rising sun. Come to me through your breath and take me by force. Come, drift upon me, and spread. Bring me the means of life. Come to me like the creeping of lava, and may this sacred ceremony of the *ali`i* bring me meditation and release.

I pull my pillbox out of my pocket and stare at it silently. I take two pills each day: one every morning, one every evening. But the doctor said no meds tonight.

Dad smiles. "You ready to do this?"

A monumental moment at a Costco food court.

"Just remember"—Dad puts his hand over mine—"if something happens, you'll be safe in the clinic. Totally private."

I usually just black out, but my mind sometimes fills in the scenes later. I vividly remember the sensation of watching myself on that afternoon in the cafeteria, along with the rest of the school.

"We're doing this together, okay?" Dad says. "We're right here with each other all the way through."

I look at him and nod. I put the pillbox away without opening it.

CHAPTER 4

The drive back to Waikīkī takes ages. Rush-hour traffic. I watch the sunset from the passenger window as we exit the highway and get stuck in gridlock. This cityscape doesn't feel like my Hawai`i. Each island is very different from the next. O`ahu is all stores and glass and glamour. It's much friendlier to outsiders and visitors and tourists. Probably because it's those kind of people who mostly live here. Military people, business types, retirees. The Big Island is more my style. Jungle. Lava. Volcanoes. Nothing over three stories high. Nobody honks on the Big Island; no one's rushing off somewhere. Funny how I miss Hilo, even though I could fit right in in Honolulu, disappear. But I don't want to disappear.

We check in to our fancy hotel on Waikīkī Beach. Dad scores us some free bottles of water and access to the VIP-floor courtesy bar.

Our twelfth-floor suite has an oceanfront lanai and a view of Diamond Head off to the left, visible now only as a dark silhouette against a starry horizon. The bay is dark, but the beach hotels cast a gentle glow onto the water, causing a strange green shimmering. We unpack, piling climbing and camping gear on the floor so we can get to our crumpled clothes.

Dad offers me the first shower, but I want to spend a few minutes in the hot tub before the pool closes.

He eyes me. "Is that safe?"

I look away. "I'll only go in if there are other people there."

"Sounds great," he says to that. "Don't forget we're supposed to video chat with Mom before it gets too late."

"I won't be long."

I linger at the pools, though. There's a family with small kids in the Jacuzzi. They practice dipping their heads underwater, just like Kai did at that age.

Several brilliant falling stars dazzle my eyes as I lean my head against the lip of the spa. It's sinking in that I won't have much time to myself for the rest of the week. I'll be on a hospital bed, enjoying the flavor of a bite stick—a wooden tongue depressor that keeps the airway clear during a seizure.

When I return to the room, I find Dad kicking back on his bed, a tall drink in one hand and the remote control in the other.

"President's about to address the nation," he announces, as if he's personally arranged it. He must be in heaven. We don't have cable at home, or even broadcast TV.

There's a hum in the room I can't quite place. I see a plastic wrapper discarded beside the microwave. "Are you making *popcorn?*"

"Yeah. Should be a good show. Don't forget to buzz your mom. She called. Tami too."

"Cool. But ... wait, isn't the president recovering from surgery? Isn't it, like, four a.m. on the East Coast? Who addresses the nation at four a.m. in a hospital gown?"

"Someone who's woken up from surgery to discover half the country gnawing at his carcass, that's who."

"Dad. How much have you had to drink since I left"—I look at my phone—"thirty minutes ago?"

"I'm fine. Don't worry about me."

"Tragedy of the commons," I say.

Dad grins. It's an ecology phrase that describes how people stockpile goods when they're afraid someone else will hoard them if they don't. It happens with timber in unprotected forests, fish in international waters, and, apparently, liquor in hotel VIP courtesy bars.

The microwave hums along, but the popcorn bag inside never inflates. Dad looks through the little window. "Ring your mom before the speech begins," he says. He pulls out the bag. "Not even hot." He tosses the popcorn back in and resets the timer for five minutes.

I open the laptop and see Mom's avatar active on the sidebar. I click on her and a window pops open on the computer. I can hear the insufferable pleas of the coqui frogs even before she and Kai appear, sitting by the desk at home. He's in pajamas, sleepy. Mom is smiling firmly.

"Hi, sweetie."

"Hi."

"You're off your meds already, huh?" she asks.

"Yeah."

"You feeling okay?"

I roll my eyes, forgetting that I'm on a video chat, not a phone. I smile. "I'm fine, Mom."

"You're so strong, Lei. I'm very proud of you."

I blush. "I love you, Mom. Where's Tūtū?"

"He's already in bed," Kai says.

"What did you guys have for dinner?" Mom asks.

Dad shoots me a look and vigorously shakes his head.

"Uh, you know, just . . . Thai."

"Fine, don't tell me," Mom murmurs. "Say something, Kai." She nudges him.

"I did more back handsprings today!"

I laugh. "You still have to practice before you catch up with me. Land your first backflip on a balance beam!"

"Whatevah. Boys don't *do* balance beam."

"Boys *can't* do balance beam."

Kai just grins.

"Anyway, Lei," Mom interrupts, "we don't mean to keep you. It's late."

I glance over at the TV. A somber anchorman is stalling: "The timing of this address is highly unusual. . . ."

I turn back to Mom. "Dad's Command Center seems to be fully operational now."

"Mike, turn it off!" Mom yells into the computer. She looks at me. "Don't pay attention to all that stuff, Lei."

"It's fine."

Mom smiles. "We really should be going. Kai's—"

The television set flashes to a close-up of the president. Dad and I gasp. The president looks haggard and uneasy. Behind him is a plain blue drape. Not even an American flag. I've never seen him so . . . I don't even know what the word is.

"Malia, honey, wait!" Dad shouts toward the laptop. "Stick around. He's on. You should see this. Lei, turn the computer, would you?"

I do, making sure Mom has a good view of the television.

The president's voice is strong. "My fellow Americans, and my fellow citizens around the globe: I apologize for the deceptions of the past twenty-four hours. Well-intentioned advisors have counseled me to keep secret what we've recently learned. My conscience and my heart will no longer allow that. I have made the determination that you have a *right* to know about the extraordinary—"

The flatscreen turns blue. A small text box bounces about the monitor:

Weak or no signal.

"What!" Dad shouts, leaping to his feet.

I stare wide-eyed at the television.

"I can't *believe* this!" Dad pounds the remote keys. Nothing. All blank.

I turn to the laptop and notice that Mom and Kai are frozen on the screen. I click the connect button. "Hello? Mom? You still there? Can you hear me?"

Nothing.

I can close the program, though, and open others. The computer's fine. I try clicking on my browser's home page and get the white error screen. "Internet's down, too."

The microwave dings. Dad and I stare at it. The bag inside is still flat. "Cable with no cable, and now a microwave with no microwaves. Just great," Dad says.

The broadcast returns. I whip around to the television. The president is still talking in front of that blue curtain.

"—uncertain of the exact effects. But we do know there's no reason to be alarmed. We all have a responsibility to each other to remain calm, and to continue to go about our lives in an orderly fashion. There is much we don't yet know, but I am making a commitment to you, from this moment forward, to keep you informed of developments on an hourly basis. We . . ."

An unseen, muffled voice distracts the president. He turns for just a moment, nods, and returns to the camera. "I understand we're already experiencing some glitches. Some satellites are cutting in and out. So, let me repeat, it's important that you—"

The image goes blank again.

Dad and I wait, motionless. A minute or two crawl by like hours. The TV screen remains blue. Dad seizes the telephone. He dials zero and waits.

"Wow," I say. "What's going on?"

"It's busy," Dad says. He tries again. This time he gets through. "Hello?" he says. "Hey, our cable and Internet are out. It just dropped right in the middle of the president's . . . Well, okay, but . . . Fine." He hangs up.

"They're working on it," he tells me. He fetches the remote and sits down, running through the channels. Still all blank.

"Hey, we can watch it online as soon as things are back up," I suggest.

"Good idea. You should grab a shower. I'll give Mom a call while you're in there."

"Yeah, sure." I turn to close the computer. But it's already off. And it won't even turn on. *Battery?* I plug it in. "Night, Mom. Night, Kai," I say.

I hope Mom's not flipping out.

These islands and their sacred tides call me forth.

The wave rises. I paddle, catch it. I spring up on my board, rush over the waters. Everyone on shore watches, agape. *I've done it! I'm riding the surf!* They all laughed, thought I was crazy, but here I am, the inventor of surfing, drifting on the sea, the gods whispering in my ears through the salty breeze. I'll be lost to history, but for me, this moment will last forever.

Come, drift upon me, and spread. Bring me the means of life.

"Honey? Come on back, sweetie. Wake up." Dad's voice cuts in and out, like a lighthouse beacon twirling through heavy fog. "Hey. There we are. You okay?"

"What? Yeah. I'm fine."

"You just blanked, kiddo."

"Huh?"

"Petit mal, maybe. Little too much excitement."

My elbow hurts. Did I bang it on the nightstand? Did I fall? "Oh, no."

"It's okay, honey. We were expecting this, right? Why don't you take a quick shower? Freshen up and get to bed."

"Okay." I feel like crying, but I gulp it down. I get ready for a shower in a sort of stupor. I can't believe this is actually happening. I can mentally prepare for it all I want, but when it finally comes . . . I feel robbed of my hopes.

I don't want to take a shower. I run a shallow bath instead. Before I get in, I poke my head out the door. "Dad?"

"Sweetheart? Need something?"

"Just . . . thank you." I pause. "Hey, what do you think he was about to say?"

"Lei." He takes a deep breath. When he answers, his voice is kind and patient. "There's no point in speculating. There's nothing to worry about; I know that much."

I close the door. He looked as though he almost believed that. I text Tami:

Strange things are afoot at the Circle K

I smile, knowing that she'll get my *Bill and Ted's Excellent Adventure* reference. It's one of Dad's favorite old-timer

46

movies; he forced us to watch it during a sleepover. The text doesn't go through. I stare at the error symbol on my phone and then plug it in to charge.

I try not to think about anything when I'm in the bath. I read from my Hawaiiana book. I've memorized lots of the mo'olelo. There are many versions of Hawaiian stories, because they're based on oral histories told on isolated islands. I love them all. I run a warm washcloth over my skin and study the tan along my arms. I drain the bath, rinse off under the shower, run my long black hair through two treatments of conditioner. My room at the clinic the rest of the week won't have such luxuries.

I paint my toenails with my favorite polish: spearmint pearl. But it takes me ages. *Why can't I hold my hands steady?*

I get ready for bed, suddenly hearing the voice from my seizure dream: *Come, drift upon me.* . . . Never heard that before. Seizures are just . . . blackouts. I never dream or hear things during them. Add it to the list of weirdness today. Also, while I'm at it: I scarfed half a Costco pizza tonight. How come my stomach feels empty?

When I come out, Dad's on the lanai with the door wide open. He looks out on the bay, the blue screen still glowing across the room. I join him. The nightscape is as beautiful as ever. Waikīkī is ablaze with the checkered light from skyscraper hotels, tiki-torch-lit pathways, and busy streets. Another shooting star highlights the faintly jade horizon. The singing and drumming of a touristy luau party waft up from below. Everything looks normal.

"You ready to call it a night?" he asks me.

"Yeah. I wanted to call Tami back first."

"Phones aren't working."

"Still?"

"I wouldn't worry about it."

"I'm only worried about Mom worrying about us."

"She knows better than to do that, hon. Put it out of your mind."

"Okay."

"Do you feel all right?"

"Dad. Yes. I'm fine."

We turn out the lights. I climb into bed. Dad says, "Love you, Lei. So proud. We'll have it all behind us in no time."

"Love you too, Dad."

He goes out on the lanai. As I lie in the dark, I realize what's been nagging at me.

It was fear I saw in the president's eyes.

CHAPTER 5

Muffled sounds from the luau invade my restless sleep. Drumming, the whipping sound of fire flung through the air. Performers grunt the *Kumulipo*, the epic chant of Hawaiian beginnings, and call out to their Hawaiian gods. The tales celebrate the link between all living things. Earth, sea, sky. Flora, fauna. Man, woman, gods. All is connected. All is sacred.

O ke au i kahuli wela ka honua
O ke au i kahuli lole ka lani
O ke au i kuka`iaka ka la
E ho`omalamalama i ka malama

In the beginning there is only *Po*, disorder, churning throughout the deep.

Out of the universe come the gods. Kāne, the creator god, appears in the darkness, holding aloft a great calabash. He tosses the gourd high into the vast emptiness. It breaks in two, its curved shell becoming the dome of the sky and its scattered seeds the stars, and the remnants drifting downward to form the Earth.

Out of the oceans rise the shores, liquid fire roiling in the void. Ai, Ai, Ai. Rise up.

Kāne fills the land and the sea and the air with creatures of every kind. He crafts the *honu*, the great turtles, to pass between earth and sea.

There is new heat within my belly, and I yearn to spill the urge. Precious and majestic, the sea foam rocks me awake, and I stir with life.

Kāne crafts the first human, Wākea, with a mound of red clay scooped from the sea cliffs. Wākea is made son of Papa and Rangi, Earth and Sky. He is joined with his wife Lihau`ula, and from them all the *ali`i*, the chiefs, and the kahunas, the priests, of Hawai`i shall descend.

* * *

The hum of the air conditioner reminds me where I am. A resort hotel on the shores of a sacred land. Dad hangs up the hotel phone.

"Learn anything?" I ask.

"Go back to sleep, hon. Everyone's as clueless as we are."

The night is silent. I drift back to sleep. I dream of shores beyond contact with modern man. I see the sacred *honu*, the sea turtle, heaved ashore, bridging sea and surf, pushing back the sand to lay its eggs. I see the face of a mother and father, betrayed. My mother and father, Papa and Rangi. Earth and Sky. They suffer an unthinkable disorder. They weep, white with death.

Kāne has fled, and in his absence billows *Po*.

Chaos.

* * *

In the morning there is no alarm. I rise out of sleep slowly, to a distant chirping of car horns. I glance at the alarm clock. It's blinking twelve o'clock. I push the covers back from my clammy skin and begin to drift back to sleep.

Then I spring awake. No alarm? I look around. Dad is asleep. The lanai doors are closed and the room is stifling.

I wipe sweat off my forehead. The curtains are open, and the bay is bright with pastel sunlight. Honking. Honolulu is supposed to have horrible traffic—there aren't enough highways, no rail system—but this is ridiculous.

"Dad. Dad, what time is it?"

We're due at the clinic at eight.

"Dad!"

Dad shoots up in bed. He glances at the alarm clock and frowns. He checks his watch. "We're fine. Almost seven. You're not supposed to eat breakfast anyway."

He's still gathering his bearings, scanning the room and rubbing at his eyes. "Why's it so *humid*?" He reaches above his headboard and tinkers with the air-conditioning. It blasts to life, and I immediately feel its cool relief.

Dad tries the remote. The flatscreen turns on but remains

blue. He slips into a pair of shorts and steps out onto the lanai. When the door opens, car horns assault my ears, and I recognize the grumble of generators.

"Power's actually out," he says. "This is crazy." He turns the air conditioner and television back off, habit guiding him to save energy.

I join him on the balcony. Nothing looks particularly out of the ordinary, but we're facing gardens and pools and beaches. There are a couple of surfers on the waves, and paddleboards, kayaks, canoes, and sailboats farther out. A helicopter hovers to the north. To the left, gridlocked traffic along the roads leading toward Diamond Head.

"Jeez," I say. "We may want to head out soon if that doesn't let up."

Dad wears a look of deep concentration. Finally, he says, "Honey, I'm beginning to wonder if they'll be able to do any tests today."

"But I already missed my meds last night!" My voice rises.

A flash of worry in his eyes. "Right."

"We have to go, Dad. I don't want to have a fit sitting here in the hotel."

"Sure. I'll see if I can call the clinic. Grab me a glass of water, would you?"

He shuffles over to the nightstand for his cell phone. When I emerge from the bathroom, he has the hotel phone to his ear instead. I place a glass of water down next to him, and he shows me his cell. "Thanks. Look: zero bars. The network's not even activated."

I take the cell phone and study it like it's a piece of art.

"Yeah, good morning," Dad says into the phone. "Hey, do you know what's going on? Have you guys heard anything? . . . Everywhere? . . . I was wondering if I could place a call. . . . Allen Medical Group. . . . Well, why is *this* working?"

Dad hangs up and shakes his head. "Net's down. No phone books. Landlines aren't working anyway. The hotel's old switchboard works, but that's it."

"Did they say what's going on?"

Dad shrugs. "No. Power is off and on. Satellite signals, too."

"Should we just get to the clinic?" I ask.

"Yeah. Let's go."

"Why does all this have to be happening *now*?" I say.

"It's okay, hon. It'll all work out. Go ahead and get ready."

"Are you going to have breakfast first?"

"I'll grab something I can bring."

Dad snatches up a *Honolulu Star-Advertiser* lying at our door. "Finally." There's a close-up screen-capture of a grave-looking president with the headline:

DISCONNECTED!
Satellite Networks and Electronics Down;
Commercial Flights Grounded

I'm able to read the front page over Dad's shoulder during our trip down in the elevator:

HONOLULU—Satellite signal losses and electronic failures were reported throughout O`ahu last night during a 10 p.m.-local-time address by the president.

The failures started during the president's remarks and continued overnight. The cause was unknown.

The article details the president's speech—just as we heard it. I skip ahead:

No advance copy of the speech was issued to the media, so the rest of his statement remains unknown.

Without GPS signals, all flights out of O`ahu's airports were canceled. Widespread electronic malfunctions were also reported on aircraft, cruise ships, and some motor vehicles.

Officials have not been able to make contact with the mainland. "Obviously, we're concerned about the loss of communications," Governor Leonard Mills said. "We're doing everything we can to reestablish contact. We're working with the military and engineers in every field."

He urged everyone to remain calm.

"Dad, I'm worried," I say as we walk through the lobby toward the parking garage.

"Yeah," Dad says. "The best way to create panic is to tell people not to panic. Don't worry about it, though, Lei. We'll just play it by ear, okay?"

"Sure," I say, anything but sure.

Dad eyes the crowded restaurant across the atrium. "I'll meet you at the car," he says.

When he reaches the garage, he's carrying two small bags filled with apples, bananas, bagels, bottled water, granola bars, and yogurts from the breakfast buffet.

"You bring the whole buffet with you?"

"It's for later," he says.

"Ah." I frown. Is this one of those *tragedies of the commons?*

Once we're in the car, I read more of the article aloud:

> "As crews repaired blown power transformers around the island, rolling blackouts were initiated throughout O`ahu under a conservation plan ordered by the governor.
>
> O`ahu mayor Terry Kalali said, "Hang in there, O`ahu. We'll be up and running in short order."

I ask, "How are we supposed to get home?"

Dad smiles briefly. "It'll be sorted out by the time our flight rolls around. Can you imagine if you were a tourist trying to fly home today?"

"Is the power out in Hilo, too?"

He pauses. "Probably not."

We stick to residential side streets to avoid the jammed intersections. Pedestrians and cyclists also crowd the streets. We all study one another on this strange morning.

We arrive at the clinic right on time. I stare at the building's front door from the car. Maybe I'll have a seizure right away, end the trial on the first day so we can just get out of here.

The lights are off inside. The receptionist greets us. "Dr. Makani hasn't arrived yet."

"Are they going to be able to run any tests?" Dad asks.

The receptionist doesn't know, but someone has left to get gas for the emergency generators. They need power before they can determine whether the machines are fried.

Dad and I wait outside and watch mynas and other birds flitter among the trees like any other day.

Dr. Makani run-walks up the steps from the parking lot, his dress shirt half tucked in. He listens to our report and suggests we stick around. "You're off your meds now, Leilani. And you already had a small seizure. We might be on schedule if things get resolved quickly."

We settle down in one of the rooms. The doctor takes my blood pressure and pulse. Dad asks, "Any read on what's happening?"

Dr. Makani shrugs. "Rumors. My neighbor's with the National Oceanic and Atmospheric Administration. He said something about a geomagnetic storm, but I think he was just guessing. Space weather. Solar winds—or something—interfering with the Earth's magnetic field."

"That's okay, let's just look it up on the Web," Dad jokes.

We share a joyless laugh.

Dr. Makani continues, "He told me a story about a big geomagnetic event back in the 1850s that zapped early telegraph operators and affected compass needles. Sounds about right to me, but there wasn't enough in the way of electronics back then for the impact to be widely felt."

"So it's a storm of some kind? It's going to pass?"

"Should be temporary, he thinks."

"Except for blown transformers and equipment malfunctions," Dad adds. "Fried parts at the power plants will take time to replace—especially around here."

Dr. Makani hands me a paper cup with a fat yellow pill in it. "Here's your new dose."

I pop it in my mouth and chase it down with some water.

Two hours pass. I'm starving. The lights come on. Dr. Makani enters. "It looks like we can proceed. Generators working, EKG seems okay. The MRI is a paperweight, but we'll get by without it. No need to fast every morning anymore."

"Yay," I say.

Here I'll stay, my head attached to electrodes, until I either have a seizure or make it to the end of the week.

Today, the whole world is on the fritz, and I'm working just fine.

The power goes on and off during the tests. I read magazines and check my phone for incoming texts from Mom or Tami. Nope. I try to read, but I have no focus. I can only listen to Dad scratching his chin as he grades, the crinkle of his homework papers, and the clicking sound of my own thoughts being etched onto reams of paper.

Dad eats some of his breakfast loot when my dinner is served. The sun sets, and a sudden calm descends upon Honolulu. Dad sits with me until a nurse asks him to respect visiting hours. He looks at me questioningly.

"Go," I say. "Your beard scratching is driving me crazy."

"I don't have a beard."

"Exactly."

Dad chuckles. He gives me a gentle kiss goodnight and heads out. "I'll be back first thing in the morning."

Two minutes later he's back in the doorway.

"Lei, come here. You need to see this." Dad's face is full of . . . awe?

"What is it?"

"Come outside."

"Now?"

"Yes."

He gets the nurse, who strips the electrodes from my head.

We step outside into a crowd, murmuring, looking upward.

It's so dark. No streetlamps. Very few buildings visible. And the stars . . . they smear the sky with milky whiteness all the way to the horizon.

I look up higher and gasp. I feel the warmth drain from my face.

"What is it?"

Dad whispers. "Geomagnetic . . . solar flares . . . ?"

Vibrant, yet cloudy and frozen, a hazy green knot dominates a quarter of the night sky.

"Aurora borealis?" I ask.

"Not really." Dad's been to the arctic, and he always returns with amazing photos of the northern lights. "Sort of. But this is less ribbony and more like . . . a pinwheel."

"Well, this has to be what's messing up the satellites and stuff, right?"

"I wouldn't bet against it."

"So as soon as it's gone, everything will return to normal."

Dad glances down at me. "That's right, hon."

"Dad?"

"Yeah, hon?"

"I want to go home."

He gives me a grave smile.

We stare up at the strange glow in the night sky for several minutes. Finally, Dad nudges me. "Come on, you need your sleep."

"Are you leaving?"

"I'm not going anywhere, Lei. I don't care what the nurse says."

We return to my room. None of the staff protests, and Dad makes himself comfortable in a large armchair a nurse drags in for him. We drift off to sleep in the darkness.

CHAPTER 6

In the morning I wake not from a strange dream but to a strange reality. Dad runs outside to check on the sky and returns moments later to report that everything looks normal in the daylight. He holds up a new newspaper. We read the front page together:

ASTRONOMER: GREEN "CLOUD" ENTERING SOLAR SYSTEM MAY EXPLAIN OUTAGES

HONOLULU—A gaseous green haze materialized in the night sky above O`ahu and has grown more pronounced since it was first spotted Monday night.

Hovering high in the northwest after sunset, the celestial anomaly is believed to be the cause of satellite disruptions and other electronic failures that began at about the same time the haze was spotted.

Upton Donnell, an astronomer at the Bishop Museum, observed the green light the night of the initial blackouts in Hawai`i. He says it is too early to confirm a causal relationship between the events or to speculate on why the anomaly might have disrupted satellites, shorted electronic equipment, and grounded airplanes throughout the state.

"It's not an aurora," Mr. Donnell explained. "It's too far away to be ionized atmospheric gas. It's not acting like a comet, either. This is something new to me."

Mr. Donnell and his colleagues studying the phenomena say most of their telescopes and equipment are not working. They know that some metal composites and alloys are reacting differently. For example, cell phones, tablets, and computers from some manufacturers no longer turn on at all, while similar devices from other manufacturers experience only network communication failure.

"We're dusting off old scopes and our slide rules, and we'll keep the public informed as we learn more," he said.

Mr. Donnell asked all amateur astronomers and backyard stargazers to share their findings and contact him at the Bishop Museum.

Mr. Donnell addressed growing support for an electromagnetic-pulse theory, in which damaging voltage surges result from certain varieties of high-energy explosions. He cautioned against making "wild guesses."

"There are a number of possible explanations," he said.

"I want to see it again," I say.

"Let's hope it goes away," Dad says.

He reads the entire newspaper to me as the morning

slowly unfolds. Apparently, whatever's happening in Hawai`i is happening all over the world. Some satellite signals have returned, but they're weak and erratic. A resident of Pearl City reports that one television station in the Balkans was broadcasting on his satellite receiver for almost half an hour before the signal was lost, but he had no idea what was being said. Some ham radio operators have made contact with peers on the mainland, but they're only able to swap stories of mass power outages and confusion.

The power at the lab keeps going on and off, but the generators bridge the divides. Dr. Makani visits about once an hour. Being off my drugs feels like floating on a life raft in the open ocean, with no idea what's coming over the horizon.

Mom and Kai. What are they up to? I keep seeing their pixilated faces frozen as they stare into the webcam.

At least Grandpa's with them.

I go to charge my cell phone late in the afternoon when we have a power "on-age." The network is up! I have full bars. "Dad! We can call home!"

Dad snatches up his own phone. He raises his eyebrows and dials Mom. "See. Things are on the mend, just like that!"

His phone never connects to a dial tone, though. We try my phone. Nothing.

"There's no way to route a call," he says.

Fifteen minutes later, my phone shows no network. Landlines don't work, either.

I've never missed anyone so much that it hurt before, but

right now I'd give anything to be back with Mom and Kai and Grandpa.

"I hope they're not too worried about us."

Dad smiles. "I'm sure they're fine."

"What do you think they're doing?"

Dad shifts. "Probably not much different from usual."

"Satellite issues wouldn't only affect O'ahu. Mom and Grandpa must be as clueless as we are."

"Probably true. But there's no reason to worry."

Afternoon rolls into evening. I work on my homework and pepper Dad with trigonometry questions. I eat dinner while Dad snacks on hotel loot. We go outside and watch the green cloud. It's brighter, nearer, but somehow less menacing. Does it seem familiar already? Or just less mysterious, like the sound of thunder after the first big storm of the season?

"Dad, go back to the hotel."

"You sure?"

"Yes. You smell."

"Ha!" He punches my shoulder lightly. "Sure that's not you? It would be nice to check on our room, make sure it hasn't been given away."

"I'll be fine. Go."

"You must really like this place." He's joking, but I wonder—is he impatient?

"Maybe these trial meds work," I say hopefully.

"It's all going to come around, you'll see." He kisses me good-night and departs.

The power goes off shortly after he leaves; the generators have finally run out of gas. In the new silence, I hear the rhythmic sounds of a Christian revival ceremony up the hill. Preaching, singing, weeping. The off-key laments and bass-guitar riffs comfort me. I think of home, and Kai's laughter. I set my cell phone on the pillow next to me, willing it to ring, with Mom on the other end.

A nurse hangs out with me by candlelight until I fall asleep.

* * *

Thursday morning the power is off, and now other equipment is busted, too. A technician is on the way, but I'm not holding my breath. Dad arrives at six a.m. with a bag of buffet goodies, including stale donuts.

"Only the finest at your five-star accommodations," I joke, chomping on the donuts. "Howzit out there?"

"Getting weirder."

Today's paper pokes out of his bag. I point at it. "Anything new?"

"The paper's dubbed it the 'Emerald Orchid.' I guess it does kind of look like a giant Georgia O'Keeffe painting."

I kind of like the name. It reminds me of home. The Big Island is also known as the Orchid Isle. And the green cloud did look like a flower. I wonder what they're calling it in New York. The Big Apple Blossom? "Who cares what they name it? I want to know what it *is*. Can I see the paper?"

"I'd rather you didn't."

I feel my chest rise, my pulse pounding. "Why?"

"Just . . . please? It's nothing."

"The best way to create panic is to tell people not to panic," I snap.

Dad hems and haws. "Fine. Here." He hands me the paper. "Remember, there's no reason to think they're not perfectly safe."

TSUNAMI STRIKES EASTERN SHORES
Damage Reported on All Islands

HONOLULU—The ocean rose as high as 20 feet over a period of hours, sending tsunami waves along O`ahu's Kailua Bay early yesterday morning.

Extensive damage was reported in Kailua and to the piers along O`ahu's eastern side. Speaking on condition of anonymity, a military pilot described tsunami damage on each of the islands between O`ahu and the Big Island yesterday evening, and severe damage along the Big Island's Hamakua Coast in and around Hilo.

Officials have not released specific information.

Theodore Thompson, a seismologist at the University of Hawai`i at Manoa, said the tsunamis are evidence that the green cloud entering the solar system is shedding meteorlike objects capable of striking Earth.

"The timing of the arrival of these large waves could easily correspond with a large meteor impact in the Pacific," he said. "A confirmed meteor impact south of Alaska on Sunday makes this a compelling assumption."

Mr. Thompson declined to speculate on how meteoric activity could disrupt global communications. He said his team was working on several theories.

"Dad! Dad."

He squeezes my shoulder. "They're fine."

"Yeah, but I want to *know* they're fine."

"We're mauka—high up—away from town. We've got a nice garden. We have chickens. Grandpa's with them."

"But Tami doesn't live near us! She doesn't have a garden! If power's out on the Big Island, then won't the tsunami warning system be busted? What about her? What about . . . ?"

"Lei, it's no good to . . . speculate. This won't get us anywhere."

I'm silent, but I want to scream. Not knowing . . . not being able to find out. A simple text is all it would take. *Click, click*, send.

Dad plays with the window slats and moodily wipes sweat off his face. After a few minutes, I grumble, "Knock that off."

"What, is there something in here you're trying to focus on?" he snaps.

"Yeah: calm," I spit back.

Dad freezes. "You know what, Lei, I'm the *textbook definition* of calm."

I burst out laughing. He looks startled, then joins in.

Dad sits down, resting his forehead in his hands. The silence is broken by honking horns and helicopters. Finally, he stands. "I'll be right back, honey."

"I'm sorry, Dad. I . . ."

He strokes my hair. "We need to get home. We should start looking for other ways off this island now, before things—"

"How bad is it out there?"

"I just want to be ahead of the game, that's all." And he's gone.

I stare at a bamboo-framed poster of the Hawaiian Islands on the wall. I try to wrap my head around what Dad said. *Other ways off this island?*

Does he mean finding another airport besides Honolulu International?

The main Hawaiian islands stretch away from each other in the shape of a lazy apostrophe. Hawai`i—the Big Island—is the farthest south and east of the chain. It's bigger than all the other islands put together. I've always thought it looks like a giant arrowhead with the "point" facing east. The islands of Maui, Kaho`olawe, Lāna`i, and Moloka`i are a little to the northwest. It's easy to see how they were a single island in the ancient past. As their volcanoes died and erosion took over, the sea eventually separated them.

O`ahu is next, a ribbon of mountains running through its middle, Honolulu on the western side. It's about two hundred miles from home, as the crow flies. The next islands are Kaua`i and its little neighbor, Ni`ihau. They're the tapered end of the apostrophe, way to the west. It's never really struck me how isolated each island is, or that the State of Hawai`i is so broken up and separated, because airplanes connect the dots.

I bite my lip, wondering.

Other ways off O`ahu?

CHAPTER 7

Dad returns with Dr. Makani. "How are you feeling, Leilani?" the doctor asks.

I try to smile. "Okay."

He checks my blood pressure and pulse. He pauses for a moment and then nods to Dad. "I think you guys should both go back to your hotel."

"What?" I sit upright.

"Go ahead and start your meds again, Leilani. We're going to call this off. The EKG is broken. I'm trying to make sense of your chart from yesterday. I compared it to your records from Hilo—the pattern is totally different—gibberish. They can't get the generators to work, and there's just no point in the two of you roasting in this little room."

"But what if I—"

Dad interrupts my question. "We talked that over, Lei. If

something happens, I can help you through it just as well as any of the nurses here."

"Can you tell me: Was I on the real medication or the placebo?"

"It's a double-blind trial. I don't know the answer to that, Leilani. But I'm guessing the trial medicine was working. You had episodes so easily the first night off your meds, but then nothing once the trial started the next morning."

Dad slips a packaged bite stick into his pocket. Tears well up in my eyes. I wipe them away. I pull out my normal pills and take one. Even though I've missed six doses, and I'm not out of the woods, it feels like a reprieve.

Dad fills out a bunch of release forms while I put on my clothes. When we walk out, it feels like I've gotten time off for good behavior.

The roads seem fine as we drive back into Waikīkī. People got the hint that they're better off staying at home, I suppose. We search for lunch, but everything is closed. I eat an apple and a granola bar from one of Dad's bags. I cheer up as we turn onto Ala Moana Boulevard. Dad has been quiet on the drive. I think he's afraid that I'm mad at him.

"This'll be good," I offer.

"I'm sorry, honey."

"No, seriously. I'm okay. Calling it off . . . it just makes this whole mess feel . . . *real*."

"Leilani, can I be honest with you?"

Here it comes. I know he's been worried, but now it'll be official. "Things are bad, I know."

Dad shakes his head. "It's not that. God, I hope it's not that. I just think they may get worse before they get better. We need to get out of here."

There's a police car at the nearest intersection, but no one is directing cars through the blank lights. Police officers stand in groups every couple of intersections. Most of them look just as purposeless as the few people milling about.

"How are we going to find a flight?" I ask. "Planes aren't even working."

"Well, some planes and helicopters are flying. Whatever's happening to electronics is hit-and-miss. Either way, I'd like to avoid the airport. I looked into the cruise ships that go to Hilo or Kona. There aren't any at port, they're all in Mexico or Alaska. Except one—and it capsized off Kaua'i during the tsunami."

"What?" I freeze. "Is everyone okay?"

"I don't know."

"How many people were on board? How far off shore was it?"

"I don't know. Word of it just reached the island. Maybe the paper will cover it tomorrow."

I'm silent. *Those poor people.*

"I'm hoping we can charter a helicopter. I've been thinking about this. The tour companies—if they aren't already offering inter-island hops, maybe we can convince them to. Or a boat. Find someone around here who'll agree to take us to the Big Island."

"Wait. By *boat*?" I try to imagine sailing from Honolulu

to Hilo. It would take *days* to get home. And the powerful seas are dangerous. "Why? What if flights resume in the next couple days? Our flight would beat us home."

"Lei, I've got to *do* something. It's only going to get harder as more people try to find a way off this island. We have a chance to get ahead of the game."

I take a deep breath, reading between the lines. "You're worried that if we don't go now, we won't ever get home, aren't you?"

Dad won't say anything.

"Dad, I'm not stupid. You've been thinking a lot about this and not telling me anything. You need to bring me in."

He pauses for a long time, then says, "There are a million people on Oʻahu. Ninety-five percent of the food is imported every day. If the planes and boats with the food really have stopped trickling in, well, do the math. Not to mention gas . . ."

I feel dizzy. "We can all eat pineapples till kingdom come," I say, trying to joke.

"That's exactly what we'll be doing, and I'm guessing it'll come by sometime next week." Dad isn't laughing.

"Next week! There's not *that* little food."

"Hon, it's not about when the food runs out. It's about when enough people realize that it's going to."

* * *

We sit in silence as we cross over a canal into Waikīkī, a boat harbor to our right. Sailboats of every type bob along the marina piers. I try to see us on one of them on the open ocean.

We pull into the garage and park near the lobby stairwell. "Good thing we didn't rent that electric, ah?" I joke as he shuts off the engine.

"Naw. I bet it would have worked," he says, but he's just teasing. "Good thing we didn't get a gas-guzzling, supercharged, V-8 tourist magnet. Ah?"

"Whatevah. At least we would have looked good running out of gas."

"I'm just glad we topped it off at Costco. Did you see the lines at the station back there?"

I nod.

In the hotel lobby I learn that the power is on throughout Waikīkī, but the generators will still be required regularly. Crowds surround every wall outlet in an effort to charge endless lines of phones, computers, tablets. The cords of lamps and TVs and coolers are yanked out of the wall. Guests are asked to avoid using the air conditioners and to open their balconies and hallway doors to create a cross breeze on each floor. New signs are posted everywhere, providing instructions and evacuation routes in the event of a tsunami.

Our fancy hotel feels like a Greyhound bus station. *Somebody, please tell me it's all a dream. Make it all stop.* I pick up my pace.

Families pack around the reception counters. Many are checked-out guests returning from the airport, demanding to be put back in their rooms.

"No one is flying *in*, either," one lady complains. "You must have vacancies. Just cancel the new reservations. It's very easy."

72

"We're doing everything we can to sort it out, ma'am. Just be patient. A few of our computers are up, but the records were online, and we're having to manually arrange . . ."

My attention shifts to a young husband trying to calm his wife. ". . . there's nowhere to plug into, Molly."

"I don't know how much longer we can wait." The wife holds a toddler in her arms, and she's almost in tears.

"Just . . ." Her husband glances around in defeat. He's holding on to a device connected to a tiny mask by a coiled hose.

"Excuse me," an older man says. He's guarding a phone plugged into the wall. "Is that a nebulizer? Do you need to use it?"

The parents nod. The mother says, "Our boy has asthma. He hasn't had his treatment today."

"Oh, well, here you go! Why didn't you say something?" The older man yanks his phone charger from the socket. "Use this."

We step into the elevator; the door shuts.

I try to imagine *needing* electricity to take my meds. That poor boy.

The elevator jolts but continues rising. I laugh nervously. "You sure this is a good idea?"

"No. But neither is a seizure in the eighth-floor stairwell."

"Oh." *Why did he have to bring that up?*

Dad and I pack our bags. He occasionally pauses to go out on the lanai, looking out at the sailboats and the yachts in the bay milling about like students in a crowded school hall waiting for the first bell to ring. He's deep in thought.

I examine the water, looking for signs of the tsunami. There's debris washed up on the beach, but no obvious destruction. Lucky for Waikīkī that the east side of the island absorbed most of the wave energy. But what if something happens on *this* side?

A few surfers glide back and forth on the gentle waves, and I can feel what it's like. Cool water. Breeze. Salty taste.

I can find that back on the Big Island, too, without nineteen thousand hotel windows facing me.

I finish zipping my pack, and Dad suggests that we grab one last meal before heading off. I can tell that he's as reluctant to execute this crazy plan as I am.

"I'm starving, Dad, but we have plenny snacks. We can skip it."

"Better to eat now."

Dad and I sit at a cantina near the beachside pools. Both of us face the bay. Any hint of rising waters and we bolt back up to floor twelve.

The surf looks perfect for me. Not too big, not too small, spaced far enough apart to make getting out past the swell easy.

"I should be surfing right now."

"Lei, please."

"You got to surf on this trip."

"Just . . . order something, will you?"

"Dad, I know I wouldn't actually be going out there. I just don't know why you have to get all high and mighty about it."

"How else am I supposed to react? You're an epileptic. Your mom and I breathe into paper bags whenever you surf.

74

Don't you realize that? I never should have taught you how to do it. I should have known . . ."

"What?"

"That you'd fall in love with it, just like your old man."

I cross my arms. "You use the same excuse for not letting me drive. Great."

"Lei!"

I'm silent, staring out at the waves.

"Come on," he says kindly. "Let's eat, okay?"

I open a menu.

There's a note taped on the inside of the first page:

> *Sorry for the inconvenience, but we must*
> *regrettably double the menu prices across the board*
> *in order to remain in operation today.*
> *Mahalo for your understanding,*
> *—Management*

Dad says, "Order anything you want, Lei. Eat up."

"Fine, I'll have two of everything."

"I'm serious," he says. "Meals may get scarce before things improve. Good thing we stocked up at Costco."

At the next table, four men in company polo shirts bark at their waiter for more chips and salsa. The waiter nods at them as he approaches us. A Hawaiian with a battered smile, he musters his best aloha.

Dad says, "Thanks for keeping things running for yet another day. I hope those fellows are tipping you well."

The waiter smiles. "*Mahalo*, sir."

Dad says, "We'll start with your biggest plate of nachos, and a *liliko`i* and mango margarita."

I order a hearty carnitas meal. We sit back and watch families play in the long string of pools. The kids are having a blast. The parents all look like they're Bill Murray caught in *Groundhog Day.*

When does a vacation in paradise start to grow old?

Today, apparently.

There are even more yachts anchored in the bay now, like some sort of Pacific fleet of millionaires has arrived to launch a surprise attack on Honolulu. A military helicopter buzzes low on its way toward Pearl Harbor.

"We should try those yachters," I say.

"Sounds good. I hope we can figure something out without too much hassle."

The four men are loud enough to overhear.

"That was no presidential bunker. He would have had a room set up to look like the Oval Office, if he were down in some compound. Did you see that curtain? Thrown up to keep us from knowing he was in a cave."

"Why does he get to run off to safety while we're left to . . . pound mai tais on the beach?"

They all laugh.

"He knew it was going to happen as early as Sunday night, right? Canceled big events in Miami."

"What if China has some new bug they used to coordinate a satellite attack? They could have been planning it for years."

"Or an electromagnetic pulse. But none of that explains a tsunami."

"Could nuclear bombs interfere with electronics and cause an earthquake?"

"I don't know. That doesn't sound right, either, though. We still have hair."

"There was the meteor. And lots of falling stars the past few nights. Maybe we're going through an asteroid belt, like the *Millennium Falcon*."

"Still doesn't explain the electronics."

"No. Dark matter? A black hole? Or a Stargate! Alien invasion. The green haze is spaceship exhaust."

"We're not in a movie, pal. I just want to get on a plane. I'm ready to empty my pockets to one of those boats over there."

"And how many do you think could make it twenty-five hundred miles to the mainland without GPS?"

"How could you miss it? Point east and go."

"With what fuel?" one snaps. "You going to help crew a sailboat?"

"Sure!"

"I'd rather take my chances with a native. Sail by the stars. If they could leave Tahiti a thousand years ago and hit Hawai`i on a canoe, my money's on the locals."

Our waiter arrives at their table. He drops off another round of mai tais and chips, saying, "Better watch out. What makes you think the 'natives' would help you get anywhere?" He's smiling.

The other three rock with laughter.

The first guy isn't laughing. "Jesus, what is this? Where's your manager?"

"Probably dealing with another asshole. Get your own chips next time. They're right over there." He leaves, smiling.

"Jerk!" the guy shouts.

I share a stunned look with Dad. "Just ignore them," he says. "Let's move."

We choose another table. I stare at the sea, thinking about the first Hawaiians, the ones who arrived from Tahiti, like the guy mentioned. Why did they come here? Why did they leave home? How scary the voyage must have been—and how miraculous when they found these shores.

The waiter brings us nachos and Dad's margarita. Dad gives him a high five and we all share a knowing smile.

It is a good thing.

"What?" I ask Dad.

"Huh?"

"Didn't you say something?"

He shakes his head. "No."

I rub my temples with my elbows propped on the table.

"Everything cool, hon?"

"Yeah. I'm just . . . I've been cooped up for too long."

"I know, hon. Maybe we can catch a giant wave all the way back to Hilo."

"Dad, what if they're right? What if things *never* get better?"

Dad lowers his nacho. He looks away, toward the

sailboats gathered on the bay. His neck muscles are tight as harp strings.

I belong here, and I am well. It is almost ready to come out.

I freeze. "What'd you say?"

Dad eyes me sternly.

I can feel it coming, but I can't speak to warn him. He continues as if everything is normal, but my flickering mind garbles his words. "Lei, it's tay woo early to be tax like that. Those guys are dunk. Don't let your imag—"

These islands are here for me, and I crave what they will offer. It is a good thing.

Strange trees rustle in a warm evening breeze, their shadows dancing over a mottled, black-and-white beach. Waves lap the shore, cresting gently over shelves of ropy, cooled earth. I tighten the luffing sail and push closer and closer to the land, where sleeping creatures await, oblivious to me, the newcomer, and to the transformation that sweeps behind me, the pigs and dogs and rats and breadfruit that will soon march up the dark slopes and sweep away the old world, leaving something distorted in its place.

I have dreamt of these shores. I was born here, but I slipped away. Now I have reached the shallows, at long last, guided across the endless waters by ancient stars.

A rumble grows beneath the land. I loosen the mainsheet, feeling the weight of the mountain's unrest. It trembles, vomiting toxic fire. But I will not be held at bay. My destiny is laid out before me. I have fled a troubled shore countless stretches away, restless, in search of adventure. Outcast, forced to flee. Famished and ill, in need of a new land to bleed.

I am Leilani. Spellbound, I blossom.

CHAPTER 8

I'm dizzy. I don't know where I am.

Someone's talking to me. Who is he? What's happening?

Dad. I focus now. Hotel room. A seizure. *Just relax, let it all come back.*

I close my eyes.

"What time is it?" I ask.

"It's Friday night, hon. Happy May Day."

"*Friday?*" Over twenty-four hours. A new record. "Did those test meds backfire?"

"What hasn't, these days? Lei, here. You've missed a day."

He hands me a pill and a glass of water. "Great."

"I tried to get you to take them. Sorry. Almost drowned you."

"What's wrong with me? Weren't you worried?"

"Yes! You had a big one. Two, actually, I think. But your breathing and pulse were fine. What could I do?"

"Yeah." I can hear generators humming in the near distance.

"You feel better now?"

"Weird dreams. I never dream during seizures. Remind me not to sign up to be a lab rat again. I'm . . . What's going on?" I swallow my medicine and wade through the fog in my mind. We're still in a hotel room. My head hurts, and I feel nauseated. "Is everything better?"

"Out there? No."

"We're supposed to fly home tomorrow."

"No flights. More stuff's on the fritz now. Whatever's happening is getting worse. People are wising up, too. We've officially missed the early-bird special."

My seizures have ruined Dad's plans. "I'm sorry."

"No. Don't be. We'll figure it out. In the morning. Let's try to sleep some more. You may feel pretty rested at this point, but tomorrow we need to pick up where we left off."

"I love you, Dad."

He hugs me. "We'll get through it, okay? Tomorrow we head home."

"Yeah, okay."

One way or another, we're going back to our family.

* * *

I awake in the morning with a clear mind and no nausea. Hungry. I rummage through Dad's cache of goodies and scarf down an apple and some granola bars. Even though

I've safely eaten this same brand for ages, I check the labels for aspartame. Dad moves quickly to pack, so I pick up my pace.

Dad snatches the *Honolulu Star-Advertiser* from the door while I brush my teeth and pack. Dad laughs as he holds the paper. It's only four pages long, like my high school newspaper.

A full-page photo displays giant tongues of flame leaping from the ruins of a military helicopter crashed into the side of UH Manoa's Aloha Stadium, just a couple miles from here. There are photos of gridlocked traffic, crowds at the airport, and congested gasoline-distribution plants with no gas to distribute. The articles report that there is no communication with the outside world. The National Guard and coast guard have been deployed throughout the islands. Residents have been told to remain at home to alleviate traffic and conserve resources. Oil tankers, a crippled cruise ship, and other cargo ships have trickled in, but harbors are clogging as fewer and fewer ships leave port. Tourists have swarmed the ports looking for passage; there are far too few seaworthy vessels to accommodate them all. Only a few sentences about the cruise ship that capsized near Kaua`i. Six hundred passengers. Number of survivors unknown. People in Līhu`e watched it slowly sink a mile offshore in the hours after the tsunami. The sea was too wild to attempt a rescue.

It leaves me short of breath and speechless. But the worst part: there's nothing in the paper about the Big Island.

"Look at this." Dad reads:

WAIKĪKĪ—Amid concerns about sanitation, food shortages, power supplies, and housing, a plan to relocate tourists is in the works.

The draft plan would send some tourists to Marine Corps Base Hawai`i at Kāne`ohe Bay and could eventually put them on navy ships headed for the West Coast.

"The airport and many of O`ahu's hotels and resorts simply won't have the capacity to safely house guests for much longer," said army spokesperson Stephen Tybert. "The hard fact is that everyone's going to be asked to make sacrifices if this continues."

Waikīkī may also have to be closed if the situation progresses, officials said. Already police and military have been sent to protect O`ahu's tourism infrastructure in the event that nonresidents are relocated.

"Hello!" Dad says. "Let's set up concentration camps for fifty thousand fat rednecks in Hawaiian shirts. Welcome to paradise! That'll boost morale around here."

"Makes sense to me," I say. "The natives *are* growing restless. That article is about making *locals* happy."

Dad pauses. "You're right," he says. "The governor is still thinking about votes. Screw the tourists."

I can feel myself glowing at Dad's praise as I put on my last clean shirt, my favorite cami, and white cargo shorts, looped with a campy belt that I should have stopped loving when I was twelve.

We put on our packs and share the duffels and tote bags. We file into the lobby, right into an agitated crowd. People are pacing back and forth, looking at the ground or shaking their heads, digging ruts into the filthy marble tiles. Some weep. Others are shoving each other near one of the crowded wall outlets, holding phone chargers in clenched fists.

A door bursts open and a flock of hotel employees stampedes into the lobby.

Guests surround them in an angry mob. Shouting fills the air. The employees march toward the main doors. Dad pulls me inside the circle of his arm. A fistfight breaks out near the grand piano. Guests kick at the bolted double doors of the restaurant, pour behind the reception counter. A vase is swept to the floor and shatters.

I stare. A woman is shoved our way, and her flailing arm hits me in the face. My nose starts to bleed.

"Leilani." Dad tugs me into the open elevator and pounds the close button. The doors shut. We're alone with a bald guy.

"You all right?"

"Yeah." I'm pinching my nose, but blood drips onto my favorite camisole.

"Oh, man," Dad says.

I can't believe this.

"Here." The bald guy fumbles through a pocket and pulls out a handkerchief. Loose change spills to the floor. "It's clean. Keep it."

"Thanks," I honk, holding my head back.

"Crazy out there, eh?" he says, helping to position the kerchief on my nose. "Like we're in some twisted game show. Smile! You're on *Cannibal Camera!*"

"People are starting to lose it." Dad ducks to collect the man's change. "Thanks for your help."

"No prob. Forget the coins, man."

Dad picks them up anyway and gives them to the man, who winks his appreciation. "All right, time to raid the gumball machine."

In the parking garage, brochures and flyers line the wall. Dad studies them and stuffs brochures into the bags of food draped over his shoulders. We hurry to our car and rush out of the garage.

And just like that, we're caught in moderate traffic along Ala Moana Boulevard. The sky's a bit hazy this morning—weird for Hawai`i. But other than trash piled all around, the street looks rather normal. I can't quite fathom how ordinary it feels.

We sit in silence as we cross over a canal out of Waikīkī, a boat harbor to our left. It's mostly empty, in stark contrast to a couple days ago. Still, sailboats of every type bob along the marina piers. I try to see us on one of them on the open ocean and anxiety stabs my stomach.

"Look through those brochures," Dad instructs me. "Find out which of the helicopter tours leave from airstrips other than Honolulu International. I'm not even going to go near there."

I hesitate.

"Just do it, Lei."

I scan the flyers. "Two companies leave from Kalaeloa Airport. That's past Pearl Harbor."

"That's it?" Dad looks very discouraged.

"Unless you want to brave the main airport."

"No. Kalaeloa." Dad heads for the main highway.

Up ahead, a strip mall with a grocery store swarms with looters. I gasp, sinking into my seat. Food and clothing and appliances tumble from overstuffed shopping carts, and other people quickly sweep up the items. Almost everyone is armed with sticks, bats, or machetes. Some sport shotguns. I even spy a harpoon and a fishing spear.

Dad pushes past, eyes forward and jaw clenched. He has to drive slowly through a crowd milling in the street. My eyes are glued to the spectacle. Oddly, it looks as if everyone is having fun; lots of smiles. One guy is strumming a ukulele. I recognize an expression I've seen many times on Kai's face: the triumph and wonder of getting away with something. These people seem to be looting just because they can, rejoicing in their mischievousness.

The crowd bangs on the outside of our car. I shrink into my seat, gripping the cushion. The love taps grow steadily more intense . . . and then we're through. Dad accelerates and lets out a deep breath.

"Wow. This is really happening," he says.

"They were having so much fun."

"Yeah, but this won't be a game to anybody for much longer."

We merge onto the highway and into bumper-to-bumper traffic. *Where's everyone going?* Drive three hours in any direction and you end up right where you started.

"Dad, I'm kind of scared."

"Me too, honey."

"I really miss Kai and Mom."

"Me too."

"Grandpa."

"I know."

"But—the Big Island is more rural. So this same stuff isn't happening over there."

Dad is quiet. "Right. They're safer than we are."

Something bothers me. *Safer?* I figure out my worry right away. "But they don't love haoles. If people are going nuts . . . It kills me to say it, but maybe *we're* safer *here.*"

"You're doing it again."

"Doing what?"

"Talking about haoles and Hilo."

I shrug.

"It's not *that* bad, is it? I've never really felt it."

I scoff.

"How badly are you bullied back there, Lei?"

I stare at him. He really doesn't get it. It's not his fault; I only talk to Grandpa about it. "Dad, why do you think all the other professors at the U send their kids to private school?"

His answer is practiced. "They're cop-outs. They have no faith in the public schools. . . ."

"Dad. It's because their kids *beg* them. To get away from the bullies."

"Ah." Dad frowns. He's quiet for a while, driving. "We'll figure something out. Maybe talk to Grandpa about it."

I roll my eyes.

"Be that as it may, back to the original point: we'll be much better off at home than here. Mom and Kai and Grandpa are *fine*. And we'll be back there before we know it, okay?"

"Yeah." It's home. That's all that matters.

As we pass the junction with the road that heads over the mountains toward Kailua and the Marine Corps Base, I spy six army buses caravanning up the green slope like a great caterpillar assaulting the world's biggest leaf. They're the first vehicles I've seen that seem to have a purpose: to move people away from Honolulu, and fast.

Maybe we should be on one of those buses.

The Kalaeloa Airport is bursting at the seams; there's nowhere to park. We're sucked into a vortex of aimlessly circling traffic. Dad fumes. I stay quiet. All the parking lots have broken barrier arms at their entrances and exits, but there are security guards to stop traffic.

Finally, Dad double-parks along a maintenance alley a quarter of a mile away from the terminal. "Let's go. Grab your stuff."

"Wait, we're just going to leave the car parked like this?"

"Yes." He hands me a bag.

We enter the terminal with our bags draped around us. Dad muscles through the crowd and we wedge ourselves close enough to the counter to hear a clerk talking to the guy ahead of us.

"We're already booked up through Tuesday morning."

"Doesn't matter. Put us down."

"That'll be three thousand. Cash."

"What?"

"Each. That's three thousand each."

"Here," the man says. He leans over the counter and passes the clerk a watch. The clerk inspects the watch closely. He jots down the man's information. The customer now has a bright tan line on his wrist.

"Three thousand *each*?" I gasp.

Dad shakes his head. "Hey," he shouts over to the clerk. "We're trying to get to Hilo."

"We don't fly to the Big Island. Moloka`i's the best we can do. We're booked up through Tuesday. We're charging—"

"Yeah, yeah." Dad waves him off. "What do you mean you're booked through Tuesday? There's a half dozen choppers sitting on the pad right now!"

"Most of those have tungsten circuit boards. Fried. Besides, the military is restricting our airspace. It won't be long before they commandeer our whole fleet and gut our molybdenum parts. Now, you have cash?"

Dad grimaces. The clerk turns to another couple.

"You should go to the Marine Corp Base," someone sitting against the wall says to us. He's also sporting a strong tan line on his wrist. "I hear they're collecting folks for transport. You're in much better shape than the people who want to get back to the mainland. A few of the army planes work; they're always landing in Hilo. You could hitch a ride on a cargo flight and be home in time for dinner."

I perk up, but Dad frowns. "And what's your plan?"

"I'm booked on a flight to Kaua`i later this evening. I've been here for two days."

Dad gives me a grave look. "I don't like it, but he may be right. Maybe we should head over the mountain to Kāne`ohe."

The guy who was ahead of us in line overhears and moves closer. "No, no. Bad idea. I just escaped from there."

"What do you mean?"

"They're not flying a damn soul anywhere. I've been trying to get to Maui since Tuesday morning. I left Honolulu International on the first army bus Wednesday night. And I waited, and waited. Meanwhile droves of tourists are filling up their gyms and soccer fields. If you think this place is a zoo . . ."

"They're . . . they're just shuffling people around?"

"It's like a refugee camp over there. I wasn't supposed to leave. No one is. I escaped."

"What?" Dad says incredulously.

"If they're trying to help, why are they limiting private copter travel?" the escapee asks. "Every day the Orchid hangs there, taunting us, the panic multiplies by ten. We all know this island's in deep trouble. They're just collecting homeless people to keep us from going apeshit. They didn't even evacuate for the tsunami. The military's interests are not ours. They couldn't give a rat's ass how long it takes you and your daughter to get to Hilo. The gas has stopped arriving, you know. What, you think they're going to expend all the fuel that's left to schlep around civilian families?"

Dad hangs his head, studying his shoes.

"I don't know. Maybe transport flights will start. But I was there. If you want to be back home in a couple days, or weeks—not months—I suggest you stay the hell away from the military."

Weeks? Months? I ball my hands into fists around the duffel bags I'm carrying.

"Well, dammit, what else are we supposed to do?" Dad says.

The man shrugs. "You could always try one of the ferry companies."

The Kaua`i-bound listener guffaws. Dad slouches. We're all in on the bad joke: it's been years since ferry companies ran between the islands. Environmental lawsuits and bad politics shut them down. And the water's too rough.

The jokester pats Dad on the shoulder. "Hey, I've helped you all I can. That watch will have to get me and my wife out of here. Best damned investment I ever made. We may still be in the same boat as you, if the army siphons off private fuel. Same boat. Ha ha. Ain't that the truth!" The man drifts away.

We stand and stare at the floor. There's a lump in my throat threatening to burst free. I choke it down.

Home. I just want to be home.

"Come on, Lei." Dad elbows me. "This isn't going to work."

We return to the car with all of our belongings. Our rental's almost boxed in to its parking spot. Dad jumps into the driver's seat. "You okay?" he asks, wiping sweat off his brow.

"I'm fine. You?"

Dad turns on the car and cranks up the AC. He bounces

in his seat for a second and then pounds the steering wheel. "Dammit!" he shouts. "Son of a bitch!" He wipes his forehead and leans close to the air vent.

I don't say anything. He shifts the car into drive and bangs out a ten-point exit. We leave the airport.

He turns the AC off and rolls down the windows. "*Everyone* wants to be voted off the island."

"I'm really sorry," I croak.

"No. Stop. That's not what I meant. Hindsight's always twenty-twenty, right? We would have been acting crazy if we had upped and fled a couple days ago. We may be crazy now. All of this may still end at any moment."

And what? I think. *We all just wake up and look around at each other and scratch our heads? We just agree to forget this ever happened? I wasn't really robbing a grocery store at gunpoint. Can I have my Rolex back?*

We drive in silence. On our way back into Honolulu, we pass by Pearl Harbor again. A battleship and an aircraft carrier creep toward the bay from the open ocean.

"Maybe they know what's really happening," I say. "They're in contact with the mainland, and they're just not telling anyone."

"I can guarantee you that they have a good idea what's *going* to happen."

"I wonder if that carrier is coming from the mainland."

"A little soon for that, maybe. They're probably returning to port from somewhere here in the Pacific." Dad is silent for a while, but then he says, "I doubt they know what's happened. It's been five days. The panic is coming fast. If the government knew what this Emerald Orchid was about, they would have announced when things would be returning to normal, to keep everyone calm. If they knew things weren't going to get better, they would have declared martial law by now."

"What's that?"

"When the military says, 'We're in charge now, folks! Fall in line! What's that you say? You have *rights?* No, you don't!'"

"Sounds like they're already doing things their own way," I point out.

"Ten percent of this island is armed forces. That guy who told us to stay away from there is totally right. He was an angel come from heaven. We just avoided a colossal mistake."

My guess is that while all of these terrible scenarios *could* happen, the military is filled with normal people, in the end. People like Grandpa. They're *Americans*, after all. They're not going to be monsters.

Right?

CHAPTER 9

We turn back into Waikīkī shaken. Silent. We're going to see if anyone will take us to the Big Island on a yacht or sailboat.

It's either that or take up paddling.

The Pacific Ocean builds so much force between Alaska and here. All that power grows and grows, pushed by strong winds, pulled by the moon, fed by currents, and then it hits these islands in the middle of nowhere. The only place that energy has to flow is between the islands. You don't mess with that power unless you know what you're doing.

Really strong athletes sometimes row from Moloka`i to O`ahu—Grandpa did it once, long before I was born. But the current's in their favor. No one rows in the direction we need to go. Dad once said we'd need tons of training before attempting something like that.

We approach a park swarming with pedestrians, cyclists, and clogged traffic, prophets with placards commanding *Repent*, and large prayer circles. Police and National Guardsmen patrol. Makeshift canvas tents have been set up in every direction, offering medical care, palm readings, cash for gold, emergency kits, political flyers, dried ahi, poi. Three separate guys are selling toilet paper for five bucks a roll, and people are buying. One guy is even selling silk-screened T-shirts of the Emerald Orchid. Someone who was trying to sell guns out of the back of his truck has been pinned to the ground by guardsmen. He screams about his Second Amendment rights. The strumming of ukuleles and the sound of singing float from beneath several shady banyan trees.

A grizzly old man wearing a placard covered with scribbled biblical passages catches my gaze and shouts as he reads from the last pages of his Bible.

"'When the Lamb opened the fourth seal, I heard the voice of the fourth living creature say, "Come and see!" I looked, and there before me was a horse whose color was pale green! Its rider was named Death, and Hades was following close behind.'"

He drops the Bible to his side and holds a cross. "Repent, you forsaken! You sinners! It all comes to pass! The horsemen ride. Conquest, civil war, famine, death! The pale green horse rears up to trample you!"

I shrink away even though he's on the other side of the street.

"Tune him out, Lei." Dad squeezes my hand.

"What if he's right, Dad?"

"About what?"

"I don't know. The end of the world . . ."

"Really? Hon—"

I interrupt. "No, I'm serious. Why is this happening? Why would God let this happen?"

Dad believes in God, but he has no patience for organized religion. He wants us to meditate each night before dinner, but he doesn't make us do it a certain way. I believe in God, but I've found sanctuary in the gods of Hawai`i. I pray and I learn the chants and I talk to them. Sometimes, on the wind and in the waves, He—*they*—will whisper back.

Dad twists in his seat. "Can I get back to you on that, Lei?"

"I'm serious."

"So am I. The truth is I don't know. I've been thinking about it. I'll get back to you, okay? Promise."

A thunderous crack startles me. I scream and jerk backward. The windshield on my side has shattered into a spiderweb. Dad screeches to a halt. A large cinder block tumbles from the hood.

"Jesus," Dad says. "Are you all right?"

"I'm fine. What the . . . ?"

Something strikes the car from behind. We both turn. A second cinder block slides off the hatchback onto the street. I hear cackling and whoops of delight from above.

Someone's bombarding us from the trees. "Dad, go!" I bark.

He punches the gas and our Civic peels away.

"What was that about?" My heart is pounding.

Dad races down the hill, turns a corner, parks along a curb. "I'll take that as a lesson." He jumps out of the car, opens the hatch, and rummages through his backpack. When he returns to the driver's seat, his camping utility knife is open. I freeze in surprise. *What are you going to do to them?* But he uses the blade to scrape the two bar codes off either side of the windshield.

I get what he's doing.

Every rental car in Hawai`i can be identified by white bar codes on the windshield. Tami is good at pointing them out each time we go surfing. If we were the wrong type of people, we could make a killing with all the cameras and wallets that we know are hidden below that towel cleverly placed in the footwell.

"You're going to have to pay a fine for removing that."

Dad peels back the last of the stickers. "They can have my Timex." He folds up the knife and quickly drives away.

I can't see anything out of the windshield now. The car is trashed. "This wouldn't be another one of those 'hindsight' moments, would it?"

Dad laughs. "There's nothing twenty-twenty about the state of this windshield."

I clench my teeth. *So much for feeling welcome on O`ahu.*

Dad parks illegally along the seawall.

"Should I wait here?" I ask nervously.

"No. We stick close together."

I jump out of the car. I reach for my pack, but Dad stops

me. "There's too much. Let's find a ride first," he suggests. He stuffs our packs into the trunk with the rest of our bags, glancing around.

"But what if we . . . ?"

"If there's no time, we'll leave it. But I bet our hosts will be able to spare two minutes for the extra food."

I fish out my meds and zip them into my pocket before he closes the trunk.

Ahead of us along the curb, a man and his son are siphoning gas out of a pickup truck. Dad watches them and then darts off to a sidewalk planter.

He returns with a few `a`a lava rocks, opens the gas tank, and uses one rock to hammer another one into the shaft until it's firmly jammed into place. He leaves the flap open as an obvious sign of uselessness to others.

We approach the marina. The sky is hazier than it was in the morning. It's almost like an orange filter has been placed over the sun. "Is there a forest fire around here?" I ask.

Dad pauses, studies the sky. "Let's hope so." He picks up his pace.

The boats are moored all along the long rows of piers. Dozens of groups of people move along the docks busily.

"Lei, I'm making this up as we go. Feel free to offer suggestions."

Okay, I think. But I've got nothing.

We step onto the wharf. There could be as many as two hundred sailboats. "Should we split up?" I ask. "Each take an end?"

Dad agonizes, finally shakes his head. "No. We're not separating. We'll just have to move quickly."

The first ten sailboats are far apart and vacant. Only one of them is small enough not to require a crew. "Maybe we should just take it."

"Don't tempt me. But I know enough about sailing to know that I don't know enough."

At the end of the next pier, someone emerges on a top deck just as we walk past. He steps to the edge of his boat and urinates into the water. Dad pauses, embarrassed.

The sailor doesn't let him begin. "Not interested. Unless you come with a barrel of rum, and when I say barrel, I mean a goddam oil drum."

The rest of that pier is empty.

We walk along the next pier. A family of three exits as we enter. I meet the eyes of the mother, who holds a baby, and then we quickly look away.

Dad gazes ahead, measuring our prospects. Only fifteen boats bob at their moorings. He pats me on the shoulder and marches forward. We start a conversation with two captains, but both of them tell us that they're already full.

"Maybe they'll take us if we show them all our food," I whisper.

Dad stops. "You keep quiet about that food."

On the next pier we speak with a guy looking for crew. "We're sailing for Maui come morning. But I could use another deckhand. I'll take you both if you're worth your weight. Do you sail?"

"Yes," Dad lies.

The man throws Dad a rope. "Tie me a sheet bend."

Dad catches the rope and smiles awkwardly. "Does it have another name? I'm good with knots; I just don't recognize the term."

The guy shakes his head. "If you sail, you know that knot."

Dad hangs his head for a second. I can't look.

"I'm a quick learner," Dad says. "We both are. We'll carry our own wei—"

"So am I." The yachter snatches back his rope. "The waters between these islands kill. This boat's no toy. We don't have room for errors or time for training. Sorry." He strides up his boat ramp.

Dad mutters.

Three boats farther along the pier, a sailor says that he would be happy to have us on board, but he's sailing for Kaua`i, the opposite direction from the Big Island. He tells us about Rocky, who's heading for Puerto Vallarta tomorrow. "Maybe he'll offer to drop you off on his way out to sea."

"Fingers crossed, Lei," Dad says. "We may have to find another marina out of town if this doesn't work."

We spot the boat from a short distance and jog over to it. An older haole man with curly white hair and bronze skin stands shirtless upon the prow. He's tall and skinny, but his arm muscles are big. He wears glasses, and the left lens is masked by a fitted eye patch. An older man, just as tanned, sits quietly at the tiller.

"Are you Rocky?" Dad asks.

The man with the eye patch grins briefly. "Where you going, and what's in it for me?"

"My daughter and I need to get back home to Hilo."

"Hilo! Naw, I'm not going that way. Water on that side will eat you alive. Rogue wave's always capsizing ships. No way."

"We'll take Kona side. Just . . . can you get us to the Big Island?"

"When we set sail, it's for Mexico. I'm not going close to shore over there. Get another twenty people like you screaming for passage? Forget it."

Rocky's gaze has drifted from Dad over to me.

"Can you swim?" he asks me.

I nod. He looks me up and down. His good eye pauses on my chest. I fold my arms and look down.

"I could swing close enough for you jump off. You could take your chances on reaching shore."

"That's fine," Dad answers. "I'm sure we could make that work."

"Wha' do I get for it? For the trouble?" He studies me. He turns briefly toward his friend at the tiller, and then his eye is right back on me.

There's a long pause.

Dad says, "I can write you a check. I can promise to send you—"

"No," Rocky says, eye on me. I take a step closer to Dad. "No checks. I'm not interested in Monopoly money."

I think of Mom and Kai, and my gut turns. We can't afford to let this opportunity fall apart. I squeeze Dad's upper arm and say, "I . . . I have a really nice laptop computer." My voice betrays my nerves. "We also have . . . top-notch climbing gear. You can keep our bags, too. They're good back-packing bags."

"You have climbing gear," Rocky says to me. "You want to give me your computer. That's somethin', innit, Nelson?"

The other guy nods. He's whittling a stick with a large knife. He watches me, too, but looks away each time I meet his gaze.

"Does the gear come with lessons? Gonna strap me in?" He puts one foot forward and performs an awkward little grind, and his eye drifts from my chest . . . lower.

Gross. My skin is crawling. My grip around Dad's arm tightens, and I shrink back.

Dad steps in front of me. He stares at the ground, and then he raises his chin, looking directly at Rocky. "Forget it. We'll keep looking."

"Hey, no. We're just teasing," laughs Rocky. "We're gonna be swinging by there anyway, right? Soon as Don shows up with stuffs, we can go. Leave in the morning."

"Dad," I say.

He squeezes my shoulder and I know he wants me to stay quiet.

"No, thanks, Rocky." We turn and walk away.

"Then stay here an' rot!" he calls over to us. "No one else is gonna help you without a price. We ain't askin' much!"

He didn't just say that. Kill me now.

Dad and I pick up our pace. We arrive at the promenade at the entrance to the marina, and Dad sits down on a bench.

He wipes sweat off his brow and his untamed new beard with the base of his T-shirt.

"What a nightmare," he mutters. "I don't . . . I don't know what to do." His voice rises.

I can't stand to see him so helpless. "This almost worked," I say. "It was a good idea. Come on; we can find other places to check."

He offers me a forced smile.

"Hey! HEY! NO!" A stocky man with a potbelly and a tight polo shirt thunders down the promenade from the street. He waves a pistol as he shouts. Dad instinctively shields me as the man runs past us. "Stop. STOP THAT! RIGHT NOW!"

A man and a woman jump out of the way as the runner barrels past them, turning onto a narrow dock. At the end of the dock, a young man in a tank top pushes an eighteen-foot sailboat out into the water and leaps on board. Another man yanks frantically at the rip cord of the boat's outboard motor. The boat turns slowly away from the dock.

The man with the gun reaches the end of the dock. "GET OFF MY BOAT! NOW!"

The thieves duck low, the motor roars to life, and the boat lurches forward. The man fires his gun four times. The skull of one thief pops on one side, spraying a shower of blood against the boat's mainsail. The body crumples forward. The boat veers at full throttle and plows into another sailboat.

The gunman lowers his arm and stands still as a statue. The second thief dives into the water and splashes away.

Meanwhile, the outboard motor is still on, groaning with effort as it wedges the boat between the neighboring sailboat and dock.

Large clumps of blood-soaked brain matter slide down the white canvas of the sail. I let out a whimper.

"Lei, come on." Dad tugs on my sleeve.

My whimper slowly rises. My heart is pounding in my chest. I feel short of breath. Dad says something, but the words don't make any sense. I feel like I'm underwater. It rushes at me this time.

It is a good thing. At last, I am ready. I may begin.

The bright sunlight flickers. "Oh, no. Dad . . . ," I moan. And then I'm

May the light of the gods dawn on me like the rising sun. . . . Come to me like the creeping of lava, and may this sacred ceremony of the *ali`i* bring me meditation and release.

"Lie down, honey. You're fine. Everything's going to be okay."

Dad's left hand is wrapped in a white hotel hand towel that has grown red with bloo

This is right. I am here. It is time. And this one spits fire. It oozes the heat. This one has not warmed before. I will linger, then, as I have done on other shores, and we both shall have our fill.

feeling? Better? Keep resting, Lei." Dad wipes the sweat off my brow. His left hand is still wrapped in a towel. White. I turn and grope for the sheets. The sun is shining in through a crack in the long drapes. The room feels as stuffy as a sauna, but I'm so cold. So col

I can feel it slipping. This is my privilege. This is my purpose.

I sit up and rub my eyes. It's dark. Our hotel room. The curtains are pushed aside and the door to the balcony is wide open. A gentle breeze whispers across the hairs of my arms. I can hear sirens, ubiquitous like coqui frogs, strangely reminding me of home. Distant shouts. Pops that I now recognize as gunfire. Dad sits on the lanai and faces the ocean. The moon is nearly full and the sky glows a dark blue with tendrils of green behind almost-white clouds. I see a shooting star race beyond the horizon. There are only half a dozen boats in the bay.

I approach silently. I'm almost outside when Dad notices me. He springs to his feet. "Hi," he says gently. "You sleep like a teenager."

"Hi." I look down.

"How are you doing?" he asks.

"I feel okay. But I'm *starving*. What time is it?"

"Late. Sunday."

Another long one. I'm used to being out for twelve hours or so. But a day and a half?

"You've had two seizures since the marina. Do you remember the marina?"

The image of that man's head spraying open, and the blood-smeared sail, will never leave my mind. "Yes. But nothing since then." Tears well up in my eyes. I brush them aside but they keep coming. I let them.

Dad embraces me. "You're okay, Lei. It's all over. You're fine."

"How'd we get back here?"

"I carried you. Someone at the marina helped us to the car. I got you up here myself. It was a quarter to noon, so the key card still worked. Haven't left since."

"What happened to your hand?" He's only hugging me with his right arm. I remember seeing blood.

He hesitates to answer. "Don't worry about it, sweetie. It's nothing."

"Did I bite you?" Panic wells up. *Did I bite his fingers when he was trying to keep me from choking?*

"It's nothing. Please."

"HOW BAD IS IT? What'd I do?"

He quickly unwraps the towel around his hand to show me. "Relax, honey! It's not a big deal, see? See?"

I examine his hand. The first two fingers are cut near the second knuckles. "I'm so sorry, Daddy. I'm so sorry."

"Stop it, Lei. I'm okay. Please, relax. Go back to bed. We're getting out of here in the morning. Keep resting up."

I step out onto the lanai and take a deep breath. No sound of generators. But there are sirens everywhere. Shouting. Car alarms. I look right, toward downtown, and see at least three separate fires billowing black smoke into the night.

"What happened?"

"It's started. The looting. Everything. Lei, please. Get some more sleep. We leave here tomorrow."

"Okay." As I turn to enter the room, I notice silent lightning bolts infrequently flashing across the petals of the Emerald Orchid.

"Dad, are you seeing this?"

He pats my shoulder. "The atmosphere is putting on a hell of a show."

"*Why?*"

"I haven't the slightest idea." *I'm stoking his anxiety,* I realize, and I silently step back inside.

"Eat something real quick," he suggests. "Take your meds."

I can't look at him. I can't bear to see his kindness and patience.

The bathroom light won't turn on, so I use my cell phone to see what I'm doing. *At least it's good for that much.* I shake a pill into my hand and attempt to turn on the faucet. Nothing.

"Water doesn't run anymore. Try the minibar," Dad suggests from the door. "Grab a candy bar while you're at it. It's on the house."

Our backpacks and other bags are arranged neatly in one corner of the room. Heaped beside them in a pile are my computer, our snorkeling gear, my schoolwork, and Dad's thick folders of graded exams among the now-useless junk. Dad's been busy while I was out. I wonder how many times he idly rifled through the bags, endlessly organizing and reorganizing our food and gear while he waited for me to wake up.

"Did you pack my Hawaiiana book?"

"It's in your bag. Don't worry."

I wonder what it must have been like for him to haul me off the pier and get me safely back to the hotel in the first place.

"Thank you, Dad."

"For what?"

"For everything."

He smiles. "Eat up, hon. You're wasting away. Then back to bed. Okay?"

I take a few moments to eat a Snickers and a bag of corn chips. I wash down my evening pill with a can of warm cola, and then I drift back to sleep.

CHAPTER 10

A piercing buzz rockets through my ears. White, flashing lights batter my eyelids. *Oh, no, again? Already?*

"Leilani, wake up! Come on." I can barely hear words over the buzz.

I'm being gently shaken. Dad is standing over me. It's still dark, but white lights flicker on and off at regular intervals. The lanai door is wide open, and a gentle breeze soothes my sweaty face. I hear nothing but the ungodly alarm. *A fire alarm?*

"Time to go," he says. "Now!"

I sit up, scrambling up the muddy walls of the dark, murky pit where my mind has crouched. "What time is it? What *day?*"

"Nearly five o'clock Monday morning." Dad hands me some clothes. "Come on. The bags are ready. We just have to get down to the car."

"Is there really a fire?" I pull on the shorts and T-shirt he's thrust upon me.

"Yes. They've been torching things up and down the beach all night."

What? "Who?"

"The Anti-Tourist Brigade. Please, hurry!" Dad yanks our phones out of the wall and stuffs them and their chargers into his pockets.

I swing my backpack onto my shoulder and buckle the waistband. The smell of smoke drifts into the room from the lanai.

"Now."

We dart out of the room, each of us with a backpack and a duffel and tote bags filled with our food. The neighboring door bursts open, and a mother with two boys flees down the hallway. A man shouts after them from the room, "We're right behind you!" and the door closes.

The lights in the hallway are making me dizzy.

Dad's reading my mind. "Are you okay with the lights?"

I gasp and freeze in the hallway. Dad bumps into me. "What? What is it?" he asks.

"My pills. Did you pack them? They were in the bathroom."

Dad grows pale. "Shoot. No!" He turns back to the door and tries to open it. Locked.

"Oh, no," I mumble.

Dad freezes. He laughs nervously. "I think I left the car keys in there, too."

He fumbles through his pockets with his good hand while navigating around the hip strap of his pack. He pulls the key card into view and swipes it through the reader on the doorknob. No response. Again. Nothing.

From the room next to ours, a man and another boy emerge into the hallway, rolling two suitcases. They race away into the flashing darkness.

"It's expired," Dad says. "We can't get in."

Almost without thought, I press my hand against the closing door of the neighboring room. "Do you remember if there's a connecting door we can break down?"

"Good thinking." We push into the room.

"Nothing. Dammit."

The smell of smoke is stronger. A helicopter zooms past the lanai. I gasp. "Wait," I say. My heart's pounding as a new idea takes root within my mind. *Calm down*, I think. *You have to stay calm.*

I drop my bags and take off the pack. I walk out onto the lanai, nervous and hopeful.

Dad follows me outside and freezes. "Lei. That's crazy. Stop."

I stare at our lanai, my mind strangely focused. The alarm isn't so bad out here, and I can finally hear myself think. The petals of the Emerald Orchid are brighter than ever, and they bathe the side of the tower in eerie green light. The balconies have high lips, crowned with decorative handrailings. The distance between them is about eight feet. There's a very thin molding running along the wall, but no one could sidle along it without falling off. My eyes turn back to the distance between the lips. If I stood up on top of this wall, I could *probably* jump far enough to grab on to the next railing.

Probably isn't good enough when you're a famished epileptic surrounded by flashing lights and you're twelve stories off the ground in a burning building.

"Lei, come on. It was worth a thought, but it's no good."

"I need those meds, Dad. I *need* them." Several lanai lengths to the right, I can see black smoke billowing out of the fourth- or fifth-floor windows.

"We can look for more, hon. I'm sure we can walk right into nine out of ten pharmacies tonight and—"

"And how will you get to them? Just wander around on foot with all these bags? We need the keys, too!"

"Lei, we'll find another car. This is crazy. We have to get out of here, now!" He's either angry or scared, but it all sounds the same.

I'm angry, too. "You're going to walk up to the first car parked along the curb and flip down the visor and catch a set of keys?"

"Leilani! You can't jump that gap. I can't jump that gap. End of argument!"

My idea grows wings. I smile, and when I answer, my tone is relaxed. "We still have the climbing gear?"

Dad nods. "I thought maybe we could trade it."

I run back into the room and yank what I'll need out of my pack.

Dad doesn't protest. He studies the balconies. *I won this*

one, I think, and the thought is followed by a surge of adrenaline. I throw on my harness and run a double figure-eight knot through the loops.

I rush back onto the lanai.

"That fire's crept up another flight. We—"

"Put this on," I interrupt. Dad slips into his harness like a pro.

The now-familiar pop of a gunshot startles me. *That was close.* I follow the sound across the gardens to the neighboring hotel tower. A flickering light comes from a window several floors down, followed by rapid gunfire.

Is someone gunning people down? I turn back to Dad, the question plastered all over my face. He's staring across the divide with naked shock.

"Dad."

He shakes himself back to attention. "Quick!" We check each other's harness straps, and then I hand him the carabiner and the belay device.

"No," he says. "You're crazy if you think I'm letting *you* do it."

"Dad, I can't belay your weight the way you can belay mine. And your hand's hurt. How are you going to grab on to the railing with one hand?"

"Leilani."

"No time, Dad. Just give me plenny slack."

"Oh, God," he moans.

I step onto a chair, psyching myself up to stand on the wall.

"Wait!" Dad says. "Loop the rope over the lanai above."

"Dad, I've got this. It's just like the uneven bars."

"If you miss, you could fall out of your harness. I don't—"

"I won't miss."

Dad groans. I wait until he's sitting on the ground with his feet planted at an angle up against the low wall and the rope doubled through his belay device and choked off with two loops around his good hand, and then I stand up on the edge of the lip, my feet balanced just below the railing. My chest is pounding. My senses are sharp, and I focus on my target like a sniper.

Another round of gunfire. My eyes dart to the chilling flicker of light. A different window. *What are they doing?*

Dr. Makani's voice echoes in my head: "*Seizures can be induced by stress. You need to avoid any adventures . . .*"

Way too late for that. I glance down and see tongues of flame pushing smoke out of more windows. A coast guard boat in the bay attempts to reach the hotel's burning facade with its fire hoses, falls short. The ground—I might as well be a mile high.

My pills. I can't go on like this, and we're not going anywhere without the keys.

I look at Dad. He has pulled the rope tight against his right hip, locking the belay device. Ten feet of rope dangle in a loop below me. I'm ready. Dad wears a look of pure agony.

I focus on the handrail eight feet away. *If you were doing this six feet off the ground, you wouldn't even hesitate. Piece of cake.*

I step up onto the handrail, leaning my weight forward into thin air, and I leap.

My hands latch firmly onto our lanai's railing as my feet dangle against the wall, desperately seeking purchase.

"Leilani!" Dad shouts. He can't see me because he's locked in place on the floor.

"Got it! Don't move."

"Thank God."

More gunfire. I pull up with my arms and shoulders and swing my left leg around enough so that I can jam my foot between the wall and the handrail. The rest is muscle and sheer determination. I pull myself over the edge to solid ground without a hitch.

"I'm in. I did it!"

Dad stands up. From across the gap, he eyes me with terror and triumph and pride.

"Didn't even need the rope."

"Go! Now!"

I dart into our dark room, aided by alternating red and white lights, snatch my meds, toiletry kit, and the keys. Gunfire. The alarm buzzing. Hunted. Every muscle begs to flee.

Dad and I meet in the corridor, race down the long hallway to the farthest stairwell, and spiral down toward the lobby, our bags banging after us. As we pass the fifth floor, I hear gunfire behind the stairwell door. I yelp. Dad and I pick up our pace and catch up to a logjam of people trying to pour through the final door into the lobby.

We heave forward, struggling to stay upright with our things. Unseen smoke burns my throat. In the lobby the crowd thins, and we race for the garage. Men near the main entrance tackle people as if they're felling stampeding wilde-beests. Locals. Tribal tattoos. One tosses a bag of pretzels atop a cart loaded with groceries and toilet paper.

Some sort of gang raid?

We leap across the hallway, fly down the last stairs, and run to our car.

Seconds later we're dodging other cars. Dad squeezes my hand as the truck ahead of us jumps the curb and speeds across the gardens. We pull forward and flee over the canal.

I silently study the destruction that has taken root in every direction as we slip into the dawn of a new Hawai`i. The glow of morning illuminates the city. Smoke rises like columns holding up the sky. Abandoned cars, shattered and burnt to smoldering shells, are scattered everywhere. Trash bins spill their guts upon streets and sidewalks. Storefronts are cavities of empty racks and shattered glass. All that re-mains are the postcards and souvenirs lining ABC Store shelves. The beach is empty, and the bay contains only a few coast guard vessels.

"Has it really only been a week?" I marvel.

"We're all werewolves under a green full moon."

"It's going to get much worse." I try on the words. As un-welcome as they are, they feel right. I'm haunted by the tribal tattoos of those men. Several races—haoles among them—but all locals. Attacking tourists. Attacking me. Almost certainly gangbangers, but still. I shiver and run my hand through my smoky hair.

"Lei." Dad shakes his head. "You were amazing up there.

I don't think I could have done it. You're a hero, you know that?"

I feel my cheeks grow warm. *"Heroine."* Adrenaline still simmers in my veins. I feel powerful, angry.

One week.

Right before my eyes, my beautiful islands are changing forever.

And so am I.

O`AHU

KĀNE`OHE BAY

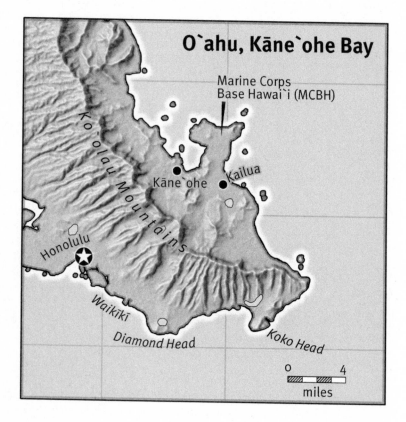

O`ahu, Kāne`ohe Bay

Marine Corps
Base Hawai`i (MCBH)

Koʻolau Mountains

Kāne`ohe

Kailua

Honolulu

Waikīkī

Diamond Head

Koko Head

0   4
miles

CHAPTER 11

The rising sun turns our broken windshield into a hundred glinting shards. The haze has intensified. For the third day since we left Honolulu, we are camped out in our car, slowly weaving south over crowded roads littered with abandoned vehicles.

Because of the reports of tsunami damage to boats moored along the north and east coasts, we've focused our attempt to charter a ride south of Honolulu, along a bay called Kaupa Pond. It's rimmed with houses, each with a dock. There must be a pier along here that will offer us a way off Oʻahu. But the only boat traffic beneath the bridge that leads to the open ocean belongs to coast guard patrols, which intercept unofficial ships like sparrow-hungry hawks, commandeer gasoline, and turn sailboats back to shore.

Dad pulls into a strip mall, zigzags across the untidy

parking lot, and stops in front of a busted-out grocery store. "Give it a try. Quick."

I jump out and trot over to the newspaper vending machines. We're scavenging for information. But every rack is empty. *How did things unravel so fast?* No news. No food. No medicine. We've tried seven different pharmacies in the past forty-eight hours, all ransacked, nobody on duty. I have enough pills to last the month, and a few dozen more back home, but what happens when they run out?

I return to the car and shake my head. We pull back onto the main road.

I glance at our gas needle: down to a third of a tank.

Why are there so many ditched vehicles? Have the cars run out of gas? Or have the drivers run out of steam, tired of circling?

Most of the abandoned cars seem newer. *Too many electronic parts?* Our no-frills rental is acting strange: radio dead, but all the warning lights lit up. We have to pull over when it rains, because the wipers don't work. The headlights randomly flicker or dim at night. Dad's worried about the fuel pump. He closes his eyes and whispers something every time he starts the car.

To my left, the caldera of an extinct volcano sinks into the ocean, creating a deep-blue bay teeming with coral. Straight ahead, singed by a crown of fiery morning light, is the tall peak of another cinder cone, Koko Head.

According to one of my favorite Hawaiian myths, it was at Koko Head that Pele made her last stand on O'ahu. I try to remember the whole story.

122

Pele seduced the husband of her sister, Nā-maka-o-Kaha`i, the goddess of water and of the sea, so she fled to the Hawaiian Islands. Pele thrust down her o`o, her shovel, in Kaua`i, claiming the land as her home, but her sister flung the sea at her. Waves filled the fiery hole made by Pele's o`o, and she escaped to O`ahu.

Each time Pele dug a new fire pit to call home, Nā-maka-o-Kaha`i commanded the rain to wash her away. Koko Head was her final dwelling on O`ahu.

Finally, she arrived on Hawai`i. She ascended Mauna Kea, the world's tallest mountain measured from seafloor, and dug her o`o on the summit, far beyond the sea's reach.

Nā-maka-o-Kaha`i used Poli`ahu, the goddess of snow, to best Pele on the mountaintop by freezing her out, and Pele retreated one last time to neighboring Mauna Loa.

The Mauna Loa and Kilauea volcanoes remain her active homes to this day. Mauna Loa last erupted in the 1980s, almost erasing Hilo. Pele could command the lava to bubble out of there again at any moment.

I feel closer to her than ever. She was kicked off each island, not accepted anywhere. Even on the Big Island, she was forced to fight for her place. But she won her home. And now she belongs. She's the pride of the island, the envy of the entire archipelago.

When I get home, I will follow her lead. Fight back. Stake my claim.

"Oh, crap." Dad taps on the brakes, and I jolt in my seat. "Military checkpoint."

I stick my head out to get a clear view. We've slowed to a

complete stop. A fleet of military vehicles crowds the road; armed military police patrol the line of cars.

"Why?" I ask.

"Tightening their grip." Dad tightens his own grip on the wheel.

Behind us, a truck does a U-turn. The driver is pursued by a camouflaged army van waiting along the shoulder of the road. Our view of their encounter is blocked by a bend in the highway.

"So much for that idea." Dad straightens up.

MPs stop at each car as they advance along the road. Most cars are released after a brief interrogation. One vehicle ahead of us has a square of colored paper tucked beneath the windshield wiper, and an MP motions for it to pull forward into the parking lot of Maunalua Bay Beach Park.

"Let me do the talking, Lei."

I stiffen. We pull forward and an MP leans into Dad's window.

"Good morning, Officer," Dad offers.

"What happened here?" the MP asks, tapping on our shattered windshield.

"Looters."

The MP nods. "Where are you going?"

"Home."

"Where's home?"

Dad points off to the left. "Home."

"What's your address?"

Dad doesn't hesitate. "Nineteen-oh-one Apoke Street."

The MP looks through the back passenger window, studying our backpacks. "What day of the week is your trash pickup?"

Dad scoffs. "Never, I'm guessing."

The MP cracks a smile. "Well, what day of the week *was* your trash pickup?"

"Tuesdays."

"Where are you coming from?"

"Her mom's house." Dad indicates me with his chin.

"What's her address?"

"Twenty-one ten Kanini Drive."

"What are the backpacks for?"

Dad pauses for a second, then says, "Look, we're just staying prepared. It's food and stuff. I want it all packed up in case we have to leave the car in a hurry. We don't know what the hell is going to happen next."

"I understand. Any weapons?"

"No. A couple utility knives."

"May I have your driver's license and registration?"

My heartbeat picks up. I bounce my knee up and down, force myself to stop.

"Sure." Dad reaches awkwardly into the pocket of his shorts. "The looters cleaned everything out. But I have my ID still." He hands the driver's license over to the MP with a hesitant smile.

"This has your address as Hilo."

"Yeah, I know," Dad answers. "I'm a professor at UH Manoa. I recently moved from UH Hilo. You won't be the first person to give me stink-eye for not getting to the DMV."

The MP is very still. He studies my father and me with a trained eye. "If you're trying to get to Hilo, you should just report to the right. We're making arrangements for civilian transport at the Marine Corps Base."

"No, sir, that's all right."

He leans in on the window and peers sternly at Dad. "Everything's different now, Dr. Milton. You'll get instructions up ahead. Stability is our primary concern. If everybody follows instructions, we'll all get through this."

He puts a red card on our windshield.

"Wait a second!" Dad raises his voice.

The MP walks away. Another MP urgently motions us into the right lane.

"Shit," Dad gasps. "What do we do?"

My cheeks are cold as death. I don't even know why.

The MP in front of us beckons again. Dad obeys, staring forward, in shock.

"Maybe it's okay, Dad. We've tried on our own long enough. What if they *are* sending people home?"

"I hope you're right."

Dad veers to the right. We continue into a parking lot full of military buses. A chill goes down my spine: dozens of reluctant people are being herded aboard the transports, and there are men with guns at every corner.

We park as an MP approaches. "Come right this way, please."

"Hold on," Dad grumbles. "Our bags."

He hands them out as I struggle to buckle my backpack. The MP looms over us.

126

"Now, please. The bus is waiting." The MP shuts the hatch, stepping between the vehicle and us. Dad takes a step backward. We're shepherded away from the car, dragging all our stuff.

"Hey, we don't even know what this is about," says Dad.

"You're being taxied over to the Marine Corps Base. What's your destination?"

Dad hesitates. I pray that he won't lie.

"Hilo."

The MP nods. "Lots of folks were caught on the wrong island. We're sorting it out, though."

"That's not what I heard." Dad tries a smile.

The MP escorts us across the length of the parking lot to the waiting buses as other soldiers siphon gasoline from cars with hand pumps.

"Have you heard about the two hundred sea rescues the coast guard has done in the past week?" The MP's voice carries an edge. "They're about done with that nonsense. You weren't planning on taking your daughter out on the ocean alone, were you?"

Dad remains quiet, steaming mad.

We board the bus as the driver turns on the engine. The first-row bench is waiting for us. The rest of the bus is full. I steal a look at the endless rows of apprehensive people, luggage piled on their laps.

Soldiers with automatic rifles stand in the aisle.

Dad and I take our seats and hug our backpacks and duffel bags. A soldier storms up the steps and takes a waiting handset from the driver. "I'll keep this brief, ladies and gentlemen; gas is wasting. Whether or not you believe you're being inconvenienced right now, you are on your way home. Our mission is your safety and security."

"You can't keep us here," someone shouts.

"Efforts to find your own way off this island are ill-advised. You are not Sinbad of the Seven Seas," the soldier answers, his Southern drawl thick. He gestures at the driver. "These soldiers could be AWOL with their own wives and children. Instead, they're doing their duty to God and country, whatever's left of each, and you need to buck up and do the same. We'll all get through this if we work together. Aloha."

He tosses the handset back to the driver and steps off the bus.

People begin shouting, in English, Japanese, and a couple of other languages.

"Asshole."

"Hey, what's happening? What's the Emerald Orchid?"

"But my FAMILY! We've been separated! I have to find them first!"

"This is unbelievable!"

"When will it get back to normal?"

"You can't do this to us!"

"Why won't you tell us what happened?"

Dad releases the bag on his lap and puts his arm around me, squeezing me tight. "Stay together, okay?" he whispers. "No matter what."

"Maybe if you smelled better."

He offers me a wry smile. "You're not a rose garden yourself right now, either."

Dad's right: I haven't really scrubbed clean in days.

I'm not really sure how bad I look, but I doubt I'm as well off as Dad. He *always* looks a bit scraggly with his ancient T-shirts, five o'clock shadow, and sandy mop.

The bus pulls forward and the voices dwindle and fall silent. Someone is weeping behind me. I don't turn around to investigate. I don't think I could manage to move my head if I wanted to; we're stuffed in tight. It's almost comforting. The floundering freedom of the past week has been a disaster.

Maybe our luck has finally turned.

We could be back home by tonight, I tell myself over and over again. I know it's wishful thinking, but I can't stop the voice. *Even tomorrow, or the next day. We're going home.*

The bus takes us around the westernmost point of O'ahu and turns. Twice, the steel-plated monster carrying us pushes abandoned cars out of the way. One tumbles down a cliff to the sea.

The sky is a mellow orange, and the bronze disk of the sun is soft—I can stare at it through the bus's tinted windshield. I feel like I'm stuck in an old, grainy movie where the film itself has started to fade.

"Hey, what's going on? Do you know? What's happening on the mainland?" I quietly ask the driver.

He's wearing sunglasses, but I see his eyes drift toward the rearview mirror. He studies me and returns to the road. He says, "If I knew the answer to that question, do you think I'd be sitting here on this bus with you?"

"Does anybody in the military know?"

The driver shrugs. "I don't know, ma'am."

Ma'am?

"I honestly don't know." Now he's rueful.

I turn to Dad with a whisper. "Dad, why is the sky doing that? Is the Orchid doing it?"

He shakes his head. "I don't think so. The Orchid's in space. It set before dawn. It's not surrounding us, at least not its visible features."

"Could be more meteor blasts. Hitting land. Or volcanic eruptions."

"Lei, stop. Try not to worry about it. Did you know that the Big Island is where climate scientists measure the rise in atmospheric carbon dioxide? It's because there's no cleaner air on the Earth—"

"Unless Mauna Loa exploded," I say. "It's overdue, isn't it? All these meteor strikes could have jarred it awake. Or what if it's radioactive fallout? Or—"

Dad sighs. "No. Please, Lei. Stop."

We enter the town of Kailua. As we drive by the beaches, I see where tsunami waves tore through the eastern coast. My view is partially blocked by buildings and trees, but I can see overturned boats, giant tree skeletons, driftwood, and endless trash.

I remember Kailua Bay full of paddleboarders, rowers, kite surfers, and surfboarders. Today, a few fishermen stand in the surf, casting nets among waterlogged boat hulls and tangled globs of plastic.

The bus stops at a gatehouse and then passes over a grassy field into the Marine Corps Base on the bay. The tsunami left low-lying areas flooded or trashed. Crews of soldiers gather junk into large piles.

With rib-cage-rattling intensity, a cargo plane rises swiftly into the air, heading out over the ocean in the direction of the Big Island. The aircraft looks old, maybe even World War II era. I tap Dad's shoulder. "Off to Hilo."

Dad shrugs. "We'll see, honey. I hope so."

We pull into an open area with baseball fields, a football field and a track, and several tennis courts. Everything is compartmentalized with chain-link fence. Big canopy tents have been erected at large intervals and are connected with orange netting and long rope barricades. The grass has been trodden into great bogs of mud.

A collective gasp runs through the bus.

CHAPTER 12

The entire complex of sports fields and parking lots and roads is swarming with people, most milling about in small areas or sitting on cots and overturned buckets. Long lines of waiting zombies curve toward the large tents and around buildings in the near distance.

We stop. I step off the bus and my hiking boots sink into the black soup of mud. A faint odor of ammonia eddies through the wind. A soldier behind a long table instructs me to spread out my bags and open them for inspection. Another soldier pats us down.

The private glances at our duffel bags, half-stuffed with food, and confiscates them.

"Hey! You can't take that," Dad barks. "That's ours."

The private ignores him, already making motions to pull another of our duffels off the table. Dad snatches one of the straps and begins a tug-of-war. The officer wins.

"Stop it!" Dad is shaking. He pulls back the last of our food bags before the officer can react. People disembarking from the bus slow and stare.

"Sir, calm down. Food items are not allowed within the waiting areas. It's for your safety. The bags are still yours. Meals are provided while your travel arrangements are processed."

Dad studies his adversary. He glances at me. I realize that I'm staring at him wide-eyed and temper my expression.

"Lance Corporal!" the private shouts to another soldier overseeing an inspection far to the right. The soldier turns, sees Dad clenching his food bags, and strides over.

"Dad," I whisper, using my voice to try and calm him down. "It's okay." But is it? We've done a good job of rationing this food. It would be ridiculous to lose it.

The officer nods to the private and steps between Dad and the table. "Good afternoon, sir. I'm Lance Corporal Billings. What's your name?"

"Uncle Sam. And you're customer relations, or something?"

"Something like that."

"Where are my balloons and free hot dog? Do I get a raffle ticket?"

Billings laughs. He ushers us to the side of the table. "Listen, *Sam*, this whole thing is *crazy*. We're all adjusting. Everybody's a little on edge."

"And I'm killing the mood, right?"

"No worries. Here, I'll walk with you over to your . . ."

". . . cage?"

". . . terminal. No, it's not like that! That's what I'm trying to say. Did you hear stories out there? Have you been trying to avoid us?"

Dad says, "I haven't been trying to avoid anything."

"What's your name, really?"

"Dr. Michael Milton."

"Okay, Dr. Milton. Can we finish inspecting your bags? We're only checking in food and knives so fights don't break out. You can keep everything else with you."

Dad loosens his death grip on the duffel. "Why would fights break out over food?" A cargo plane marked with a white star inside a blue circle roars into the sky behind us. "Is everyone starving?"

Billings chuckles. "It's not like that, Dr. Milton."

He turns to me and asks brightly, "And what's your name, young lady?"

I look at the ground. "Leilani."

"We're going to get you two home, okay? Where are you going?"

"Hilo."

"Hilo! That's all? You folks kama`āina?"

"Yup." My eyes flick up to his. "Mind if we snag a quick snack from the bags first?"

Billings holds my gaze. Finally, he gently takes the last duffel bag from Dad and gives it to the private. He turns back to us and hands us each a string cheese and several ticket stubs. "Not exactly a raffle, but hold on to it tightly. This is your bag tracker, okay?

"Here, I'll take you over to the interisland line." He takes my backpack and hoists it up onto his shoulder.

What a gentleman.

We follow the lance corporal through the mud. "I won't lie to you," he says, "no one looking to get to the mainland has left yet, and interisland transport is happening slowly. But it *is* happening!"

Relief washes over me in a wave.

"You've gotta remember: we're all reacting to a scenario no one ever imagined. It's been a messy process, but we're getting there."

"And what scenario is that?" I ask, biting into my stolen snack.

Billings stops. "I call it the 'this thing isn't going away' scenario. My superiors have other labels for it, but my job is to calm you folks down, not rile you up." He smiles.

"Wonderful," Dad groans. "You're so comforting."

"But we're dedicated to the displaced, don't you worry. The governor was here yesterday!" Dad gives me a *who cares?* expression, which I return.

"What does the governor have to do with the Marine Corps Base?" I ask.

Billings shrugs. "Nothing. Power play he's sure to lose." He pushes ahead of us.

"That may be the first thing he's said that I believe," Dad says, to me.

We arrive at the end of a very long line. It's several people thick, and it hugs the walls of a large swimming-pool complex and wraps around the corner. My hopes of getting home today nosedive.

Billings says, "Here you are, Dr. Milton and Leilani. Thank you for your patience and cooperation. Just remember that you're probably in the safest place on the island right now. We'll get you home as soon as we can."

"Wait a sec," Dad says. "Really, that's it? You have to give me *something*. Come on, what's going on? What did you mean by 'it's not going away'?"

"Mike, I'm not going to bullshit you. Fact is, I don't have any facts. Your guess is as good as mine. The higher-ups don't share. And it's not my job to ask. My job is to keep everyone safe and maintain order so that we can all pick up where we left off once things return to normal."

"Please, Lance Corporal," Dad begs.

The officer's expression chills. "Mike, I'm sorry. I don't know what to tell you."

Billings steps away. Immediately, he's eye level with an agitated Asian American woman, distracting her from her tirade about the mud.

"That guy was born for this," Dad says.

"You should finish your tantrum now anyway."

"Oh, I'm hardly done."

"That may be the first thing you've said that I believe."

We both laugh.

We're on our own again, behind an elderly Hawaiian couple and exposed to the intense heat of a sickly sun. Thanks to the constant cooling presence of O'ahu's trade winds, we survive a miserable three hours waiting to proceed through the line. We talk story with our neighbors as we constantly shift on our feet to catch the breeze.

"Where are you folks off to?" Dad asks the couple ahead of us.

The old man gives Dad a hard look, and then leans in close. "Lāna`i, by way of Maui."

"Our son's family lives out there," the woman adds.

The husband scowls at her. "You gotta be more careful."

"With these two? Relax, Kani." She smiles past him. "We live here, but luckily we pay some of the bills on the farm, so we can show paperwork. A ticket to ride."

Someone comes down the line with Dixie cups of luke-warm water, and we greedily guzzle them.

"Keep your cup," the soldier orders. "You won't get an-other."

"We're trying to get back to our family, too," I say to the old couple. "On Hawai`i."

"The Big Island. Good," the old woman says. "If this goes on, that'll be the best place to be. Big Island's four times big-ger than O`ahu, ah? With one-tenth the population. And there are more cows and wild pigs and goats than there are people. Pressures over there will be different."

"You haoles better watch it," Kani warns. "Pressures will be different for *you*, no doubt."

"Doesn't matter," I say. "We're from there. Not gonna let anyone push us around."

"It'll be hard," Dad admits. "A lot of folks are going to try and spread out if things don't return to normal. The pressures will build."

"That's what we're hoping to do once we've gathered," the wife says. "I'm glad we have a ticket off this island. We're out of food. We tried everything short of thievery. There's nothing honest left here."

"Oh, there's food," the old man says. "We just weren't the ones to hoard it. If only this had happened twenty years ago, I'd've been right out there scooping it up early."

The woman slaps his upper arm. "Knock it off, *lōlō*. You'd've grabbed nothing but Spam and Cheetos and boxed wine, and we'd've died of malnutrition."

Finally, we arrive at the front of the line. The private asks for Dad's driver's license, jots down a couple of notes, scribbles out two blue name tags, and waves us through.

"That's it?" Dad asks.

"Now you wait until your number block is called. Be ready to go at any moment."

"We just waited for three hours!"

The soldier actually chortles. "Get used to it."

"In there?" Dad almost groans. "District nine?"

The soldier nods. "We can't have folks wandering around the base. It's for your safety."

Dad glances at me and then leans in on the officer. I can hear what he's saying, though. "Hey, my daughter has epilepsy. She's had a couple big seizures lately. Is there . . . ?"

"I'll make a note of it." The soldier looks me up and down, notes my medical bracelet. "We have good medics around; don't worry. If something happens, you'll be taken care of."

He brushes us to the side and motions to the next people in line.

"What were you after, handicapped parking?" I say.

Dad sighs. "I don't know, hon. Some sort of leg up, that's all."

We shuffle forward along another muddy path lined with orange plastic netting and arrive at a field draped with a dozen massive camouflage tarps, under which hundreds of people are crowded, cowering from the sun.

A low chain-link fence runs along the perimeter of the field. Stretches of it look like they've always been there, but some are new. Silvery-white razor wire is looped along the top—a long, stretched-out Slinky from hell. Shiny new.

"District nine? What's that?"

Dad feigns shock. "I haven't shown you *District 9* yet?"

"No."

Dad's tried to introduce me to all the great science-fiction movies of his time, showing me the films and television episodes that meant so much to him growing up. I tease him that I only play along because it gets me out of doing homework, but I've really enjoyed the "lessons." I almost died of embarrassment when he made me and Tami watch that old Bill and Ted movie—but it *was* funny. Those days now seem long ago, in a galaxy far away. And I might never have them back.

"It'd be a good one to watch right around now," Dad says. "About aliens stuck in a refugee camp in South Africa."

I laugh dryly. *Is that what we are? Aliens on our own islands?*

We pass into the camp and search for shade. Departure announcements come about once every two hours. Each time, only a handful of people dash away with the escort. All of the announced flights are for Maui.

I watch a truck filled with luggage pull up to a warehouse across the street, our duffels visible in the pile. Soldiers haul the luggage into the warehouse through a side door.

As I walk the perimeter, I pass beneath a plumeria tree overhanging the fence. I freeze. I raise my hands to my temples and squeeze my eyes shut. After a moment I open them. I reach up, pluck a yellow-white plumeria blossom off the nearest branch, and tuck its stem behind my ear. I hold the flower in place for a second and drop my gaze down to the damp dirt sprinkled with countless petals, holding back tears.

* * *

The next group is called up. Maui, again. Dad and I have been sitting cross-legged at the edge of a tarp's shade. He rises and jogs over to the announcer, the barbed wire doing its endless loop-de-loops between their faces.

"Hey, when do you guys do runs to the Big Island?"

"Whenever we need to. Please, sir, don't hover."

"But we can go to Maui, too. Can we specify that we want to go to Maui?"

The soldier shakes his head. "You have a blue tag. Big Island. You don't want to be sitting around in Maui any more than here."

The sun drops toward the jagged, razor-edged slopes of the green Koolau Range, and I have never seen such a beautiful sunset. Above, thin scallops of raked clouds hover bloodred, like a ceiling consumed in flame.

The gorgeous colors.

I look across the fields and beyond two parking lots at another, larger makeshift camp. No wonder the trade winds smell like body odor and human waste. They must be the out-of-staters, separated from the rest of us like the lepers who used to be sent to Moloka`i.

We're issued two cots to set up under the open sky. Good thing there hasn't been rain today. Someone nearby sneaks some mosquito repellant, quickly stuffing it back into their suitcase. *Good idea.* I share my own canister with Dad.

Dinner is served from giant stew pots along a row of tables. People spring to the front of a mad dash that takes us by surprise. Dad and I wait half an hour for the crowd to thin. We ask about aspartame in the food, and the server rolls his eyes. An unsavory stew is poured into our Dixie cups, and we go back to our cots to eat.

Later we lie on our cots, clothing piled beneath our heads, and watch the stars twinkle dimly behind the Emerald Orchid. Someone nearby weeps as meteors drizzle down faintly, like tear streaks, fading to spent dust far above the mountains.

CHAPTER 13

The next several days, we wait.

We exercise to pass the time. I'd rather avoid the dirt and sweat from doing sit-ups and push-ups three times a day, but I play along. I think I know what Dad's doing: training for that big canoeing adventure. Just in case it comes to that.

The portable toilets overfill by the end of each day. We're given a couple of squares of toilet paper every time we want to go. The food is getting worse, and water is available for shorter stretches. I've only taken one shower in the swimming pool's shower rooms. The pool is useless—the tsunami filled it with sand and mud and junk.

We write Mom a letter, and I give it to a soldier at our camp. He pulls the rolled-up letter through the chain links and assures me, "It'll make it to Hilo eventually, but you know they can't play post office." He's young, Hawaiian, and very handsome. Maybe I didn't pick him out randomly.

"Thanks." I can only hope that Mom will think to visit the airport and ask if she has any letters waiting for her; she must know by now that civilians are arriving from Oʻahu each day. Perhaps she goes there to look for us.

"It's all good," I continue. "I understand. Gotta try, though, yeah? `Ohana.`"

Family.

"`Ohana,`" he agrees. "Where you from?"

Heat rushes to my cheeks. "My mom's native Big Islander. Dad's from New Mexico."

The soldier offers me a shy smile. "Gotta name?"

"Leilani. And you?"

"That's one of my favorites. I'm Aukina."

"What, you straight outta cadet training or something?"

"Ho!" He laughs and shifts the letter in his hands. "Way to see the world, ah?"

I laugh. "Hey, you know what's going on out there? The mainland?"

"No. Wish I did. Communications are completely out. But talk is the whole world's without power. Plenny problems everywhere."

I frown. This doesn't come as a surprise. But hearing it out loud—it sounds really serious—really *bad*. Who could possibly have time to spare a thought for Hawaiʻi?

"Hey," I say. "You guys have extra medicine? I'm running low and can't run out."

"What do you need?"

I tell him my brand and the generic name.

"I'll see what I can do."

"Thanks."

"Hey, good luck with this, ah?" He waves my letter to Mom. "I'll keep an eye out for a reply."

"Thanks." I blush again and turn around. I return to Dad, and for a moment I wish he were Tami. We'd already be talking up that *cham*—our secret word for a good-looking guy. I suddenly miss her with a sharp pang of . . . loss.

But it's not forever, I tell myself.

I kill some time by removing and reapplying my spearmint-pearl polish. I usually don't do my fingernails, but I add them in to the mix tonight. If I can't get rid of the dirt, at least I can hide it.

I wonder if Private Cham over there would like spearmint pearl. I shrug. Can't be worse than my current cellblock brown.

We often hear gunfire across the bay. Single shots or short bursts. I think of that man's head bursting open against the white sail. As miserable as we are in camp, the fence that surrounds us keeps the madness at bay.

Sunday and Monday come and go. Two weeks since we last talked to Mom and Kai. It feels surreal—and painful. I'm angry all the time. Or sad. Or numb. I never just feel normal anymore.

Tuesday. I've counted about fifty lucky people with blue name tags called to board a plane bound for the Big Island. Meanwhile, four new tarps have been hoisted up inside our

144

pen, and hundreds of additional interisland travelers have arrived.

Would we already be home if we'd come here right away?

I have a cot, but now Dad sleeps on the muddy ground next to me, using the canvas of our tent as a ground cloth. There were no more cots to go around, but the people in the camp redistributed the ones we do have among the women and children. It was a good moment. Started with one guy insisting that a new lady take his. She tried to refuse, but he won. Then a few more got up and did the same thing. And suddenly everyone was passing cots around, like some weird square dance without music. People were laughing, chatting with each other. It took a while for the excitement to die down. Thinking of it now, I'm reminded of Saturday-morning soccer games.

I turn to Dad sitting beside me on the cot. "Anyone around here have a soccer ball?"

Dad's eyebrows go up. "Let's find out."

We ask around. Finally, a soldier passes a ball over the fence. It doesn't take long before we have a game going. Coed. All ages. People move camp and squeeze together to give us room to play. We're on a soccer field, after all. The game gets crowded, so someone suggests teams and rotating matches. Everyone who's not playing watches. Even the guards spectate during their patrols. Every time there's a goal, cheers ripple through camp, inside and outside the fence.

We play until just after dark, and we agree to do it again every evening.

* * *

I've been leaving my phone off. I turn it on now and switch off airplane mode. It finds a network and shows full bars. I dial Mom, but the call fails. Before I can shut it off, it dies. I'm certain it still had power. I sit and stare at the blank screen.

"Dad, my phone's fried."

"Weird how things are zapping out so randomly," he muses, sitting cross-legged on the flattened tent next to the cot. "The Orchid's . . . aura . . . must have folds and knots that miss things as it churns around out there. Like pancake batter that still has balls of dry flour even after you whisk it. It may only be a matter of time before *nothing* works anymore."

A chill runs up my back. "Well, when it goes away, though . . ."

Dad shakes his head. "When the Orchid goes away, everything will still be broken. It'll take a long time for factories to get up and running. This thing goes away right now, we've still entered a new era, Lei. Nothing will ever be quite the same."

The truth of his words lingers like cigarette smoke; it stinks, and I'm not ready to breathe it in.

Dad squeezes my shoulder. "Mine's charged and still works."

"Yeah, but you don't have any music."

"What was the last song you listened to?"

"I don't remember. Why?"

Dad shrugs.

I force a smile, try to make light of it. "Oh, now I remember what it was."

"What?"

"John Denver. 'Leaving on a Jet Plane.'"

"That's not funny." Dad shakes his head.

"It is when you try to sing it."

We both laugh.

It's just dead weight, but I place the phone in my backpack.

Now and then it rains for several minutes at a time as dark purple clouds drift quickly by, but mostly it's stayed sunny and humid in the strange light filtering down through the sky. Occasionally, a bus offers to take people—mostly families with young *keikis*—to the nearby beach. The kids and their parents love it. Dad and I never go. Even though it would be good to replace running laps and dribbling soccer balls with actual swimming practice, we don't want to miss a flight while we're away.

If they were taking folks to the Kailua beaches, maybe then I would go. A chance to surf.

When the "beach bus" returns on Saturday afternoon, the families file into the camp, looking fresh and rather cheerful compared with the rest of us. *We should have gone this time,* I think. Only one flight was called all day, not for the Big Island. A little dip in the bay, in spite of its floating trash heaps, would have done my spirit a lot of good.

Two *keikis* run by me—a small Hawaiian brother and sister—covered in mosquito-bite welts. Their mom chases after them. The mosquitoes have found her, too. They settle into their space a few yards away from us and the mom says,

"I said stop scratching! They're making you bleed. It's gonna get infected!"

I watch the three of them for a moment, grimace at myself, and unzip my backpack. I pull out my smaller can of repellent. I hesitate, put it back, and take the larger one.

Before I can change my mind, I trot over to the mother and present her with the bug spray. "Here, take it."

"Fo real?" She reaches for it.

"I've got . . . you know . . . I got plenny," I whisper.

"*Mahalo.*"

* * *

The weeping at night has been replaced by coughing, and every day that we've been here, older people have been carried away on gurneys. One body is taken away beneath a sheet, the lumpy, shrouded gurney hauled through the gate over a muddy path and out of view.

CHAPTER 14

We've been in camp for a full week. This morning the soldiers are wearing masks.

The masks are the soft, white kind—the type dentists wear. But where's mine? I feel like the only passenger without a parachute on a plummeting plane.

I sit down on the cot, lean over, and draw a map in the dirt with my finger. Kaua`i, off to the left. O`ahu, bigger, right in front of me. About the size of those masks. Moloka`i, a long finger to O`ahu's right. Then Maui, a figure-eight shape, slightly lower. Then the Big Island. Mom. Kai. Grandpa.

I study the distances *between* the islands. *Can I do it? Can I swim that?* No way. *But could Dad and I row it?*

The answer has to be yes.

I start my next set of push-ups, my eyes fixed on the gap between O`ahu and Moloka`i. One island at a time. If we have to, we'll do it. We'll make it work.

One. Two. Three.

I've seen Grandpa canoeing like a frigate bird over the water in Hilo Bay. He could do it. *Then so can I.*

Four. Five. Six.

Moloka`i—once famous for the old leper colonies. The government's quarantine policy ended in the sixties, but before that, people were sent there to live out their lives. Never to return.

Seven. Eight. Nine.

Moloka`i doesn't like outsiders. Surfing, for example— don't even try it if you don't live there.

But you have the right *to belong. Fight for it, like Pele.*

Ten. Eleven. Twelve.

We'll make it work. We'll get there even if we have to paddle on surfboards.

Thirteen. Fourteen. Fifteen.

And then we'll keep going.

* * *

On Thursday I see Aukina patrolling the perimeter of the far side of the fence. He's. So. Hot! It's still obvious how young he is compared to most of the soldiers. In my mind's eye I catch a glimpse of Grandpa—straight out of high school on a battleship. Looking like that. It makes me smile. I head toward the fence.

I attempt to brush my fingers through my tangled black hair, for all the good it will do, as I catch up to him. "Hi, Aukina."

He turns. His mouth is covered with a mask, but the

smile shows in his eyes. He waves. "Hey, Leilani. Howzit? Been watching you on the soccer field. One mean forward."

"Really?" I float into the air, a flush rises into my neck. "Um, thanks. You should play!"

He raises an eyebrow. "Oh, I've been meaning to tell you: I asked around about your meds."

"Yeah?"

He shakes his head. "Sorry. Nothing like that on base. What's it for?"

I shrug uncomfortably. "No worries, just . . ." *Only forty left.*

"Sorry, didn't mean to pry."

I change the subject. "Hey, what's up with the masks? Why do you get to wear them and we don't? It's creeping everybody out."

Aukina looks down at his feet for a moment before a muffled answer comes. "There's a nasty flu spreading at the other camp. I don't like that we're supposed to wear them in front of everyone."

"It's not more than that, is it? Like, radiation?"

"No. That would mean creepier masks. The day we march out here with those . . . it's all over either way."

I slouch forward against the fence. *That's encouraging.*

"Hey, trust me," he offers. "Folks are monitoring radiation. This isn't about that. People are getting sick in that camp. You can't put thousands of people in one place in the tropics without issues, yeah?"

"Well, even so, didn't your mother tell you not to bring out your toys if you weren't willing to share?"

He studiously scrapes his muddy boot over a patch of grass. "I'll mention it to the sergeant, Leilani."

"Good."

"Dang, are all girls from Hilo as *tita* as you?" he asks.

He just called me tita. Does that mean I finally belong? I laugh. "'No. Just me, baby. Just me.'" That's a line from the film *Army of Darkness*.

He doesn't seem to pick up on the reference, and I'm mortified. *Dad and his movies!* An awkward silence falls. My cheeks grow warm. *Of course he doesn't know that movie, stupid.* "I was joking," I try. "I'm actually the nicest person from Hilo. In Hilo, I mean. I'm not from Hilo. Well, I am now, but . . ."

"Lei," Aukina says. I fall silent. "It's all good. I was just teasing you."

"Oh, yeah. Well . . . anyway, I better go."

"K'den. See you around."

"I'll be . . . here." I turn to leave but whip back around when my stomach grumbles. My embarrassment fades. "Hey, Aukina?"

"Yeah, Lei?"

"I'm so hungry. Do you have any real food?"

Aukina shakes his head. "I'm hungry, too."

I turn, but whip again as he adds, "Hey, Lei?"

"Yeah?"

"You see this?" he says, hefting his rifle with a wry smile. I frown. "Yeah. So?"

"'This is my boom stick,'" he begins. I laugh. That's the

most famous line from *Army of Darkness*, when the time-traveling hero Ash shows off his twelve-gauge Remington shotgun to King Arthur and a crowd of "primitive screwheads."

Aukina continues, grin widening, "'S-Mart's top of the line. That's right. Shop smart. Shop S-Mart. You got that?'"

I march away, beaming. *Oh. My. God. He's an even bigger nerd than I am!*

In the early afternoon, the rest of us are issued masks. I doubt I had anything to do with it. Apparently, someone dredged up a dusty box of medical supplies. They look like they've been in storage since the days of Pearl Harbor. Most people eagerly strap them on, and now only their wild eyes show their fear.

Dad and I put them on.

I pace for a bit, then disappear into my book. I read about King Kamehameha, who united the islands and abolished the bloodthirsty *kapu*, or system of taboos. And he won his later wars with a little help from Captain Cook and the other Europeans who "discovered" Hawai`i. Kamehameha's rule was foretold, and the kahunas prophesied that his arrival would be marked by a fire in the sky. Turned out to be true. Halley's Comet.

Maybe the Emerald Orchid is just a sign of good things to come.

Yeah, and maybe I'm a Chinese jet pilot.

I laugh out loud. Another quote from *Army of Darkness*. Where's Aukina when you need him?

* * *

In the evening our soccer match is interrupted by the sound of gunfire from the camp across the road. Everyone rushes to the fence. I hear screams and shouting and see something that nearly stops my heart. A body is draped over the top of the other camp's high fence. A group of soldiers scurries about, devising a plan to pull it down, while other soldiers push onlookers back.

Dad searches for his next words as we peer across the distance. "These camps aren't going to hold together much longer."

Our own wardens appear outside of our fence, blocking our view. "Turn around! Move away from the fence."

I spot Aukina. "Hey!" I shout through my mask. "Did you guys *shoot* that guy?"

"Lei," Dad begins, but his muffled protest dies as others around me take up the chorus. A yelling match ensues. The soldiers hold their position. Aukina and I share a glance before my view of him is blocked by another soldier. He looks sad . . . maybe even frightened.

Dad pulls me back from the fence by the sweaty collar of my raggedy blouse. "Someone tried to escape."

We slouch back to our cot. "You okay, Lei?"

I force a smile, hoping Dad can see it in my eyes above the mask. I want to rip it off. It itches and it's stuffy and it scares me. But I'm more scared to not have it on. I pat his arm. "Don't worry, I won't break into a seizure *every* time someone gets shot in the face."

Dad presses his palms into his eyes, mumbles something. "What?"

"Maybe you should," he finally says.

"Huh?" A prickle of adrenaline shoots up my back.

Carefully, he says, "Have a seizure."

"You're asking me to go through that on purpose?" The question is calm, but I want to scream.

He presses forward. "I could play it up. We'd get short-listed. Wake up in Hilo. This place is eating me up from the inside, Lei. I'm desperate. Aren't you?"

"Dad." My heart's pounding. "I . . . I can't just turn them on. We waited all that time at the clinic and . . ."

"You were on an experimental dose then. When you weren't, they came fast and furious. Besides, I found this." He pulls a pink artificial-sweetener packet from his pocket.

"Dad." *He didn't just* find *that. He's been looking for it, planning this.*

"Or you could even fake one."

"Stop it. Stop it." I stand up and take a few steps away from him.

Dad closes his eyes, shakes his head. "I'm sorry. Forget it. I'm just . . . thinking out loud. It was dumb." He tosses the sweetener packet in the dirt.

I sit back down on the cot. "Don't . . . feel bad."

"I'm sorry, Leilani," Dad says with a crackly voice. "I haven't handled this very well."

"What are you talking about?"

"I'm not James Bond. I'm . . . Mike."

"Oh, Dad." There's so much I want to say. I remove my mask and I sit with him. I reach out and gently touch the raised skin on his hand, a scar he'll probably always have as thanks for keeping me from choking.

"You're . . . exactly the dad I want you to be. We're in this together, remember? You said that to me. We're both responsible for each other, okay?"

He nods, but I wonder if he heard. He pushes his mask up against his forehead. "I can tell you all you need to know about biogeochemical cycles, why rare Hawaiian plants aren't getting pollinated anymore. What good is any of that? The birds and the trees won't need my help once humanity dies off. I couldn't even get us off O'ahu. God, I miss Malia so damned much. Kai, too."

"Dad." I bury my head in his shoulder. *Humanity dying off?*

"Day after next, it'll be three weeks since we flew out here. Three weeks! We should have—"

"Hindsight's always twenty-twenty. Right?" I say. "Unless you're one-eyed Rocky the Randy Pirate," I add, laughing. "Then it's just . . . twenty."

He cracks up, and it makes my heart sing.

"It's still so surreal," I say. "I just want to take it all back, go back in time, not get on that plane. Stockpile food and put up a fortress in time. Live somewhere else, where this nightmare isn't happening."

Dad wraps his arm around my shoulder. "I should have let you bring the board."

"Huh?"

"Your longboard. I should have let you bring it. If I could go back in time, that's what I'd change."

"What?"

"Well, I'd change everything else, too. But—weirdest thing—that's been on my mind. I was wrong."

I laugh. "I actually think you were right."

"Really?"

"Yeah. If I had brought it, I would have lost it. Now it's waiting for me back home."

"Good point."

Dad absently draws in the dirt with his finger.

"We can't stay here, Lei. These . . . meals . . . we're getting weaker, not stronger. If we don't get a plane tomorrow or the next day . . . things aren't going to hold together here. So many people want out. I'm going to speak to some of them tomorrow, see if as a group we can . . . ask to leave."

"What will we do instead?"

Dad releases an explosive sigh. "We waited too long in Honolulu, and I don't want to make that mistake again."

"They just made it real clear that we can't leave."

"We have to ask. If they still say no, then . . . I want to get out before things deteriorate."

I look at the fence. The shouting has only gathered steam. *Before* they deteriorate?"

Dad grins ruefully. "We'll have a new moon in a couple days. It'll be darkest then. We have to find a way out during that window."

"Maybe we'll get on a flight before then."

Dad turns away. I reach down and snatch up the artificial sweetener while he isn't looking.

When a new tank of water is put out, I take my epilepsy medication and a bottle of painkillers over. I've been having headaches, probably because I'm dehydrated.

As I wait for my turn at the water jug, my mind is on fire with escape plans and the echoes of gunfire. I imagine trying to row thirty-plus miles over open ocean against the current and feel sick to my stomach. Nothing comes to mind that isn't high risk. It's finally my turn at the water tank. I pop the ibuprofen. Only a few left. My epilepsy pills: forty total. Twenty days' worth.

Leilani, I think. *Do your part.*

I put the pills away, my hands trembling. I pour Dad's packet of sweetener into my cup, close my eyes tightly, and drink. Then I race back to be close to Dad.

CHAPTER 15

*Y*ou *are Leilani. I am Leilani.*

It is a good thing. It passes on and my purpose is done.

The kahuna warns King Alapa`i, "One day a boy will be born who will kill every chief, rule every isle. Look for the sign of your doom—a great fire in the sky—and kill the newborn while he suckles."

Suckle. Gather your strength.

When Halley's Comet flares above the ocean, Alapa`i orders the baby Pai`ea murdered. But the infant's parents secretly pass his care to a friend.

Leilani. It passes. Time to linger and grow strong on the heat.

Pai`ea grows into a skilled warrior. Alapa`i dies, and Pai`ea slays the rightful heirs. He becomes the first to reign alone over the entire island of Hawai`i. He schemes with false gods to rule *all* the islands.

We are together now, but we will drift away, as I once did. For now, we linger.

He is forever known as Kamehameha, and of him the prophets sang:

> *E iho ana o luna*
> *E pi`i ana o lalo*
> *E hui ana na moku*
> *E ku an aka paia.*

> That which is above will come down
> That which is below will rise up
> The islands shall unite
> The walls shall stand firm.

I slowly come to. I'm lying on the same cot in our same muddy spot.

"Hi," Dad says, muffled by a face mask. "You back? You've been in and out for a while now, dazed."

I sit up. Dad's cross-legged in the mud beside me. I lift my own mask over my forehead. "Hey." After another moment of dialing in to my surroundings: "This isn't Hilo."

"I can't believe you did that."

"I'm so hungry."

"Here." Dad offers me a can of Spam.

My eyes grow wide and I peel it open and dig into it with my fingers. "Where'd you get this?" I ask between gulps.

"Well, it's your consolation prize. I tried everything. Apparently grand mal seizures are pretty low on the triage list these days, if you would believe it."

My memory grows clearer. The seizure happened Thursday night. "What day is it today?"

"Who cares?" Dad says. "It's Friday evening."

"Well, that was dumb."

"No. It served a purpose." Dad leans in close. "I'm convinced we're really on our own."

"What do you mean?"

"A bunch of us are going to petition tomorrow. And you'll scan the perimeter while I'm with the others. Look for any weak spots in the fencing along the ground that you and I could crawl under."

"Dad, this is insane. We can't just break out of a military camp. What about our bags and—"

"Tomorrow night, if they won't allow us to walk out of here, you and I start looking."

"Dad . . ." I begin. He watches me closely, waiting. But I don't really have anything to say.

"We can do this." He hugs me. "Eat your Spam. And drink as much as you can. You missed your doses. Today's, too. Take them both, and take them from now on."

"Okay," I say. "Oh, hey, Dad?"

"Yeah, hon?"

"Who won the round robin?"

He shakes his head. "No one's played soccer since the shooting."

* * *

In the morning dozens of people are vomiting and complaining of fevers and diarrhea. Very few eat the mush at breakfast; we all fear contamination. I'm so hungry, though; I force down some pasty oats mixed with ground-up Spam. While I'm psyching myself up for each bite, I grow clammy, thinking about scurrying under the fence.

I search for Aukina and find him standing guard near a part of the fence that's about to be converted into another gate. A second large pen has been constructed, and a chain-link corridor will connect it with our camp. Aukina stands alone with a pile of fencing supplies and tools. The sight of his face perks me up, a little. So. Damn. *Cham.*

"Aloha."

"Hey, Lei. Howzit? You feeling better?"

"You know what happened to me?"

"I think the four-star generals know what happened, the way your dad was . . . getting attention."

"You think it's funny?"

"No! Man, you're always giving me the stink-eye."

I sigh. *He's not to blame. Cut him some slack.* "It's just 'cause I know you know all of this is BS."

I see Aukina's knowing expression in his eyes above his mask.

"We want to leave, but no one will let us."

"I know it's bad, Lei. But be glad you're here, ah? Have you heard about the factions forming?"

"No. We don't know *anything*."

"The corporate farms keep getting occupied by new

162

militias, so we're taking them over. That's easy to deal with. But part of it's about a free Hawai`i. The Sovereign Nationers see a chance to secede from the States. Hawaiians are ganging up. The haoles are ganging up. The Asians are sticking together. The Filipinos . . . You and your dad are better off staying out of it. Especially since—"

"Ho. The Sovereign Nation folks?"

Aukina shrugs. "They're part of it, yeah. But it's messier than that. It's about `ohana, yeah?"

We're quiet for a moment. I hear the sound of gunfire somewhere across the bay again. The pops and cracks of distant bullets are just background now. Now it's about territory? People splitting into racial gangs? At least it's not just about Hawaiians and haoles. But . . . *What group am I in?*

Stop. That way of thinking is the problem.

"And there's some weird religious stuff behind some of it, too. Creeps me out."

"Aukina . . ."

"A few Christian 'armies' are drunk on hellfire."

"Aukina . . . People are dying in *here*. *You're* shooting us. Everyone's sick. The flights have stopped."

He just looks at me.

"I want out. My dad and I need to get home. Can you help us get on a plane?"

Aukina stiffens. "I have absolutely no sway over that kind of thing, Lei."

"Can you help us get out, at least? We'll swim the bay. Once we're back in Kailua, we'll figure out what's next."

He opens his mouth to protest but then falls silent, and finally says, "No, Leilani! I . . . No. What you're asking is . . ."

"Where's your family, Aukina? Where's your `ohana?`"

"My parents are here. Pearl City. My brother lives on base."

"My mom, my seven-year-old brother, and my grandpa are in Hilo, going through God knows what. We're broken, Aukina. I don't care about the turf wars. I don't care about the blackout. We need to get home. We'll swim if we have to. We need your help."

"Do you know how many people have died trying to get down the island chain? It's unbelievable, Lei. The ocean is powerful. We're saving lives. That includes you and your dad."

My hands go up to my face. *I'm not going to cry. I won't!* I just want to hide. "This is . . ." I can't find the words.

"I know," Aukina says.

"I had that seizure on purpose."

"What? You *faked* it?"

"No. It was real. I triggered it. And it showed that nobody gives a rat's ass about us."

"You want out *that* bad?"

"Are you honestly surprised?"

Aukina shifts his weight around. Silence settles between us. He hesitates, and then fishes through one of his breast pockets. His hand emerges with a small tin canister, like an Altoids box, but plain and dull. "Here. Take this. Quick. For your dad, too." He hands me the tin, urging me with his eyes: *Hurry! Hide it.*

"What is it?" I whisper as I fit it into my shorts' pocket.

"Iodide tablets."

"What're they for?" I know that most salt is iodized because it's such an important vitamin, or something, but I've never heard of tablets.

Aukina grimaces. "Don't ask. We're all taking them. You should, too."

I look him in the eyes. "I don't understand how your good intentions went so bad."

"Someone thought this camp would be a good idea. Someone else who doesn't care was put in charge of making it happen.

"But now problems *everywhere* are bigger. These camps are so low on the list, Lei, that—" He stops himself and readjusts the rifle strapped around his shoulder. He takes a few steps toward the pile of construction materials, picks something up, and then continues talking in a hushed tone.

"Lei, I want to tell you a secret. But don't repeat it. I'm trusting you."

I look him in the eye.

"So, our carriers and subs operate on nuclear fuel, right?"

I didn't know that, but I nod.

"There's a few in the . . . neighborhood. They're not acting right, though. There doesn't seem to be any danger, but who knows? Anyway, on top of that, we're out of gas. Unnecessary flights have stopped. We need what's left for something big. Our orders are to . . . I'd take you and your dad with us if I could. But I can do the next best thing, I guess."

"What?" I whisper. I've forgotten to inhale.

"I like you a lot, Lei. You're strong and you're . . . eye-catching. You're way older than your age. Hawai`i's going to need people like you. I really hope you'll be okay. I hate good-byes, but this is it, okay? Don't come find me again."

"I don't understand. . . ."

He tosses something at my feet. "Your shoe's untied." He turns away, stiffening to attention.

I look down. A foot-long bolt cutter is lodged in the mud at my feet, its red handles blaring in the sunlight. I kneel and pretend to tie my shoe. Without looking around, I snag the tool and, grimacing, slip it under my shirt and into the band at the bottom of my bra. My heart is pounding. I feel like a fugitive.

I catch Aukina's eye for a second. I want to say thank you, but his eyes shoo me away as if his gaze were a kick in my rear. I rise and walk away, hunched over, trying with all my might not to hurry or look suspicious.

Our ticket to ride.

I fasten the top two buttons of my blouse and roll my shoulders forward, praying that the handles aren't obvious.

CHAPTER 16

Thirty-two pills left. Past midnight on Tuesday morning. Very dark. The Orchid is slightly fainter tonight through the thickening haze. Still, it casts soft shadows from its shimmering perch in the sky. Dad's group petition took several days to organize, and it was a spectacular flop. With the blurry stars twinkling heartlessly above, we're finally ready to take matters into our own hands.

Crouched low, my knees in the mud, I slowly buckle my backpack, grimacing as its quiet click seems to shoot through the silent camp. Dad hefts his pack on his back, adjusting its weight, and nods to me. My heart thrumming in my chest, I abandon our cot.

We circle the perimeter of the canopy. The mud squishes beneath my boots.

We've accounted for the five guards patrolling inside the

soccer field. It doesn't look like they wear night-vision goggles, but we're not taking any chances. One thing about a field of people is that when everyone spreads out to sleep, it's easy to drop down and blend in—even with packs on our backs. That's what we're betting on, anyway.

We know there are guards stationed outside the fence, as well, but we don't know where or how many. At least there are no watchtowers, unless you count the bleachers beyond the track. I remind myself: we're trying to break out of a soccer field, not a high-security prison.

I drop and lie still, alerted by the muddy squish of an approaching guard.

A baby screams beneath the next tent, providing us cover to scurry forward several yards. I resist the urge to dash; no room for error. We must take our time weaving through the dense masses. We have all night, and our target position along the fence—the southeasternmost end nearest the bay—is only sixty yards away.

A flashlight scans in our vicinity, and we drop like possums again. Did a guard see us? I wait, breathless and motionless. Dad goes limp and relaxes his breathing somewhere behind me.

The light draws nearer, sweeping the ground in broad strokes. Someone *is* looking for us. I shift my position slightly, to be sure my pack will appear to be lying flat. An older Hawaiian man is lying next to me, no more than an arm's length away. In the dim light, it looks like he's staring right at me.

I smile sheepishly and give him a small wave with my fingers. *Please don't do anything,* I urge him with my thoughts.

The flashlight draws nearer still. As its beam searches our area, the old man's face is bathed in a flickering glow. I recognize him as the guy we talked to in line the first day. Wasn't he going to Maui, then Lāna`i? He should be long gone. His eyes are wide open. His mouth is slightly agape. *Stop staring at me; they're going to notice!* In a sudden, cold sweat, I realize that he's not looking at me. He's not looking at anything.

He's dead.

No breath comes and goes across his stiffened lips. His eyes are vacant, his expression frozen upon a dirt-streaked face. His gray hair is tousled and bristles gently in response to the eddies of the wind.

The flashlight continues its greedy search. A cockroach casually emerges from the V in the old man's button-down shirt, and I stifle a gasp. It crawls up onto his cheek, and then darts into his hair and out of view.

"Shhh!" Dad whispers from behind me. I bite my lip and close my eyes.

The light switches off. We wait. Eventually, the footsteps drift away. We raise our heads, gather our bearings, and continue toward the fence. I can't help glancing back at the dead man in the mud. He will never reach his son's farm. Above him, his wife sleeps peacefully on her cot.

I blink back tears.

Dad and I reach the edge of the field. The fence is only twenty feet away, across the hard-packed dirt track. It's so dark, with nothing but faint starlight and a menacing green glow to guide our sight. Still, the gap ahead feels awfully exposed.

"Ready, Lei?" Dad's breathing is short and fast.

I nod. "We have to be quick."

"Once we go, we're committed."

We wait for several minutes, listening, watching the shadows for signs of movement. Another baby cries somewhere far behind us.

"Now," Dad whispers.

We slink across the track, hunched over as low as possible without getting to our knees, and crouch at the base of the fence. Dad pulls the bolt cutter from the loose sleeve of his jacket and sets its jaws against the lowest link. He's trembling.

The tall fence will take at least a minute to cut through. But I picked this route during my scouting so that we'd have an easier out.

"Dad." I tug him away. "Over here."

Five feet to the right, the fence ends at a pole. The links are hastily lassoed onto the pole with five wire clips. I point to the clips and he smiles. "Excellent."

He snaps the five loops and the entire fence curls back like wallpaper. We squeeze through the gap without removing our packs, ducking beneath the intact Slinky of barbed wire, and we're free.

We cross a road and creep over to the side of the nearest building, the warehouse where our bags were stored. It's so dark that we have to go slowly to stay surefooted. I still feel exposed. Anyone with night-vision goggles could look from any direction and see us brazenly darting away from the camp. *This must be what rats feel like as they scurry across a field.*

An old Humvee in the near distance turns onto the road we just crossed. We duck behind a bus parked parallel to the warehouse.

Behind the bus hides a door to the warehouse. I try to open it. Locked tight. *Our bags are in there somewhere—with all our food.*

I look up and study the open windows that run along the wall, about eighteen feet off the ground. All of the wooden shutters, hinged from the top, are open, tied to a sprinkler system suspended beneath the high awning. Without air-conditioning it must be the only way to ventilate the building.

My mind races. *We have to find our bags. I can get up there. I can get in and out. We have the time. It's either get food now or fight for it later.*

"Dad, wait," I whisper, pulling him back as he marches onward.

"What?"

I don't tell him what I'm planning. He'll say no. "Just give me a second, okay?"

He watches, dumbstruck, as I remove my bag and scale the side of the bus, searching out hand- and footholds among the partially open windows and specialized armor plates.

"Leilani. Stop!"

"I'll be right back." On top, I pause, resting. The climb shouldn't have been that tiring, but my shaky weakness only reinforces what I need to do.

Okay, hurry up.

There's just enough light from the Emerald Orchid for me to see my target. From atop the bus, I leap for the sprinkler bar. A piece of cake after throwing myself from the hotel lanai. My hands grasp the bar and hold tight. I let my body swing, dissipating the energy of my jump. I heft my hands on the bar, catching a tighter grip, and a bolt somewhere yanks loose. I grunt but don't lose concentration.

"Lei!" Dad shout-whispers. "Dammit! Get down here."

"Aren't you hungry?" I call down in a low voice.

I start a controlled swing and catch my foot on the lip of the open window. Ignoring Dad's panicky pleas, I walk my hands up the wooden shutter and finally put all my weight on the windowsill. Now I can rest for a second.

"Dad. Quiet."

He grunts. I turn and inspect the interior of the warehouse. It's very dark inside. The ground seems awfully far away. But there's no activity in there—and I can *smell* food, like in a musty convenience store. It smells like a dragon's lair stuffed with endless treasure.

"Does your cell still have any charge?" I whisper.

Dad nods.

"Toss it up."

He complies. I almost feel guilty for bossing him around, but . . . whatevah. I catch his phone and turn it on. The old thing still runs. "Wait at the door." I stuff the phone in my pocket, and then I slip inside the warehouse.

"Hurry, Lei. Someone's going to see the hole in the fence."

Good point. I patiently dangle from the tips of my fingers, taking a deep breath. My feet are only going to be about twelve or thirteen feet off the ground.

You can do this.

I let go of the sill and slide, kind of controlled, down the inside of the wall. Luckily, I land on a box with a muffled thud.

I pull out the cell phone and shine its light. I'm sitting on a suitcase. Surrounded by luggage. *Our bags are in here somewhere.*

But the warehouse is chock-full of baggage. Piles of it. I'll never find our duffels. I begin to rifle through the nearest bags, looking for food that I can quickly haul away.

The suitcases are all empty. Other bags are empty.

They've taken the food out. We were never going to get our stuff back.

I creep forward, amazed at the limp bags stacked in high piles. Each has a numbered tag, just like the one that Lance Corporal Billings handed us when we arrived.

All lies.

Shelves materialize with the help of Dad's phone. Crackers. Jars of peanut butter. Boxes of cookies. Powdered-drink packets. Fruit leathers and dried fruit. Granola bars—maybe the ones we bought at Costco. Every bit of nonperishable food that anyone brought with them is here. I follow the shelves toward the front of the warehouse. The food becomes higher in protein as I advance. Bags of jerky. Waxed cheese. Salami sticks. Mixed nuts. Canned food. Towers of Spam and Vienna sausages.

I race back to the luggage, snag two large suitcases with rollers, and run back to the shelves, dumping in lots of fruit and granola bars, preserved meats, canned goods, cheeses, shrink-wrapped bags of jerky . . .

My hand stops on the shelf closest to the front of the warehouse. Hundreds of boxes line these shelves. The labels say: POTASSIUM IODIDE (KI).

The medicine the soldiers are secretly taking. I swipe dozens of boxes. I don't know why Aukina gave me his, but I know a lucky strike when I see one.

The suitcases fill quickly. *Go back for a third suitcase? A fourth?* Dad and I can each drag two. My thoughts spring back to the camp. That dead old man. His frail-looking wife, who's going to wake up in the morning alone. Hungry *keikis* asking around for food, nursing mothers with screaming babies, fights in the food line and at the water coolers. I see myself returning to camp, a superheroine hoisting bags of food, shouting the truth.

A grinding screech echoes through the warehouse, and light floods the aisles. I freeze.

A large garage door is rising at the front of the building. The headlights of at least two rumbling trucks pour in. I bolt with my suitcases and crouch behind a pile of luggage.

Voices echo. Flashlight beams whip along the rafters as

people jog forward. I slow my breathing, fending off faintness. Keeping low, I poke one eye around the luggage. Soldiers load the trucks with pallets of stacked food. Guards are stationed along either side of the garage doors. Have they been here the whole time? Sleeping? The thought makes me tremble.

I keep my eyes on them. One soldier pauses, so close. I could reach out and touch his leg.

Stay calm.

Dad must be jumping out of his skin. *Don't try anything,* I mentally warn him. The door where I told him to wait remains quiet.

Finally, the soldiers get back into the vehicles, and the rolling steel doors begin to lower. I watch the guards closely while I still have light. They're standing outside the warehouse, but they don't move as the door slams shut.

They would have seen us leaving here for the bay. I shudder.

The echoes of the rolling doors still reverberate as I wheel my two suitcases over to the side door. I wait for the lights of the trucks to glide by before opening it.

As the rumble of the vehicles drifts out of earshot, I press on the door latch, then freeze. *An alarm?* With the light of the phone, I inspect the doorframe for wires or anything that would indicate a trigger. I don't see anything.

Wincing, I press the door open. Slowly. Pause. Nothing. I open it farther. Pause. Finally, I poke my head out.

Dad stands behind the door with a two-by-four raised in his hands. He sets it down. "Are you out of your mind? What—"

"Food." I pull both suitcases into view. "More than we came with."

Dad's eyes widen. I think he's about to praise me, but he whispers, "How are we supposed to swim all this stuff across the bay? And we can't wheel all this down the open road past the base's main gatehouse. You need to consult with your father before breaking into guarded military buildings."

I bite my lip. How to get all of our stuff over the water never crossed my mind. We were going to float our backpacks beside us ... they're made for wet canyon hiking and river crossings, with inflatable compartments. But these suitcases?

Then I see the bus we're hiding behind.

"Dad, this is the bus that takes the *keikis* to the beach, right?"

"They all look the same."

"Can you open these compartments? Boogie boards. Floaties. Things like that."

"Ah," he says, popping open the first compartment under the bus. Nothing. All of the compartments are empty.

"Lei, let's go. We'll keep an eye out."

I pull on my pack. "So, do we leave this food here?"

He eyes me sternly, shakes his head. He picks up both suitcases. I try to grab one.

"No. I'm balanced this way; it's actually easier. And I don't think we should risk the sound of rolling them."

"Wait, Dad. Not that way! They're guarding the front of the warehouse."

"When did you become a ninja?" He follows me on a

winding route as I carefully scout out the path ahead. We can hear voices and boots on gravel behind buildings up ahead, but our course is remarkably free of patrols, and soldiers.

Gunfire sounds across the bay, a long, sustained burst. A machine gun? Is the military out on the island, securing the towns?

Who knows? Doesn't make any difference right now. I peek around the next corner. We dart for a bit of cover.

A flurry of flashlights from far behind catches my attention. I glance backward and my heart leaps into my throat: they must've discovered the hole in the fence. A dog barks. Another.

I hate dogs.

"Lei, go!"

We scurry into a grove of trees. I can hear the gentle lapping of water ahead. The thin strip of forest abuts some sort of compound, a water-treatment plant, maybe. I can just make out a parking lot through the foliage, and I smile.

I see the familiar silhouette of a surfboard on a roof rack. I point it out to Dad.

"Perfect."

The barking in the distance becomes more excited.

Please, God, no dogs.

We leave our bags and scurry to the SUV, free the longboard with quiet efficiency, and then duck under the trees.

The strip of forest ends in a pebbly beach, and the bay stretches out before us, only twenty yards away. With the built-in tubes of our backpacks already inflated, we tie the suitcases onto the longboard with my climbing rope.

Searchlights whip through the sky. The barking grows frantic—and closer.

"Ready?" Dad asks.

I peer across the dark at a few distant fires burning in Kāne'ohe. Calm as this bay is, protected from the ocean by the large promontory of the military base, it's still two miles across. Our plan is to arc to the left beyond the tidal sandbars in the mid distance and scope out a safe place to beach along the foot of the peninsula that connects the base to the rest of O'ahu.

The barking is nearer.

We sneak out into the water, carrying the suitcase-laden surfboard into chest-deep water. We remove our packs. Lying flat on the surface of the water, they bob gently on our little waves. We dog-paddle farther out into the gentle surf, pushing the floating packs and surfboard ahead of us.

Five minutes later, a pair of flashlights appear along the shore, accompanied by excited barking. The flashlights scan the bay, but we're out of range on the mild waves. After a few minutes, our trackers move back toward the base.

"First thing. When we get to the beach." Dad's teeth chatter. "We eat. Real food."

We pause intermittently to gather our strength as we dodge tsunami debris—mostly plastic trash—and then turn left, heading for the nearby shore. At one point I almost tip the suitcases.

"Don't soak our steaks," Dad jokes. It makes me wonder if the tins of tablets are waterproof. I should have checked.

Our feet touch the nearest beach of Kāne'ohe, still very dark. We haul our belongings up the beach and into the trees, free the suitcases, and ditch the longboard. Wordlessly, dripping wet, we each scarf down half a stick of salami and some dried fruit.

"Dad," I whisper, forcing down a strip of leathery mango the best I can without any water. "What's potassium iodide?"

He raises a dramatic eyebrow. "Nothing we want to be dealing with."

"Why?"

"It prevents radiation sickness during nuclear disasters."

"*What?*" I listen in cold shock.

"Iodine is processed by our thyroid glands, in our necks. Nuclear meltdowns produce radioactive iodine isotopes, and they enter our bodies through the thyroid. If you take potassium iodide, though, your thyroid glands can only process so much iodine at a time, so you coat the glands with safe iodine. The radioactive stuff won't enter the bloodstream. It can burn your mouth and throat and stomach, but it beats getting cancer. Why do you ask?"

It takes me a moment to find words. "Aukina gave me some, told us to take them. All the soldiers are taking it. I found boxes and boxes of the stuff in the warehouse, and I grabbed a bunch."

Dad is silent.

I whisper, "Was this whole thing . . . a nuclear war?"

Dad doesn't answer for a long time, but he finally shakes his head. "There are over five hundred nuclear plants around

179

the world, Lei. Not to mention submarines and aircraft carriers. If the power is out everywhere . . . it would be hard to pump fresh water into cooling tanks. With that many chances for something to go wrong, it could—*somewhere*—only take a couple weeks for used fuel to become exposed and sizzle through containment structures. Gas generators could hold off the situation for a while, but what happens when the gas is gone? A lot of plants could already be melting down. The radiation could render parts of the earth uninhabitable for millions of years."

I stop chewing.

Dad brushes sand off his hands. "The Three Mile Island disaster in 1979 was caused by a stupid pipe valve. Fresh water couldn't enter the cooling tanks, and fifteen minutes later the core was exposed. It turned into . . . it was like volcano lava. Oozed down to the bottom of the tanks and melted through six inches of solid carbon steel before anyone noticed. A few more minutes and there would have been an explosion that ripped the dome apart. It could have scorched the entire region. Something similar happened at Chernobyl in 1986, but they didn't contain it in time. It *did* explode. Parts of that region are still radioactive. And the Russians actually prevented the worst-case scenario.

"Can you imagine what's happening to all those five hundred plants without power? Without hundreds of employees running around at each of them turning dials and rerouting systems?"

"Stop. Please."

He pauses. "Hawai`i's probably the safest place on the globe, if it comes to that."

"Aukina said—" I cough, wishing desperately for water. "Aukina said something about aircraft carriers and subs 'in the neighborhood' dealing with issues."

"What kind of issues?"

"I don't know."

"Start taking the iodide," Dad says a minute later.

We each dry-swallow an iodide tablet—each fortunately sealed within a waterproof blister pack. I can feel a headache coming on. How will we find fresh water to drink?

"Lei, you snagged enough of this stuff to last us a year."

"Bleeding throats for a whole year. Yay."

"You might have just inadvertently gotten us our tickets home."

"What?"

Dad rubs a hand through my sopping wet hair. "Something to trade for passage. Infinitely more valuable than an effing Rolex."

The thought makes perfect sense. It lifts my spirits, in a mad sort of way. I wonder: *Is* that *what we're doing? Are we trading cancer prevention to get home? So that the five of us can slowly die together?*

CHAPTER 17

W e work our way through the houses along the beach to the nearest road. In spite of the tremendous effort that went into our escape, the entrance to the Marine Corps Base is only three-quarters of a mile away, across a thin causeway that stretches over the bay. We were so intent on getting out that I never really thought about the next steps. Get off the island . . . but *how*, exactly?

"I know where we should go," Dad says as we head inland along the side of the road. "It's in Kailua, but it's in the same direction as the beaches there. I think we can get there before morning. We hole up for a day and find a way off this rock."

"You make it sound so easy."

We march along the outskirts of Kāne'ohe, staying within sight of the road to Kailua but sticking to the bushy slopes of

the hills that separate the two towns. Cars occasionally putter along the road. After grueling hours of hauling our gear,
we come upon a flickering glow in the woods.

Cautiously, we approach the edge of a steeply sloped
clearing—and then we stumble back in shock. A pile of three
bodies lie in flames at the center of a bonfire. As we watch, a
fourth, naked corpse is tossed onto the pyre by four men. I
turn away, shutting my eyes tightly, but not before I see a bullet hole right between the eyes of the final body.

"Lei, you all right?" Dad pulls me close.

"I don't . . ."

"Stay with me, hon. Breathe." He looks into my eyes.

"It's not that, Dad."

"Follow me." We back away, lifting the suitcases as the
powerful roar of a vehicle comes from up ahead. Lights jostle
into view over the nearest hill, scattering the shadows of trees
like elongating claws. We dash into the brush as a van rockets
past. A half-dozen men burst from the van with handguns
and fire on the pyre builders.

The four pyre builders dash for their weapons. Within
seconds they crumple, dead.

The newcomers race toward the pyre; they struggle to
pull out the burning bodies and beat out the flames.

I'm frozen in place, and my headache throbs with my
pulse. It looks like they're trying to rescue people they know.
Others raid the enemy truck, hauling away milk crates filled
with food.

"Come on. Now." Dad takes my hand and we scurry away

until we're over the next hill. As we slide down, Dad whispers, "You okay?"

"What the hell . . ." I catch my breath, dizzy.

"Christ—that was the worst thing I've ever seen," says Dad.

Why did we leave the base? I want to scream. My headache tempers my panic, though. *Focus on that pain, not what you just saw.* We march onward, jumping at every shadow and sound. Finally, we arrive on the streets of what used to be a well-to-do neighborhood on the slopes of Kailua. With the sky already pink with approaching sunrise, Dad weaves us through trash heaps and burnt-out car shells with the same caution we used to escape the base.

Just as the sun peeks over the edge of the ocean, Dad relaxes his white-knuckled grip on the suitcase handles. "Here we are. Quick," he whispers, and tells me that we're at the Oʻahu home of the chancellor of UH Hilo. Dad's been here. The chancellor and his wife were in Hilo when we left. The place should be empty.

Dad cautiously knocks on the front door of the little yellow bungalow. "Hello?" No answer. We slip into the backyard, broad leaves and tall ginger blooms providing cover.

Dad snatches up a garden gnome near the back lanai and punches the red pointy hat through the window of the porch door. Carefully, he reaches through and unlocks the door.

"Dad, I need water so bad."

"We'll find some in here."

In the kitchen he opens the fridge and steps back, holding

his nose. "So much for *that*." He slams the door. "Try the cabinets."

The cabinets are empty. I glance at the door to the garage. Pried open. "We're not the first people to snoop around in here." I pointlessly twist the faucet.

"You're dehydrated," he says.

"I think so."

"Why didn't you say anything?"

I shrug. "You'd've had me licking leaves or something."

"You're right." He snaps his fingers together. "I've got a better idea."

He snatches an empty water bottle from his pack and walks into the bathroom.

He lifts the toilet-seat lid and stares at the water in the bowl.

"Dad. You have got to be . . ."

"Just teasing." He drops the seat cover and removes the lid along the tank. "Bingo!"

He dips the water bottle into the back of the toilet and presents it to me as if he's offering frankincense to baby Jesus. I stare at it, and then I guzzle down the water. Once I've emptied it, Dad refills it for himself. He fills it again and hands it back to me.

He checks the medicine cabinet and tosses a big bottle of aspirin to me. I greedily flush two tablets down.

"Don't ever tell anyone about this," I command. "Ever."

"Not a word."

We go into the master bedroom. Dad ducks under the

bed and surfaces with a black security box. It's locked. "Who-ever broke in didn't know to look here."

"What's that?"

"Something John shared with me. At the time, I did not approve."

He hefts the box, places it on the bed, scratches his head. We find a hammer in a kitchen drawer. Dad claws at the box. Useless, I wander the rooms. I take off my shoes and socks and curl my toes against the soft throw rugs. Just to be indoors—a roof to block the sun, no mud on the ground, warm colors on the walls—I could be in Buckingham Palace. I roam, savoring every moment, studying the photographs of Hawaiian flowers and coral reefs and the portraits of the chancellor and his family.

What I wouldn't give just to see a *picture* of Mom and Kai. I grab my phone to look through my pics—and remember that it's zapped. My longing hits me like a bout of nausea. I pace the hall. *Not even a hundred miles between us.*

I'm coming, Mom. Kai. Grandpa. Be strong. I blink back tears.

Dad is still working.

I return to the bathroom. A clean toilet seat: I imagine it's like a first-class bed-chair on a long flight. I've never enjoyed sitting on porcelain so much. I feel like a queen. I turn to flush and stop just in time. Do we need that water?

When I see myself in the mirror, I gasp. I look like what an Egyptologist might see when she unwraps a mummy. Thin. Disheveled, tangled hair. Dirt—everywhere—mixed with scratches and endless mosquito bites . . .

Aukina called this "eye-catching"?

You'd think I'd recently had several seizures, jumped from a burning building, languished in a prison, broken out of a military complex, death-marched through the jungle, and survived the OK Corral. I shouldn't be so surprised. I find a brush, go to wet my hair, and then stare at the brush. *I need water.* Such a basic thing, just one turn of a knob away. *Dip the brush in the toilet tank?* No. That's our drinking water.

I can't even brush my hair anymore.

A dismal understanding begins to descend. Brushing my hair—it's nothing, really. But I finally see that this disaster is going to have consequences I haven't even dreamed of.

Numbness settles in. *My entire future—gone.*

If the world really is broken, I'll never go to prom. I'll never finish watching *Star Trek* with Dad. I'll never pass a driver's test, go to college, or have a boyfriend. I'll never backpack in Europe. I'll never have another ice shave.

I'll never refill my seizure medication.

Dad cries, "Aha!" I run to see.

He holds a large pistol.

"I've never seen you with a gun," I say in a near whisper. "It . . . doesn't look right."

"I'm from New Mexico, hon. My childhood had plenty of guns."

"I thought you didn't believe in violence."

"I never believed in Armageddon, either, but guess what?"

"It believed in you?" I offer.

Dad laughs, then grows somber. "If God won't play by the rules, then I don't have to, either."

187

I watch him, incredulous. He cocks the hammer, flips open the chamber, loads the gun, and snaps the chamber back into place. He knows what he's doing.

"Won't that . . . make us less safe?" I say.

His eyes are stern. "My *only* concern is your safety."

I stare as if seeing him for the first time. He's in charge now. I look at the pistol.

"Don't touch," he orders. "Not for you."

I resist the urge to step back. He has nothing to worry about. I see that man's head explode outward, painting the sail red. Four rapid, hollow pops—nothing like in the movies. A man is erased.

"Why did God break the rules, Dad?"

Dad places the gun on the coffee table. I follow him into the bedroom, where he rummages through the closet, emerging with a holster and a belt. He runs the belt through his trouser loops and the holster and then tightens the belt all the way to the final hole. "I still don't know how to answer that. But I owe you a response, don't I?"

We go back to the living room and sit. "There's a couple easy outs. One is to say 'There is no God.' Another is 'This was always His plan; we've always known about Revelation and we were supposed to be prepared.' But both try to fit a square peg into a round hole, yeah?"

I shake my head, clueless.

Dad rubs his rough chin. "Think of it like a scientist. When I design an experiment, I make guesses based on my best understanding. When what I'm studying does something unexpected, I conclude that my assumptions were wrong. I don't just give up on science altogether."

"Dad, I'm lost."

"The world has changed, right? Our understanding of a loving God is being challenged by new variables. But what are we supposed to do, reject the entire notion of God, just because the new scenario doesn't match what we anticipated? Or do we decide to keep exploring? Keep asking new questions to understand something we still have a lot to learn about?"

"I think I get it."

"Kind of ironic, isn't it? I'm angry. But it's my very nature as a scientist that keeps me from rushing to convenient conclusions."

"Well, what about the other thing you said? Meltdown. What if this *is* the Apocalypse? Judgment Day? And other Christians had it right the whole time? You were just too proud a scientist to take the Bible literally?"

Dad laughs. "Ever thought of being a trial lawyer? Your cross-examinations are tough."

Yes. But that future is gone.

Dad takes my hands. "I just think that if you rush to that conclusion, you're guilty of confirmation bias. When you really want an experiment to give certain results, you tend to ignore evidence that might invalidate your conclusion.

"I've witnessed nothing to suggest the miraculous. Why should I ignore the possibility that *we're* responsible? I'd be missing out on some powerful lessons if I absolved humanity."

"How are we responsible for this?"

"Easy. Don't forget, the only thing that has happened here is a power outage. A hundred years ago this thing's arrival would have resulted in a global hiccup. We became too reliant on an unsustainable resource. Right?"

"Well, why didn't God stop it from happening, even if it's not His fault?"

Dad shrugs. "God is acting as He always has, you know? Why didn't He stop hurricanes from killing people, famine in Africa, the Holocaust? Acts of terrorism? God has always let bad things run their course. His response to this disaster actually reinforces our current understanding. All the more reason not to let this shake your faith."

"Well, I'm still mad."

"You *should* be angry. You have every right to be. I am."

I let my head sink onto Dad's shoulder. He pulls me close, says, "In the back of my mind, I always wonder if there's really a deity out there. God. Gods. Akua. But my faith is a comfort to me, just as your Hawaiian heritage is a comfort to you. It's a comfort to believe that there's an afterlife that we'll go to. That there's a place my parents are, even though they're gone from here. If I reject that whole system now, in the very moment when I need comforting the most, what else do I have?"

"We have each other."

Dad nods. "I hope so. I hope to God you're right."

It takes me a moment to realize he's not concerned that I'd ever ditch him. He's coming to grips with something that I've been refusing to consider.

He's scared that Mom and Kai are gone.

CHAPTER 18

We nap late into the afternoon on opposite sides of a king-sized pillow-top mattress covered in soft linens. We could have our own rooms, but we need to be together.

I dream.

I stand inside a big plant nursery on the outskirts of Hilo. Several hundred different species of orchids are on display along narrow counters, an elaborate garden project turned tourist trap. I wander the aisles, looking for the Emerald Orchid among the potted plants.

Kai darts between the aisles and ducks beneath one of the counters. I chase him, but he's gone. Mom's on the far side of a table, an orchid resting above her ear. She's talking to me, but I can't hear the words. A *tita* from school stands in my way, a pistol gripped in her hand. She raises the pistol at me. "Stay away, haole."

I take a step backward, but freeze. *No. I won't run.* I clench my fists and stride toward the girl.

She flees.

Kai and Grandpa are next to Mom. They race toward the gift shop. I chase them, but I can't reach the end of the orchid aisle. No matter how fast I sprint, the gift shop only grows farther away.

* * *

It's early evening. The dream rests on my chest like a lead X-ray apron. I nudge Dad awake.

"Bad dream."

"I'm right here, Lei." He puts his hand on my arm.

Later, Dad ventures outside and finds a drum of rainwater in the backyard. No more toilet tank. I know those tanks have clean water, but still. We drink as much rainwater as we can, and fill our water bottles. I finally brush my hair. We wash up—*yes!*—and I shave my legs—*double yes!* We collect the dried contents of our packs from the backyard clothesline. I change into new clothes. A small thing that has a big impact. I even smile when I look in the mirror.

I should just cut my hair; it'll be way easier. I open drawers, searching for scissors. I find a pair, turn back to the mirror and put them down. I have my mom's hair. I drape it over my shoulder and run it through my hands. Silky, velvety black hair. It'll be a rat's nest before too long, but I can't cut it.

I braid it tightly. Cornrows would be even better. Mom would have done them well, but I'm not going to bother asking Dad. There's a new tube of lip gloss in one of the drawers.

The color is called "Kiss." A light pink, almost natural. Perfect. I try it on and smile. I tuck the tube into my pocket.

I can't shake the image of Mom talking with no sound; of me, sprinting to catch my family.

"I'll get home. Nothing will stop me," I say aloud.

I escape to the chancellor's study, where I pore over shelves of books like I'm Kai in a candy store. A good book will distract me. After I redo my nails—I'm getting bored with spearmint, but oh well—I settle into reading a novel that I started at home, hunched over a quivering candle flame. The hours melt away, just like in the olden days, when candles were things you only used for nice dinners and fragrance.

* * *

Before dawn we eat a breakfast of crackers and waxed Brie. Dad shaves his feral beard. With just enough light to see by, we switch all of our food and the potassium iodide into the backpacks and put everything else in the suitcases. The packs also hold a few changes of clothes, our two-person tent, and essentials like my medicine.

I pop my morning pill. Twenty-nine left.

The packs are incredibly heavy, but if we have to ditch the suitcases, we won't lose the food.

We pore over a large map of Hawai`i and examine the terrain between us and our family. I can't believe that we flew here from Hilo in forty minutes while I listened to music with my eyes closed.

Dad says, "Looks like Moloka`i is about thirty miles away from Kailua Beach Park. The park is only an hour's walk from here. Moloka`i should always be visible once we're on the water."

"And then Moloka`i to Maui. Ten miles? A cinch."

"I hope so. Then we have to get through Maui. Launch for the Big Island from Hana. Another thirty miles on the water. But first, Hana. Don't forget: eastern Maui is a ten-thousand-foot-high volcano. Better to skirt the coast on a boat."

As Dad is talking and pointing at the map, I rub my eyes. It sounds like we're planning an old British expedition to discover the mouth of the Nile, or something.

An urgent knocking at the door. We share an uncertain glance. The knocking continues. We've shuttered all the front windows, but I can see a pair of eyes through the remaining gaps. They know we're in here.

"You're not safe here. They're coming!" a man shouts. "Please, John, hurry."

Dad moves to stand flat against the door but doesn't open it. He holds the gun tightly in his hand. "Who's coming? Who are you?"

"It's Haku. I saw you in the garden last night. They're sweeping the block. If they find you, they kill you."

Dad unlocks the door and holds it open just far enough to peer out. "Which way are they going?"

"Who are you?" Haku asks, startled. He takes a step back. He's an older fellow—Hawaiian—with wire-frame glasses and gray hair.

"John's in Hilo. I'm a professor at the U. We were just leaving. Which way?"

"Go out the back," he says, looking over Dad's shoulder at me. It's clear he's risking a lot by rushing over to our porch. "Go right—makai. I gotta go."

"*Who's* after us?" Dad says.

"The Filipinos, and some others, are after whites." Haku darts down the driveway.

"Come on," Dad says.

I snatch the road atlas, roll it, and stuff it into my backpack. We yank our possessions through the dark brambles. Dad pushes our gear over a wooden fence and we scramble after it, emerging on a winding residential street. I realize that I've been trying to hold my breath, and I take in a lungful of air. We rush along the dim sidewalk, finally able to roll our suitcases. I'm terrified, but what else are we supposed to do? A Jeep rumbles down the nearest cross street, and we dive into someone's yard. But who was in the Jeep? I'm not even sure who we're running from. They can't be everywhere, can they?

I feel like a ghost lingering among the living—or maybe it's the other way around. I imagine the eyes of wary monsters watching us from the shadows of every window. I'm just as frightening to them as they are to me.

No one belongs anywhere anymore.

It's only a matter of time before somebody decides they have more of a right to our things than we do.

Dad often rests his hand on the grip of his pistol, as if it brings him comfort. It just makes me more anxious.

I look at a map of Kailua. A canal runs the entire length

of the neighborhood, splitting in two about three miles from here. One branch curves south into a large pond beside hundreds of homes. The other branch darts north and dumps into Kailua Bay. If we can find someone with a boat along the canal or the pond, we can avoid boating past the Marine Corps Base before looping right toward Moloka`i.

And if none of that pans out, we look for an outrigger canoe.

We turn right onto the nearest canal access path, leaving the houses and their invisible spying eyes behind. We're in a strip of unkempt grass that separates the houses from the canal. The banks of the waterway are lined with tall trees and bushes that offer more cover. Dad and I take turns darting into the bushes to steal a glimpse of the canal. Not even a kayak.

Our prospects for escaping O`ahu are probably worse than ever. We're twenty-three days out from the president's severed speech, we're on foot, and the marinas along this coast have suffered the wrath of a tsunami. Who cares if we have iodide to barter? Everyone who wanted to leave O`ahu and had a way to do it is long gone.

There was a widower in Hilo who lost his wedding ring in the Wailuku River. He returned to the pool where it had slipped off his finger every afternoon for ten years, diving, swimming, sifting, endlessly turning over stones. He breathed his last one fall afternoon, suffering from pneumonia, and was buried next to his wife without the ring. I couldn't understand his compulsion then. Now I do. There are some things you never give up on, no matter the odds.

"Dad!" I call. It's my turn to peek through the underbrush while Dad babysits the suitcases. A rickety pier juts out from a cobbled bar along the near bank of the canal. Moored to it is a fifteen-foot, center-console fishing boat with a sunshade and an outboard motor. The sort of boat tourists charter when they want to go deep-sea fishing for a couple of hours—it looks quite capable of a run between the islands. And I can see three large, red tanks of gasoline stored under the canopy beside the wheel. It's idling, motor in the water.

Dad appears and gasps. "This is our boat."

CHAPTER 19

After shuffling onto the decrepit dock, we stand dumbfounded, as if we've just discovered a living, breathing dodo bird.

Dad jolts into motion, tossing his suitcase into the boat. "Give me your bags."

"Dad," I whisper. "We're just going to take it?"

"Do you want to go home, Lei? This is it. Now or never. Quick."

I hand him my suitcase. I can't believe our luck; I can't believe we're five minutes away from being in the open ocean, when I was just despairing.

But I pause.

This is someone else's boat. Someone nearby. They have their own plans for it. They've made preparations. *What if they're trying to escape from O'ahu, too, and they've spent days gathering the gasoline?*

"Lei, now!"

"Maybe we can all go together."

Dad stiffens and leaps back onto the deck, squeezes me tightly against his left shoulder and faces the trees. I freeze. A thirty-ish haole man watches us from the shadows of the trees on the far side of the dock. He steps forward hesitantly, eyes on the gun on Dad's hip.

I flashback to the boat thief's head exploding against the white sail.

"What're you doin'?" He's muscular and tall. He runs a hand over the top of his sunburnt head. His T-shirt says "Volcom Pipe Pro."

Oh, man . . . he's just a surfer.

"Get away from my boat, will ya?"

"We need to go to Moloka`i," Dad says, a tremble in his voice. "We've been trying to leave here for three weeks."

"Will you take us?" I ask. Dad shakes me, but I don't care. "No one wants to steal your boat. Will you take us? We have food. We have iodide pills to stop the radiation. We'll help you find more gas when we get there."

"I'm not going anywhere." The guy takes another step closer. "I'm getting goddamned sick and tired of this. Can't come ashore without someone begging for help. Get away from my boat. Grab your stuff and move along."

Dad pulls the pistol from his hip. I can feel his quickened breathing. The gun wavers in his outstretched hand. The man hops backward and then steadies himself. He puts his hands up and smiles thinly. "Hey, come on, man. Don't do this. Your daughter . . ."

"Dad," I say.

"Shut up!" Dad shouts. The gun shakes at the end of his stiff arm. We fall silent. "Now, you can take us to Moloka`i, and then keep your boat. We'll pay you in iodide. Or we'll just take it. Up to you."

"I don't want this to end badly any more than you do, man. Just chillax, okay?" He's slowly advancing. "Is there . . . is there radiation? Where'd you hear that?"

"Stop right there." The surfer doesn't listen. Dad raises the gun skyward and clicks the trigger. Nothing. The man rushes to tackle Dad. But Dad pushes the safety off with his thumb and pulls the trigger lower. A thunderous crack pounds against my ears. The bullet fires high over the surfer's head. He stumbles backward. "Jesus Christ! All right."

He looks behind him and glances at the boat, deliberating. "I'll take you. Don't screw with me, though; I need this boat. Okay?"

"We just want to get off O`ahu." Dad unwraps his hand from around me and wipes his brow. "I promise. Now, we're going to get in the boat. Don't try anything like that again, okay? Once we're in, you can come on board."

"It took three days to siphon all this gas."

"You can sit up front," Dad continues. "I'll drive. I'll have the gun trained on you all day."

"No worries, man. You win, all right?" The man stays back, glances nervously behind himself into the trees, and stands with his arms upraised.

My ears are ringing fiercely. I had no idea how loud a gun

is close up. Dad directs me onto the boat, keeping an eye on both of us. "Stay at the back," he says. I crouch in the boat and drop my backpack.

Dad steps into the boat and takes the console, his eyes on the surfer. He still has a shaky grip on the gun as he uses the other hand to flip the motor from neutral into reverse. The boat's rear pulls away from the dock, and Dad steadies his free hand on the steering wheel. "Now jump onto the nose if you're coming, and untie us."

The stranger carefully walks forward, hops on, and turns his back to us, glancing at the trees, stalling.

"Now!" Dad cries.

The surfer loosens the rope from the pier and starts to pull it in.

Another man emerges from the trees with a heavy red gasoline tank. He drops it and reaches for his own pistol.

"Dad! Gun!" I shout.

The surfer yells, "Hurry!" and turns, rising, about to fling himself at Dad.

Dad ducks, punches the throttle downward. We're in reverse, and the surfer falls backward into the water. Gunfire echoes in my ears. I have no idea where it's coming from.

A bullet hole materializes next to my foot, and I yelp. Dad flips the throttle all the way forward. The boat slams to a halt, churning the water behind me white, and then accelerates forward. I grab on to a compartment to keep from tumbling out.

The gunfire continues. Dad crouches low but never lets

go of the wheel. He reaches across his body and fires blindly at the shore. I glance back as we race away. The gunfire pops continue, and I stare dumbly at the man on the shore with his arm outstretched, too confused to realize that he's firing directly at us.

The canal is straight and narrow. We race down the center. Dad slows only when a sharp bend approaches. He takes the turn and then pushes the throttle forward again.

My heart stops. There's a wet stain spreading outward from a small tear in the back of his shirt.

"Dad, you've been shot!" I cry.

"Lei, sit down!" he shouts. "Sit down."

"Oh, my God. Oh, my God," I whimper, hands to my mouth.

"I'm okay. I'm not shot." Dad glances back at me. "You're spooked, that's all."

I shake my head. The back of his shirt near the right shoulder has grown a dark, tear-shaped stain.

We come to the fork in the canal. Dad turns left and speeds up. Soon we fly under a road, past Kailua's formerly famous white-sand beach, and out into the bay. Dad cranks the throttle and we scream away from shore.

Ten minutes later he slows the boat to a crawl on the open ocean and checks the back of his right shoulder with his left hand. His fingers come away red.

He half smiles, stunned. "I'm shot."

I can't believe this is happening. No. Take it back!

"You're right." He looks around, as if checking the rest

of his body for holes. "Are you okay? Are you hit?" His voice rises.

I shake my head, but then I check. "No, nothing. Dad . . . is it bad? We need to get you to the hospital."

Dad shakes his head. "We're not going back. We're finally out."

"Dad! Don't be stupid." His image grows blurry as my eyes well with tears.

"I'll live. We'll make it to Moloka`i."

"Dad . . ."

"Lei, please, *sit down!*" He winces.

I plop down and run my hands through my hair. The waves are big, and the boat, crawling forward, rocks back and forth. "Is it still in there? Aren't you going to get infected?"

Dad doesn't answer. I wait for what feels like minutes. He's deep in thought, at war with himself.

"Please, Dad."

"There are no hospitals to run to, Lei!" he shouts. He sits down next to me. The boat rises over a giant wave and sinks down into the next rolling trough. "I don't think I'm hit anywhere important. We have to gun it for Moloka`i, okay? See it, there?"

He points east, to a faded mound of land that looks farther away than thirty miles.

"If we gun it, we can be there in an hour and a half. Twenty miles an hour, give or take? Right? I'll take it easy, okay? We'll find help there."

"Dad, the base is only ten minutes away. We know they'll

have equipment." My heart is pounding. He'll say no. There's nothing I can do.

He stands up, trying to hide a grimace, takes the wheel, pushes the throttle forward, and steers toward the distant break in the horizon.

"We could've gotten away if I had listened to you."

"Look, we got away, Lei. We did it." He pauses. "Your way would have been better."

I search the boat. Empty, aside from the three gas tanks. No life jackets, no water, no first-aid kit. I don't see any oars. Dad can't swim now. And even if he could, he's covered in blood, which would delight the sharks. If we don't make it to land on our first attempt, we'll be at the mercy of the tides and the currents. We could drift out to sea.

I approach Dad, try to examine his shoulder tenderly. His shirt is sticking to his skin.

He barks. "Ow. Please. Don't touch."

"I just want to try to stop the bleeding."

"No. Not right now."

Forty-five minutes crawl by, and though O'ahu has grown distant, Moloka'i doesn't look any larger.

The waves are taller than our boat. I never could have guessed that the open ocean would be *this* powerful. I'm sure that every swell that rushes toward us will capsize us. The boat muscles through but sways alarmingly.

Moloka'i is far out of reach. "Twenty miles an hour? Maybe that's what the current is doing *against* us."

Dad is stiff at the wheel.

The motor sputters. Dad shuts the engine off and instructs me while I refill the gas. I do my best to pour a full canister into the tank. The rocking of the boat on the high swells makes me slop gas all over the motor. I lean my head away from the tank as the fumes engulf my face.

"Careful, hon; we can't afford to lose any—"

"I know!" I yell, panicky.

I take a deep breath. *Slow down.* Finally, I train myself to pour a little at a time, syncing my tipping with the rolling ocean.

Dad fires the motor back up. We cut through the enormous, choppy waves like an ox driver plowing a lava flow.

The motor dies again. I pour in the second red tank.

I've never been to Moloka`i. "What's it like over there?" I ask above the wind and the roar of the motor.

"Not sure."

I refill the motor. The last canister is only half full. Dad winces at this news. We veer northward and head due east as the nearest tip of Moloka`i approaches. It's obvious that Dad's hurting, and the strain of talking over the noise requires effort, but he explains, "If I didn't have a hole in my shoulder, we might play this safer. But we're going to shoot the moon." He wants to situate us so that we'll drift toward land and not away from it if the motor fails. He thinks we might be able to reach Kalaupapa, halfway along the northern coast of the island. That's the famous refuge of Father Damien. It's the nearest town that we can reach along the north shore. Kualapu`u is technically closer, but it's perched a thousand feet up sheer cliffs.

Though we're half a mile offshore, we're finally alongside a new island. Finding help for Dad is no less urgent, but relief blankets my anxiety. Home feels nearer, the horrors of O'ahu distant.

The coastal cliffs rise ahead of us, and the ocean grows angry. My grip on the bench tightens as we pass our last obvious landing before the coast becomes a wall. We're asking for too much. Dad knows; his left fist is clenched around the steering wheel.

With the low-lying shelf of Kalaupapa visible miles away, our motor dies. We have nothing more to feed it, and no way to steer the boat forward.

We drift toward the rocks at the base of the cliff face.

Why was I fooled into hoping?

I hear Dad stifle a moan of frustration or despair. He circles the boat, gripping his right shoulder, searches the cabinets, finds nothing new to help us. I watch hopelessly as he ducks over the port side of the boat and attempts to paddle with his good arm.

"Dad," I plead, but it comes out as more of a gulp. He sits up and wipes the ocean spray away from his eyes—or is it tears?

"Lei, we can't get there."

Kalaupapa: I can see it. It's within our grasp, maybe four miles away. But we'll never reach it now.

A giant wave lifts our boat and carries us toward shore like a surfboard. I cry out in alarm. Dad stumbles over and wraps his good arm around me. We rebalance and brace for the next wave.

"Inflate the packs," Dad says. "We may need to abandon ship."

"The suitcases?"

"Forget them. That's why we rearranged things. Hurry!"

I jump to work, watching the waves crash against the cliffs. The current is carrying us backward as the tide pushes us in. There's no way around it: if we try to scramble to shore by leaping off the boat as we reach land, we'll be crushed against the rocks for sure. We're going to have to beat the boat to shore. If we can find high ground on the steep slope, crouched atop a boulder or tucked into some crevasse, maybe we can escape the onslaught.

Maybe we can walk a strip of land during low tide.

Dad's shoulder oozes. Sharks . . . *Stop*. No second-guessing. We will jump. No Dad heroically staying on the boat to keep sharks away from me. If we bail, we go hand in hand.

"Dad, can you swim?"

He hoists his inflated pack loosely up on his left shoulder. "We're both strong swimmers, Lei. We'll stick close, but if you can scramble onto a rock, do it. Don't come for me. Don't. I'll make it. We'll meet up as we can."

I can hear what he's actually saying, but even so, panic recedes. My senses focus. My mind clears of doubt. I see what we must do, and my muscles are ready to act, with or without my blessing.

We watch the wall grow nearer. Among the jagged rocks are occasional inlets clattering with tumbling stones. If it's the only beach, we'll take it.

"Lei, go!"

I look into Dad's eyes. I see a bravery that sears itself into my knowledge of my father. The pain eats at him. He knows he can't swim. The forces churning below will swallow him. He knows that we must jump. He wants to send me to safety.

"Go, Lei. Go! I'm right behind you."

He won't give up the act. I see the good-bye on his face. He hasn't given up, but he knows that only a miracle will save him.

But this is the end of the world. God has run out of miracles.

I dive into my suitcase. The climbing rope springs out.

"Lei, go! No TIME!"

I invent a slipknot, hand him the loop of my lasso. "Under your shoulders!"

He drops his pack. "Stubborn as your mother!"

I pass the loop through the shoulder straps of his inflated backpack and hand it to him. He slips it tenderly over his arms. The boat surges toward the cliffs. We will dash against a jagged outcropping within another wave or two.

I tie the rope around my waist, seize my inflated pack by a strap, bunch up the slack rope, hold it in one hand. "Swim with the current. We can make that cove." I point with my chin. "Hold your pack. Kick. I'll do the rest."

"Promise you'll free that knot if you have to."

"Okay."

One shared look. We leap.

A wave swells up and nearly knocks us against the hull

of the boat. I scramble to secure my pack. Dad is beside me, chest up, holding on to his pack with his good hand, kicking, breathing labored. I hold on to the rope near him, reducing the slack, and swim away from the boat as hard as I can.

We rise several feet with the crest of another wave. The next one will break right on top of us. *Hold your breath, Dad, I think.* Then we're underwater.

I surface several feet closer to the rocks and study my options.

I must navigate us through a narrow gauntlet, time the swell just right so that it delivers me right up to the wall of the nearby shelf without smashing me against it.

Then I'll have seconds to scurry up the rock face before the next wave pounds, loosening my grip. Meanwhile, how to hoist up Dad and two packs?

The boat slams into the rocks with a deafening crunch, as if they were the jaws of a sea monster. The hull scrapes along the ocean's sharp teeth, splintering open. I don't look; my sights are set on the lava shelf before me. I detect a crude natural stairway a little to the right, and swim feverishly to align with it.

The next swell carries me up to the low wall. I seize a handhold in the volcanic rock as the tide reverses, my pack hooked in the crook of my opposite elbow. The rope disappears into the water, but it's still tied to my waist. Beneath the surf, my feet scramble for purchase, hindered by the weight of my hiking boots. Finally, my toe grips a ledge and I pull myself up the crude stairway, racing the next swell. My leg is tangled in the rope, but plenty of slack remains. Just as I reach the top of the shelf, the waves break on the wall, and a geyser of ocean water pummels me.

I crawl farther ashore, gasping for breath. And then I'm tugged backward by my tangled leg. My forehead smacks against the rock and I grope wildly for a handhold as my pack and I slide toward the ledge, Dad rushing away with the reverse tide. I turn and lock my free foot into a deep pock and, now on my back, whip my arms out behind me to grip the rough rock.

The tugging finally stops. I spring up and free my leg. Blood drips into my eyes from my forehead. I wipe my face and search for Dad in the swell.

I see the bag. Not him. *Is he already gone, sunk below the waves?* Then I spot his head behind the bag. His good hand grips a shoulder strap. His face is contorted in agony, and he's struggling to keep his head above water.

"Hang on!" Frantically, I reel in the rope.

I'm blasted by another wall of water; the tide reverses. I loop my hand around a bight in the rope and pull fiercely. Nā-maka-o-Kaha`i wants Dad for herself, but I want him more. *Jealous witch!* I sob with rage. *Pull. Pull.*

I drag him up to the base of the crude stairway. "Ditch the bag!"

He releases the backpack and clutches the same handle I used. The bag bobs away, but the rope is still looped through the shoulder strap. As the swell relents I stoop down the shelf and grab the strap of his empty gun holster. He pulls himself upward with three good limbs, and I yank him forward with all my might.

We tumble into a heap atop the shelf as another wave punishes us. Dad crawls forward, coughing violently, while I pull on the rope to reel in his backpack.

A moment later, we huddle together just out of reach of the spray, our packs piled beside us amid a nest of tangled rope.

"No way I could have done that alone," Dad pants, coddling his shoulder.

Emotions swell and wash over me. Nausea.

The boat has capsized thirty feet away, pinned against jagged boulders. The monster sea feeds on its prize, grinding, twisting, cracking, and splintering fiberglass with each lash of its watery tongue.

Dad coughs, looking around. I follow his gaze. We're on a thin shelf of volcanic rock, pinned against a cliff wall at least five hundred feet high. There's no path forward, no path backward, and the tide is still rising. The village of Kalaupapa sits serenely in the mid distance along a low-lying plain, but it might as well be on the shores of New Zealand. Our packs are waterlogged. The suitcases and the gun are lost. My head hurts, my eyes sting with salt and blood. Dad bleeds from his shoulder—it's been like that for two hours now, which can't be good. I have no idea what our next move is.

"That's one island down," Dad says. Every word is painful. "Two to go. Welcome to Moloka`i."

MAUI NUI

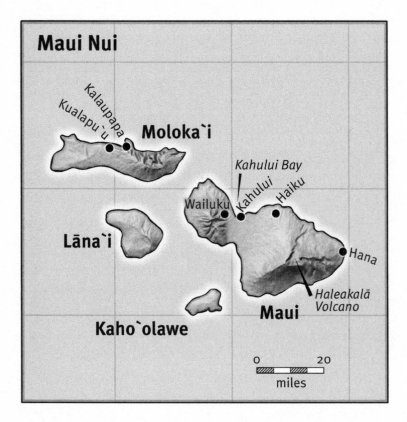

Maui Nui

Kalaupapa
Kualapu`u
Moloka`i

Kahului Bay
Wailuku
Kahului
Haiku

Lāna`i

Hana

Haleakalā
Volcano

Kaho`olawe

Maui

0   20
miles

CHAPTER 20

WEDNESDAY, MAY 20

We sit as far out of the reach of the rising tide as we can, our backs right up against the cliff face. No way to know whether the shelf we're on will eventually be submerged. Our wrecked boat continues to grind and splinter on the rocks like a bone gnawed by a hungry dog. We're just barely shaded from the sun by the high cliffs. It's getting warm. And Dad is growing sleepy. I shake him out of another trance and he sits up. We have no plan. I'm on the brink of despair.

But perhaps there are a few miracles left.

I watch with confusion and then with mounting hope as an outrigger canoe materializes against the churning sea from the direction of Kalaupapa. Its crew of three is aiming toward us.

"Dad! Look!" I nudge him and he drowsily follows my gaze.

They *have* come for us. I can scarcely believe our good fortune as I watch the outrigger stop sixty yards out from shore, directly in front of us. The middle rower stands. He lifts up two life vests and a rope, and then dives in.

Dad and I watch as he swims over. I help the swimmer get his balance on the edge of the shelf. He's haole, in his fifties. Strong.

His eyes are kind. "Are you all right? Is everyone here?" He speaks with some sort of accent—French?—long ago worn smooth.

I nod. "It's just us. My dad is badly hurt."

"What's wrong?" He hands me a vest and glances over at Dad.

Am I supposed to say that Dad was shot? How will he react? Will he guess that we stole our boat and leave in disgust? I could make up a story. . . .

"Quick. What's wrong?"

"Shot in the shoulder."

"You? Deep cut."

"It is?" I raise my fingers to my forehead.

"No biggie: you'll wear it well. Can you follow the rope back to the canoe?"

"Yes."

"Go. I'll take care of him."

I turn to dive, but remember: "Our bags. They float. We need them. . . ." I stop. *Is it wise to confess that we have food and medicine? How much can I trust these people? But why would they row all the way out here if their intentions weren't good?*

216

"I'll tie them to the end of the rope. Your dad's the priority."

I pull myself along the rope, struggling against the water. One of the rowers rises and hauls in the line while the other steadies the oars, maintains the canoe's position. I hold on tight and let the puller do the work. Behind me our rescuer, Dad, and the bags are reeled in.

The man pulling the rope helps us all aboard the canoe, and we turn toward Kalaupapa. The front rower has only one leg.

"We've been averaging a rescue a day," the middle fellow says as he rows. They push hard to increase speed, but they haven't even broken a sweat, and none are short of breath. "We all saw your boat stop. You're very lucky to have made it to solid ground—both of you."

Dad and I are tucked into the hull of the long, narrow canoe, covered in towels to protect us from the blazing sun. I'm behind him. "Keep pressure on his bullet wound," says one. I see to my task, even though I'm afraid of hurting Dad. "She did it all," Dad says. "She saved my life."

"*You* saved our lives." I try to change the subject. "Thank you. Thank you."

The one-legged guy says, "That's what we do now. In Kalaupapa, we vowed to serve the distressed. Traffic has been heavy, and so many don't make it."

"Lei. I'm . . ." Dad's thought stalls.

I pat his good shoulder. "Hang in there. We're getting you help. Don't go to sleep, okay?"

He nods.

We land at Kalaupapa within the hour. A handful of people help us to shore. When they realize the extent of Dad's injury, we're ushered into an old Land Cruiser parked at the beach. Someone fires up the engine, and we're off. I don't know what's going on, what's happened to our bags. I don't care. We're racing now—and it feels like we've just lapped Death.

I melt into my seat. I'm in the middle, with Dad on one side and a woman on the other. She pulls a do-rag from her pocket and carefully pats down my forehead. "You may need stitches, darling."

"Okay, thank you." I brush her hand away, rest my head on Dad's shoulder, and close my eyes.

Relax; they're trying to help. Everything's okay now.

We skid to a halt. The driver jumps out and helps Dad out. We've arrived at an urgent-care clinic near the beach. Dad is helped onto a gurney and wheeled away. I follow.

Minutes later he's wheeled through the last set of doors toward surgery, and someone pulls me back as we try to cling together.

"Lei."

"Dad!"

"He's in very good hands," another stranger whispers in my ear. "These folks have had a lot of practice with gunshots lately. Come. Sit. We need to take care of *you.*"

The next hour is a blur. I get stitches in my forehead. I answer questions. Finally, I'm in a waiting room. The small clinic is busy. As I glance around I have the feeling that the

End of Days hasn't caught up to this place yet. The hustle and bustle feels normal.

Eventually, though, my thoughts catch up with my battered body.

Panic claws at me, loneliness. A black hole. I'm plummeting, tumbling. I tuck my face into my hands and weep, flooded with all of the fear I didn't have time to let in till now.

Forget all of it; it doesn't matter. But it's not even over yet. This labyrinth is real, and I'm somewhere near the center. I just want to be in Mom's arms. My feet press into the floor with enough power to budge the Earth. When will it let up? When is enough enough?

The world that worked is gone, but I'm still here. Anguish washes over me.

An older man sits beside me. He coaxes me into his gentle arms and holds me tight. I could never explain how, but I instantly feel his kindness. I weep against his chest.

I wipe my face against my sleeve and look at him. He is Hawaiian, with a potbelly, a round nose, and deeply pocked, ruddy cheeks. He has careworn, coffee-colored eyes, and the thickest mane of wavy black hair I've ever seen on a man his age. He looks nothing like Grandpa, but he reminds me of him. "Thank you."

"How are you?" He hands me some tissue.

I shrug and blow my nose. "Better."

"You guys are going to be okay now, yeah?"

I nod.

"Your dad's getting patched up. He's doing good."

"Are you a doctor?" I ask.

"I'm a healer."

We sit beside each other comfortably.

"Are those stitches under that bandage?"

"Yes."

"Good. No scar gonna tarnish that beautiful young face."

I laugh. "Do I look like I spend much time in front of the mirror anymore?"

His smile widens. "You and your dad on your way to Hilo, yeah?"

He must have been around when I was answering questions. I nod.

"Crazy out there, yeah?"

I nod again.

"I love the Big Island. Wish Moloka`i had mountains like that. Mauna Kea's, what, fourteen thousand feet high?"

"Yeah. Think so."

"All those telescopes and radio dishes." He looks at me intently, trying to connect without coming on too strong. It dawns on me that I've been hugging a complete stranger.

"Would you like to be alone?" he asks.

"No, that's all right," I say quickly. I can feel the panic even now.

"I'll stay." We sit together in silence.

"Your name is Leilani?"

"Yes."

"One of my very favorite names. I love the sound, I love the meaning."

"Thank you."

"Have you had any fits?" He points to my bracelet. "Since all this started?"

The sudden question and the word "fits" throw me for a loop. Such a casual term to hear from a stranger. "A few." I cover my wrist.

"I'm an epileptic," he says. "No shame with me."

I look up and study his eyes. His honesty shows. "I'm running out of meds," I say. "Do you have any?"

"For epilepsy? Not here."

I slump.

"Maybe it's an opportunity, Leilani. Especially now, yeah? Everything's changed."

"An *opportunity*? No offense, but no thanks." I pause. "What's your name?"

"Akoni. But I go by Uncle."

"Uncle?" A Hawaiian title bestowed upon respected elders. "Are you from here?"

"I've been on Moloka`i awhile," he says. "Maybe I was one of St. Damien's misfits. Who knows, eh?"

"Leprosy?"

"I never had the disease. I came to minister long after segregation ended." Akoni plucks at my bracelet, as if he's read my mind. "Our disease—leprosy of the mind, I used to think. Helped me fit in. Helped me belong."

"Helped you 'fit' in," I joke.

His high-pitched chuckle bounces out of his belly and makes me smile. "Exactly." We settle into another silence.

221

Akoni's expression grows penetrating, and he asks, "Have you heard them?" This appears to be a difficult question.

"Who?"

He continues to study me. Finally, his expression lightens. "The nurses, I mean."

"No."

"Hey," he says, "no worries. Do you want to get settled in while you wait for your dad?"

"Settled in?"

"Come on." He rises. "I'll show you around. Your bags will be waiting at the camp. Then we'll come right back."

Another refugee camp?

I follow Uncle Akoni outside to the sidewalk back toward the beach. We turn the corner and he leads me several blocks through a small town bursting with purpose. Everyone seems to be immersed in some task. A pear-shaped haole man, an obvious stranger to hard labor in his previous life, pushes a wheelbarrow full of sand up the sidewalk. A trio of Asian women hoist sloshing pails of fresh water across an intersection. Hawaiian carpenters assemble underneath the awning of a shop, tool belts sagging from their waists. Two Hawaiians march toward the shore with long fishing poles balanced in their fists. Nobody is suppressing them, overseeing them. No military police patrols with weapons ready; no barbed wire; no elderly people sick and dying on their moldy cots, forgotten in plain sight.

Most people wave as we pass. Many say, "Aloha, Uncle!"

He waves back and often answers them by name.

"How—didn't this town get pummeled by the tsunami?" I ask.

"A bit. The damage was easy enough for this group to make *mo' bettah*."

It all feels out of place and out of time. Like a modern-day place of refuge, akin to the Big Island's ancient Hōnaunau, where vanquished warriors and *kapu* transgressors once found sanctuary.

"I thought people from Moloka'i hated outsiders."

He smiles. "But they call this the Friendly Isle!"

I roll my eyes. *Tell that to the surfing crowd.*

Akoni gives that squeaky, bouncy laugh again. "This island never really warmed to tourists," he agrees. "Especially our hemmed-in little shelf here. But now it's different. We were made for this. People are beginning to get a little weary, but we'll make it work as long as we can. Damien is patron saint of the outcast, yeah? We're all castaways now."

We arrive at the end of the village, where a field has been mown into a rolling lawn that houses collapsible shade structures, tents, and folding tables and chairs and cots—shanty living quarters for who knows how many families. The makeshift cityscape is ragtag, but open and airy—people are free to enter and leave—and not nearly as muddy and slovenly as the ball fields on O'ahu. It feels inviting, somehow. The strumming of a ukulele welcomes me. Potted seedlings bask in the sun. They seem hopeful. Clotheslines run from one structure to the next.

Our bags are propped against a rusted electrical box at the end of the track. The box has old graffiti painted on it. One of the words has been crossed out with new paint and replaced:

eat poi
4
~~brkfst~~
evah

"Pick out a spot," Akoni says. "I'll take you back to your father. No one will bother your bags."

I wander through the camp for several minutes and come to an edge of the field that offers some elbow room. We lean the bags against a woody green bush of naupaka. I study the tiny white half-flowers blooming everywhere and think of Kai. Once we went beach camping and he annoyed me by slopping gooey marshmallow all over the sleeve of my shirt with the end of his roasting stick. So I pushed him into a naupaka bush, trapping him in the springy branches. I waited before helping him out. He then smacked me in the nose with the end of his marshmallow stick. I tossed him right back in the bush as he cackled with laughter.

I look at the naupaka's half-flowers—only four petals on one side, looking as though the other four have been plucked. I think of the myth: Naupaka was a princess who fell in love with a commoner. The two were forbidden to marry, and during their last embrace they tore a flower in two, each taking half. One headed for the mountains while the other remained by the sea. The plant grows at high elevations and along the shores, the flowers always incomplete.

I cup one of the small half-flowers in my hand. *I will make you whole.*

"I'm coming," I whisper.

I wipe tears from my eyes with the back of my wrist as I straighten. Akoni casts me a silent smile, and we turn back toward the clinic.

We pass a church on our way, and I'm surprised to see a young man with a pair of binoculars leaning out of the bell tower above us.

"Ahoy!" Akoni shouts up to him.

"Ahoy, Uncle!" the man calls, lowering his lenses.

"Any giant salamis today?" Akoni's belly laughs tumble out of him.

"No tsunamis," the lookout reports.

We continue on our way. Akoni says, "We have a constant eye on the sea. No satellite warnings anymore. And who's to say that we're not in for more Orchid debris strikes?"

"Great."

Outside the clinic we see a giant flock of large birds pass overhead, darkening the orange sky. The flock is very high up, thousands of birds stretched out over miles.

"What is that?" I wonder aloud.

"Not the first flock I've seen. I think those are mainland birds. Geese. Storks. Cranes, maybe."

"But migratory birds go north to south. That flock's aimed for China, yeah?"

Akoni shrugs. "The Orchid's scrambling more than just circuit boards."

"The birds are on the fritz," I test the notion. "Weird."

"Not just the birds."

I sigh. "Can't wait for Dad to see that."

Akoni takes me back to the clinic counter. "Now, about payment . . ."

I feel hot. I'd been wondering when the other shoe would drop. I've just been had by a slick salesman. Not that I'm disappointed in Uncle Akoni; I'm ashamed of myself, for starting to believe in a world that could run on kindness.

"We don't have any money. But maybe we can pay for all this in iodide tablets?"

Uncle Akoni frowns. "No one's going to ask you for money. What good is it? This place doesn't operate on a capitalist system. We're a commune. Trying to be, anyway."

"Oh. Really? Sorry. Didn't mean to—"

"What's this about iodide?"

Have I said too much? This old man has lowered my guard. I need to be more careful. "I . . . I don't know. I have some . . . tablets. Just in case. That's all."

"Where'd you get iodide tablets?"

I shake my head nervously. "The military on O'ahu were all taking them."

"Really? This is the first confirmation I've heard of this."

"I'm not trying to confirm anything—they could be doing it just to be safe, yeah?"

226

He leans close. "Oh, no. It's real. The *hotness*. I've been putting it together, Lei. They know about it, yeah? They like it. It's good for their ship."

I stare at him blankly. He smiles awkwardly. "You really not with me on this?"

I shake my head.

"Well, later, then. You have more pressing issues. Meanwhile, stay quiet about those tablets. This 'commune' has shallow roots. If people think you have something they'll need, you'll be a target."

"Okay. Thanks. I really appreciate your help. I can tell you're busy. It means . . . a lot." I blink back tears.

"I'm going up the cliff to Kualapu'u for a few days, but I'll be back Sunday. Have you guys been to church lately?"

Are you kidding? "I'm kinda mad at God these days."

"Aren't we all?" More of a statement than a question. "Even so, back to the matter of payment: If your father's up to it, will you come? As a favor to me, if nothing else?"

"I guess. I hope so. You've restored my faith in people, anyway."

"Good. That's where it always starts. What we say and do to each other is the clearest sign of God's presence in our hearts. But there's *more*, Lei. We just have to learn how to listen for it. You a good listener, Leilani?"

At some point his tone changed. His question is dead serious, and I don't get it. "Sure."

"You have a gift, you know," he says, tapping me on the

head. "You're not using it, though. You're not seeing it for what it is. We'll get there, though, okay?"

"Okay."

"*A hui hou*, Leilani. Flower of Heaven."

"K'den," I say, more confused than ever. "*Mahalo*, Uncle."

CHAPTER 21

On Sunday morning Dad and I stand together on the beach amid a group of thirty or so newcomers, facing the high cliffs of Moloka`i, me with my train-track stitches and Dad with his arm in a ragged sling. We are participating in a traditional *oli kāhea*, a sacred Hawaiian chant of request to enter. This password ceremony doesn't feel like "tradition"; it feels real. Dad and I don't belong here. We are guests in need, in search of mercy, in a new world where you can't count on any help. It is fitting to ask permission to enter this modern isle of refuge. We read our tattered pages and chant:

> *Komo, e komo aku hoi au maloko.*
> *Mai ho`ohewahewa mai oe ia`u; oau no ia,*
> *Ke ka-nae-nae a ka mea hele,*
> *He leo, e-e,*

A he leo wale no, e-e.
Eia ka pu`u nui owaho nei la,
He ua, he ino, he anu, he ko`e-ko`e.
Maloko aku au.

To enter, permit me to enter, I pray.
Refuse me not recognition; I am
A traveler offering praise,
Just a voice,
Only a human voice.
Oh, what I suffer out here,
Rain, storm, cold, and wet.
Let me come in to you.

Dad's breathing is a little shallow as he tries not to let his expanding lungs pull at his torn shoulder muscles. He should be resting, but he insists that he's well enough to attend this ceremony and the Mass. His surgery went really well. The wound was shallow; the bullet had lodged against his shoulder blade, not in it. He's doing so good. My relief is indescribable.

A dozen Hawaiians stand before us in a line. They chant the answer to our request:

Aloha na hale o makou i maka-maka ole,
Ke alanui hele mauka o Pu`u-kahea la, e-e!
Ka-he-a!
E Kahea aku ka pono e komo mai oe iloko nei.
Eia ka pu`u nui o waho nei, he anu.

What love to our homes, now empty,
As one ascends the mountain of Supplication!
We call!
You are welcome; we invite you to enter.
The cold outside is the hill of Affliction.

We step forward, officially welcomed. Those who have gathered to witness the ceremony clap their approval. Moloka`i, of all places. It's funny: there have been many times in the past few days here that I've felt more accepted than I ever have before. I could stay here. I could be Hawaiian here. My misfit self could belong.

But it's still not home.

"Do you see him yet?" Dad asks.

I shake my head, trying to hide my disappointment. "I thought for sure he'd be here. He'd better be at the church." I haven't seen Uncle Akoni since we arrived, but I told Dad all about him as soon as he awoke.

He would like to thank Uncle Akoni, for protecting me and getting me stitched up, and for being part of a community that saved his life.

I've wandered these streets for the past four days, scratched beneath the surface of their Brady Bunch veneer. I keep waiting to discover something awful. It's like I want to be comforted by familiar misery.

I've seen couples arguing; a fistfight; people doubled over in the agony of loss. A woman said her suitcase had been stolen. I overheard two men argue about how many people this shelf could support in the long term.

This experiment may not last. I don't know. But people are trying, and they're not fooling themselves. They're protected in a new world by a new set of rules. They're safe, and they're comforted.

After the ceremony people spread out as they chat before Mass. Dad and I walk to a nearby rocky shore with a group of four young Hawaiian men. I talked to one, Joshua, yesterday as they returned from a morning of fishing. He offered to give me some pointers on spearfishing. I don't know if he was planning on anyone else being a part of it, but Dad was eager to learn some new tips, too.

I pause for a moment on the road, let the group get a few steps ahead of me, and apply some lip gloss.

Joshua invited me out surfing yesterday afternoon. Surfing on Moloka'i! I could have died and gone to heaven. But I didn't go. Dad never left my side at the clinic, and I couldn't leave him now.

"Let's try this for a bit, eh?" Joshua says. His buddies drop their empty five-gallon buckets and inspect their poles. Joshua readies his spear and moves me through the basics while Dad watches, his arm useless. Joshua spends most of his time talking about the fish and the coral. This cove has been protected as a fishery, so there's plenty to catch.

"This island has always tried to be self-supporting," Dad observes. "God help O'ahu and the other islands."

"Yeah, they'd better figure it out. We can't feed the whole bunch," one Hawaiian grumbles. Another turns his catch bucket around to show us a bumper sticker:

SUST 'ĀINA BILITY.

Dad and I laugh. "That's *fantastic*," he says. "Why didn't I think of that?" `Āina* means "land"; *kama`āina* means "child of the land." But the word goes deeper. The play on words offers a glimpse of Hawai`i's future. I've witnessed a lot in the past few days that leaves me hopeful—at least for Moloka`i.

"The answer to our future is a return to our past," the owner of the bumper sticker says.

Grandpa always said things like that on his blog.

I laugh, and then wince: *Grandpa.* I let the pain sit there. I miss him so much. It's so sad he doesn't have his blog anymore. But he's okay. I know it. He's always been a time traveler, effortlessly shifting back and forth between the past and the present.

He *knows* so much about spiritual health and old farming and cooking techniques, he's the perfect person to keep Mom and Kai safe—and the rest of us, once we get home.

I try my hand with the spear several times, with no luck. Dad drifts away after a few minutes and sits down along the ledge of a rocky pool. I go to him. "You okay?"

"I'm fine, honey. A little tired. Go have fun. I think Joshua likes you."

"You kill the whole thing when you say it out loud!"

"Sorry." He laughs as I pretend to swat him.

A large green sea turtle surfaces just in front of our dangling feet. It watches us for a few seconds before dropping back down below the choppy surface. I lean against Dad, and we sit in silence watching the *honu* graze on the coral and pop up for breaths of air. I think I can see a kind of wisdom in its placid eyes—ancient, calm, and vast, something far beyond human intelligence. No wonder the Hawaiians hold the *honu* in such high esteem.

A church bell rings in town. "Shall we go do this Mass thing?"

"Look." He points, smiling. A second turtle has joined the first. This one's smaller. Dad makes no motion to rise. I relax and settle back down next to him. The turtles dance through the coral in slow synchrony.

"*Honu,*" Dad says. "Aren't they church enough? They kind of represent the true nature of God. For me."

"How's that?"

Dad smiles. "Did you know that some turtle species cross the entire ocean to lay their eggs? Why would they do that?"

I shrug.

"They didn't always. When the supercontinent of Gondwanaland was just breaking apart, the turtles would simply swim across a narrow strait, lay their eggs, and head back home. Over the next hundred-or-so million years, the continents drifted apart, about an inch a year. The turtles went about their business, doing what they used to, what their parents used to do, each generation unaware of the imperceptible change. Now they cross oceans. And they'll be here still, following their ancient paths, inch by new inch, long after we're gone."

I absorb Dad's story, watching the turtles feed obliviously beneath us. "And you see God in that? It just makes me feel smaller than ever."

"I do. To me, it makes Him *bigger* than ever." Dad shakes his head.

"Does everyone become a philosopher when they get shot?" I ask. The bells ring again. We help each other up. "Saved by the bell," Dad says.

"I think I'd rather listen to your sermons than some priest's."

"That's why you call me 'Father.'" He winks at me. I roll my eyes.

I wave good-bye to the fishermen, and we shuffle back into the heart of the village.

We're caught off guard by the size of this Mass. People have gathered *outside* the church. Folding chairs cover the spacious lawns surrounding the building, sprawling in large blocks out from a wide center aisle. We find seats along the aisle.

The sound of ukuleles and *ipu* drums roll over the crisp morning air, and everyone rises. We turn to watch the priest walk up the aisle and my jaw drops.

"That's him! He's the priest."

Uncle Akoni is adorned with a faded white habit, a hand-woven green stole, and leis of kukui nuts and plumeria flowers. As people sing a hymn, he advances up the aisle of folding chairs and camp stools, holding high a leather-bound gospel for all to see. Two young altar servers walk beside him. He scans the crowd attentively, offering warm smiles and a few jovial winks. He sees me and his eyes light up. I smile sheepishly. Why has he taken such an interest in me? Or does he treat everyone as if they are important?

Akoni celebrates Mass with solemn wonder. It seems so fresh for him, though he's probably performed thousands of

235

Masses. The chanting, the standing, the kneeling are all a blur. I only remember his face and his eyes—and his homily:

"Shhh. Listen. Can you hear it? Can you hear the whisper?

"Our first reading may have escaped you. Old Testament babblings from First Kings. But speaking for myself, today, I am forced to listen—and to marvel. To marvel at the profound insight we are offered into the fabric of our creator. To marvel at the wisdom of our ancient prophet Elijah, who, in the context of his time, could only have assumed that the great forces churning around him were the works of an angry and righteous hand, and yet who ignored all of it, focusing instead upon the truth so plainly etched into the fibers of our being."

Is he looking directly at me?

"I'll repeat it for you. And you should *listen* this time. For it has already been written as well as it could ever be said:

"And the Angel of the Lord said to Elijah, 'Go outside and stand on the mountain. There you may find the Lord.' Elijah did as he was told, and traveled to the mountaintops to find the Lord. There he witnessed a strong and heavy wind rending the mountains and crushing the peaks—but Elijah did not seek the Lord in the wind. And after the terrible blowing of the wind there came an earthquake—but Elijah did not search for the Lord in the great tremblings of the earth. Following the quake there arose a white-hot fire. The mountainsides were scorched in blazing flame, and still Elijah found no sign of the Lord. Yet, after all these mighty displays, Elijah heard a *whisper*. Only then . . . only then!—did he hide his face in his cloak and drop to his knees before the mouth of the cave. And at last, the Lord God spoke to him, saying, 'Elijah, why have you sought me?'

"Shhh. Listen. Listen well! Take this simple truth with you in these frightful times: the mighty God of the cosmos has no need for grand displays when His whisper will do. But can you hear it? Can *you* hear the whisper?"

* * *

Mass ends, and we linger near our folding seats while the crowd thins out. The shadow of the nearby cliffs has receded, and the sickly sun is warm against my skin. Dad's eyes look red.

"How are you doing?" I ask him. "You okay?"

"I'm okay. Thinking about Mom and Kai. I'm glad I came. How about you?"

I nod. My eyes drift to Uncle Akoni, working his way slowly through a crowd of admirers. Finally, the three of us stand face to face.

He shakes our hands and inspects the stitches on my forehead. "You have a nice memento, there. It'll heal well, though." He turns to Dad. "And you're looking good, too! Shot four days ago and you're sitting through my homilies!" Akoni laughs. Chuckles putter out of him like smoke from an old steam engine.

"Thank you for all you've done," Dad says.

"I don't deserve much credit. *All* of us want this." Akoni turns to me. "Leilani. Any fits lately?"

I glance down. "No." *Such a weird question.*

Akoni smiles at me. "I'm so glad you came. So glad you're doing better." He beckons Dad and me to move closer and lowers his voice. "Listen, I was hoping we could talk more. But I don't have time right now. Things aren't going very well up the cliff, and it's going to spill over fast. Our council needs to head back up there. Everything we've built here is at stake."

"Can we help?" Dad asks.

He shakes his head. "This isn't your struggle. If you guys want to get home, I suggest you leave now. Things are shifting. I can get you to Maui on an outrigger tomorrow, but that's it, at least for a while. I know you're still recovering, but I know you want to get home, too."

"Wait," I say. "A free ride to Maui?"

"Tomorrow only," Akoni repeats. "We need our boats."

"We'll go!" Home suddenly feels closer than ever. "Thank you."

Akoni nods. Dad says, "What's going on? More turf wars?"

Akoni chooses his words carefully. "It's getting harder to convince people of the long view."

He pauses, then leans in. "Listen, they still have a working ham radio up the cliff. There've been confirmed reactor meltdowns *everywhere*. Arizona. At least two on the East Coast. One in Japan. A handful in Russia. Europe. Australia. I doubt that's all."

Dad's expression is blank. My throat feels dry. Akoni continues. "The meltdowns will progress one after another, too. Several hundred power plants out there, yeah? As gas runs out, as backup generators fail, as local communities break down, plants will continue to malfunction. Even in the most stable places, nuclear engineers are eventually going to stop showing up for work in the morning. They're going to head for the hills with their families like everyone else. It's . . . bad. *Really bad.* Each time another one blows its lid—we're not talking *near* disasters like Three Mile Island and the Japan tsunami fiasco. Not even Chernobyl. Months from now, new explosions are going to keep happening. On a bell curve. Like popcorn kernels on a stove top. A few to start out with, then a whole bunch in short order, and then a handful of stragglers at the end."

"Jesus," Dad croaks. "Except each kernel could blow up the kitchen all by itself."

"Much of the globe could be a nuclear wasteland for the next geologic age."

"Jesus," Dad whispers again.

"It's not even bombs. It's just . . . *power plants.*" Akoni shakes his head. "Here's the mystery, though: we aren't detecting any fallout. Nothing. *Nothing.* No radiation."

"That . . ." Dad's voice cracks. He tries again. "That doesn't make any sense. What equipment are you using? Maybe it went kaput with everything else."

Akoni's eyes brighten. "No. Not that. An old Geiger needle doesn't require integrated circuitry."

"We *are* in the most isolated place on Earth," Dad says. "Stands to reason that even trace amounts of radiation would get here last. . . ."

Akoni shakes his head slowly. "No. Not that, either.

Dr. Milton, surely you understand that we'd be able to read *something*. But there aren't even *normal* levels of radiation. I think I know what's happening." He points to the sky. "*They* are mopping up the radiation."

"Huh?"

"Everyone wants them to leave. God forbid they do."

Dad frowns. "Uncle Akoni, I don't think I heard you correct—"

"Yes, you did. Listen. *Listen.* Leilani knows what I'm talking about. I'm sure she does. We can hear their communications. Something about our epilepsy. There's a kid up the cliff who's heard them, too. During seizures."

I laugh—one short bark. Dad stares blankly ahead. Uncle Akoni doesn't care. Maybe he's used to this reaction; maybe he assumes what he's saying is obvious. I don't know. Other islanders approach. He plows quickly forward. "The Orchid. I believe it's a ship. Maybe several vessels. They've touched down, too. All that 'meteor' activity. It's only a matter of time before they descend upon Hawai`i, too."

"Wait," says Dad, frowning. "Do you have *proof* of this? Or are you—"

"No proof." He shakes his head. "But I've *heard* them. You will, too, Leilani, if you just listen. Funny, right, coming from a priest? But I'm not talking about God this time. They're out there. I'm sure of it. I don't know why they've come. But whatever else they're doing, they're preventing our global nuclear winter. Makes sense, right? What's the point of usurping a wasteland?"

Someone tugs on the sleeve of Father Akoni's robe. "Get some rest, Mike," the priest says. The crowd is pressing in on us now. "Get home. Focus on your family. And Lei: one more favor, yeah?"

"Anything."

"*Nānā i ke kumu.*"

"*Nānā i ke kumu,*" I repeat. "'Look to the source.'"

Akoni starts. "You know that phrase?"

"I love Hawaiian."

"Well, you know the words, but do you *hear*? Look to the source. A wise Hawaiian proverb for seeking fundamental answers to our problems. Learn to listen, Lei. The second you reach Hilo, you go up on the mountain. Stand at the mouth of the cave. And when you hear the whisper, see if you can't answer back. You promise?"

He's not making any sense. What am I supposed to say? His gaze is penetrating, insistent. "Okay, Uncle."

"Lord knows we're running low on Hail Marys," he says. And then his sea of followers closes in and we drift apart.

CHAPTER 22

MONDAY, MAY 25

W e rush quietly over the waters at midmorning in a large *wa`akaulua*—a boat with a double hull— pushed by the powerful trade winds blowing along the upside-down triangle sail. The boat we're on is much smaller than the vessels the original Hawaiians would have arrived here in, but it still looks impressive.

The shores of Maui drift by to our right, a short distance away. As our craft rises and falls on the large ocean waves, the deeply gouged slopes of the West Maui Mountains bob rhythmically in the near distance. I study the rugged terrain that we're effortlessly skipping past with a profound sense of gratitude. The Moloka`i coast is only ten miles behind us. Maui and Moloka`i and Lāna`i and Kaho`olawe were all once connected as one island. The set of islands is known as Maui Nui by scientists and others—Greater Maui. But to me they're as isolated and different as O`ahu is from the Big Island.

For the moment, home is growing nearer at a swift fifteen knots.

Our trip will end along the bay of a small town called Paia on the slopes of Maui's grand mountain, the volcano of Haleakalā—"the house of the sun." Dad and I will head east, toward Hana. Once we find our way around Haleakalā, the nearest tip of the Big Island is another thirty miles.

We're opposite Kahului Bay now, the twin cities of Kahului and Wailuku sprawling along Maui's valley floor to our right. I see several cars driving along. The sky's sickly haze has been lifting bit by bit each day, but here there is a tall, hot fire spewing brown smoke and gray ash into the sky behind the airport.

"The Maui pyre," one of the three crew members explains in a low voice. "It's been burning all week."

I study the pillar of smoke with morbid fascination. That's *people.*

"Why?"

"Maui's nothing but tourism and corporate farming. And just like O`ahu, the waterworks—the irrigation—it's all belly-up," our captain says as he adjusts the mainsheet. He's the same one-legged man who helped rescue us on Wednesday. "Folks aren't getting along so well. Keep to yourselves if you want to hang on to those bags."

The column of ash is massive, and my understanding of the disaster that's unfolding on these islands billows. In spite of all our heartache these past weeks, we've been the lucky ones.

There are so many dead that the bodies are burned instead of buried.

I envision pillars of gray ash rising from the slopes of Hilo and bat the images back. I focus instead on the faces of Mom, Kai, and Grandpa. Tami. I'm sure things are better there and they've all been spared this nightmare. I have to believe that.

"*It's only a matter of time before they descend upon Hawai`i. . . .*"

Like a recurring dream, it keeps coming back. I don't believe Uncle Akoni's theory for one second, but I can't shake it. *He was such a nice guy. Why did he have to end up being nuts?* Harsh, but true.

Dad's already put it behind him. Of course we talked about what Uncle Akoni said. To Dad, Uncle Akoni is just one more guy with one more guess. On the weirder end of the spectrum, but just a guess, all the same. Why can't I let it go?

"*. . . I've* heard *them. You will, too, Leilani, if you just listen.*"

We near our target bay. Our crew scans the coast and the slopes for signs of danger, and then we dart in toward shore. The captain says, "I wish we could take you all the way, but this run is pushing it as it is."

"You've been a great help to us," says Dad. "Give Uncle Akoni our gratitude and our loving wishes in his efforts to unite the island."

The captain gives Dad a stern look. "You need more

strength before you march for Hana. Get into the trees and rest up for a few days. Don't trust anyone to help you."

Trust—the "spirit of Aloha." I used to think it was everywhere *but* the Big Island. But now I wonder, *Could it be the other way around?*

We beach and quickly disembark. The crew helps Dad fit his backpack around his tender shoulder and wishes us well. We travel with only our food, our tent, the iodide, and minimal clothing.

As we turn a woman and a teenage boy scramble down the embankment. "Please, can you take us toward Kaua`i?" one asks the crew. "We need to get to Kaua`i." She's haole, in her late forties.

"I can take you as far as Moloka`i."

The woman nods.

The boy and I share a glance. "Where are you coming from?" I ask him.

"Hana. Kona before that."

Kona! That's on the Big Island! His white T-shirt is stained and shredded. He looks much the same as I feel—as if he's been through hell and hasn't yet seen the finish line.

"How's the Big Island? Have you been to Hilo?"

"No. Just Kona. Things were a mess there, but nothing like here."

"How crazy is it here? The military? What's the best route?"

"No. Militant locals. We've been shot at twice. Stay off the roads. No cars. The checkpoints are airtight. Only older cars work anymore anyway. And stay off the obvious trails. They're using pig-hunting dogs. Make sure you have a gun, or at least a knife."

My eyes widen.

"Some psycho sheriff, he's gone all *Lord of the Flies* back there. He's running the passage like a drug cartel. If you surrender your stuff, they might let you by. They're taking everything, though. They'll take the fancy hiking clothes right off your back." The boy eyes my backpack. His eyes are sunken in and darkly rimmed. His face is pale. He's probably starving.

I whip off my pack and hand him an entire stick of salami. He trembles as he takes it, eyes alight with disbelief.

"Here." He hands me his machete. I take it from him gently, studying it as if I'm a cavewoman being handed an e-reader.

"Let's go, folks! All aboard!" the captain shouts.

"Jason—now!" his mother yells. The boy looks back at me twice as he climbs onto the *waʻakaulua*. I watch him until Dad and I turn onto the nearby beach road and march away.

"Dad."

"Yeah, honey?"

"You don't think Mom and Kai have left home, do you? To come find us?"

"No, I don't."

"Why not? What if . . . ?"

"Mom knows that we're on our way home. She's not going to leave. Remember the rule she taught you?"

I remember well. We had been in a mall in San Francisco. I was eight, and I got separated from my parents. In a panic,

I ran off to find them. A helpful woman and a security guard reunited us. "We knew right where we lost you, honey," Mom said. "Next time you get lost, stay right where you are. It'll make it easier to track you down."

But I'll never forget that panic. When it takes hold, all bets are off. Mom's had a month to constantly second-guess her resolutions. . . .

"Let's not linger on the road," Dad says. "If the stories about this sheriff are true . . ."

This area of Maui is largely farmland, and we stick to the rolling fields where the grasses are tallest, hiking steadily toward the tree line of the unbroken jungle, which will take us most of the day to reach.

We traverse the township of Haiku nervously, keeping to forested gullies where we can. We find ourselves cautiously climbing over fences and scurrying through a patchwork of fields, yards, and open streets. We see people, but not many. An old man sitting on his porch, who pretends not to notice us. Two kids running across a yard. An occasional old car driving up the hill from the valley. It's like we're actually *in* a haiku. But where has everyone else gone? There's nowhere to go. I could imagine hordes of city dwellers on the mainland heading for the hills, or the wild lands beyond the highways. But here, we're just rearranging deck chairs on the *Titanic*.

The echo of rapid gunfire comes from somewhere in the direction of Kahului. I look toward the sound and the plume of the pyre still burning hot and fierce near the airport.

"Come on," Dad says, following my gaze. "Got to reach the jungle before nightfall."

Just as dusk settles over Maui with a breathtaking, bloodred sunset behind us, we move beneath the canopy of full-blown jungle. Now I'm fighting with thorny brambles and giant, hairy ferns and great mops of tangled vine. I use my new machete for the first time, swinging it timidly at first, and then more confidently. "This is going to be miserable."

"Let's stop for the night. My shoulder is done."

We pitch our small tent and hop inside, escaping a cloud of mosquitoes. I already have more itchy bites than I can keep track of. Dad's in a fair amount of pain, but he's trying to keep it to himself. He swallows down painkillers. We snack briefly on our stores of food, always the same: crushed and stale crackers, dried fruit, and processed meat by-product that's been stuffed into tubes as rock hard as a billy club.

We lost our sleeping bags with the suitcases, so we pad the floor of the tent with clothing. I help Dad get his shirt off in our cramped quarters. "Dad, you're bleeding!"

"I know. Is it bad?"

I study his wound. "The stitches look fine." I re-dress the wound with the first-aid materials the clinic gave us.

"How's your forehead?"

"Itchy," I say. "No big deal."

"Let's do another mile in the morning. Then I want to lie down and do nothing for at least a couple of days."

"Sounds good."

* * *

I take my evening pill. Eighteen left. With luck, I could make it home before I run out.

* * *

"Lei. Are you taking the iodide?"

"But Uncle Akoni said—"

"I don't care what he said. Nice man, but not all there. Besides, even if he's right about the radiation—just because they can't detect it yet, doesn't mean it's not coming. Meltdowns are happening. We're lucky to be in Hawai`i. But it's only a matter of time before it reaches us."

I fish through my bag and open the canister of tablets Aukina gave me. I wonder where he is. Still taking orders on O`ahu? Helping other girls crawl beneath the fences?

I take a tablet and hand one to Dad. "Here."

"No."

"What, you're going to make me take it, but—"

"There's not enough, Lei."

"You're joking."

"Those are for you and Kai. It's nonnegotiable. Please don't turn it into a fight."

"Dad."

He offers a sympathetic smile. He's quiet for a long time, and then he says, "It's going to be all right."

I turn away and burrow into my bed of clothing.

I stare up at the Emerald Orchid through the screen mesh of our tent. It's partially covered by jungle canopy, but it's clear enough. Very bright tonight, but less crisp, as if a projectionist needs to give the focus knob a half turn out there somewhere. Is it a trick of the hazy atmosphere, the mesh tent fabric above me, or are my eyes crossed with exhaustion?

"Dad?" I say. "What if that *is* a spaceship?"

"Lei, it's not. Look at it. Looks nothing like—"

"Oh, I know. I'm just playing it out, you know? Wouldn't that be nuts? If all the major cities were dealing with an alien invasion? And here we are, out in the ocean, lost in our own little problems, totally clueless."

"*Little* problems?"

"You know what I mean."

Dad sighs. "Yeah, that would be wild. But the reality of what's going on is just as bad, Lei. We don't need to chase some priest down any rabbit holes to appreciate the severity of our situation."

"You don't have to lecture me."

Dad sits up with considerable effort. He looks at me closely. "I just meant . . . Akoni's well-meaning, and I'm sure he—"

"I *have* been having dreams," I interrupt him. *There, I said it.* It feels good to get that off my chest, but now I feel exposed, too. "Stronger than usual." Dad's listening. I continue, hesitantly. Maybe I shouldn't have admitted this. It sounds so bizarre out loud. "I've been dreaming during my seizures. I don't remember them well, but . . . *something.* A voice."

"Alien communiqués? In English?"

My eyes narrow. "No. Don't get me wrong; I agree it's nuts. But . . . remember how Grandma Lili`u would tell that story about hearing radio transmissions during the Pearl Harbor invasion? Through the filling in her tooth?"

Dad smiles. "Yeah."

"Did you believe her?"

"I don't know. I think so, yeah. There's a scientific basis for that, though. That's not an uncommon story."

"Well, neither is Uncle Akoni's. *I've* heard something. He mentioned another epileptic kid, too."

"Three people? Come on, Lei. Anecdotal. No evidence there. Remember when I talked about confirmation bias? Sounds like you want to believe this is true."

"Sounds like you want to believe it's not."

Dad lies down. "I believe that you're hearing something. It's probably a side effect of the drug trial."

"Huh," I say. "What if it's God?" I ask. "Or akua? Or aumakua—a family guardian, like Grandma?"

Dad smiles. "There you go. See! Don't you want to interpret these voices in a way that means something to you, and not in some paranoid way?"

We lie in silence, staring up at the Orchid. Just a haze. A fuzzy green cloud. No one would look up at that and think, "UFO."

But . . .

Maybe Dad's right: no aliens. Better to believe the gods are speaking to me in my seizures.

But what are they telling me?

I shrug and close my eyes. How is it that a *priest* confused me about this?

CHAPTER 23

After we move camp another mile into the forest, Dad rests for three solid days and nights, scarcely moving except to eat. He stays quiet and still, disciplined. "The more I heal now, the faster we'll go in the end," he argues. I trust his instinct, but I'm dying to get going. I mostly stay in the tent, too, to avoid the mosquitoes and the occasional rain bursts. I pass the time rereading my water-damaged Hawaiiana book—I've kept it through everything—searching for clues about the gods. Nothing new has jumped out at me.

Each day Dad and I make and remake plans.

"I don't know how we're going to get through this jungle," I say. "What if we went around the dry side?"

"Too exposed. That sheriff talk worries me. They could have all our stuff in an instant."

"We should just give it to him. Get on with it. Make our way through."

"There's no way to smuggle that much iodide. And I won't surrender it."

"Well, how will we get away from Hana, Dad?"

"I don't know."

Just like O`ahu all over again: back to floundering, waiting for the right moment. We grow silent, listening to the distant squawks of more birds inexplicably flocking west in huge clouds across Hawai`i.

I never get more than three or four hours of sleep without waking up from a nightmare. Sometimes they involve reliving the worst of our experiences. Sometimes I awake from imagined gunfire or the smell of burning flesh. Sometimes it's the white lights blinding me in a dark city. I don't know what meltdowns actually look like, but in my dreams they're always like nuclear bombs from the movies. Sometimes pale aliens with big balloon heads are banging at the door of the presidential bunker. I lie awake, trying to figure out what's going on in the rest of the world. It's easier than thinking about my family, but it's still hard. I spend hours thinking about what it feels like. I don't know how to say it. We're so cut off from the globe. I've grown up at a time where news pours in constantly from every corner of the world. If my parents weren't talking about it, it was on TV, it was on the radio, it was on my computer, it was on my phone, it was at the airport, it was in the waiting room, it was at school, at the restaurant, at the grocery-store checkout line, at the gas-station pump . . . News from everywhere, all at once, all the time. I never really noticed it. Maybe it would feel like this to suddenly go deaf in one ear. Like something you always took for granted has left you crippled and spinning in its absence.

* * *

On Thursday I count pills. Only twelve left. *Should I start taking only one each day?* I think. *I doubt it would be enough. I need the full dosage for it to work.*

I swallow my evening dose.

I must get home. This week.

* * *

On Friday morning we pack up the tent. I cough blood for the first time. My throat stings. I take my next iodide tablet in a bit of a stupor, wiping the blood spatter off my hands so Dad won't see it. Is this what I'm fighting for? A lifelong struggle to stay one step ahead of an invisible monster that'll still be around millions of years after I'm gone? Kai and I watch Mom and Dad and Grandpa waste away and die while we figure out how to fend for ourselves? I grabbed tons of this stuff, but it will eventually run out. What then? Will we be the only two civilians left on the islands?

"You okay?" Dad asks.

I nod, change the subject. "You know what today is?"

Dad searches, shakes his head. "No idea."

"Last day of school."

"Really?" Dad looks up, the calculator in his head churning away. "Wow, Lei. Congrats. You're a senior."

"Thanks. Where's my new car?"

Dad sits down. He buries his head in his hands. "Dad? I was just making a joke."

"We were going to get you one," he says.

"What?"

"A car. Not a new one. Something used. You were going to pick it out." He still won't look up at me.

A car. I don't know what to say. I sit down cross-legged next to him. He's crying. I wrap my arm around him, rest my head on his shoulder.

"Thank you." I have to whisper it so my voice doesn't crack.

He wipes his tears away. "It's the thought that counts, right?" His grin is sheepish.

"Something like that," I say.

* * *

"Look at this," says Dad. Our packs are cinched, and we're ready to press through the jungle toward Hana. He's holding out a compass and giving it the stink-eye. I glance at the instrument. The needle won't settle into one position. It spins, hesitates, and then continues to rotate in an endless search for polarity. It's as if Dad is moving a magnet around beneath the compass.

"Lovely. How are we going to navigate?"

Dad shrugs, pocketing the compass. "We're not as easily had as geese. We're on a slope that drops into the sea. We'll just cross every river and gully in a perpendicular fashion, and make sure the ocean's to our left whenever we can catch a glimpse of it."

We trudge through the tropical forest for two days. The going is torturous, especially the endless chore of climbing down deeply gouged ravines, crossing angry streams and rivers, and then struggling up their far sides as bursts of rain pelt us. We have run out of mosquito repellent. I think briefly of that mother and her kids in the military camp, but I can't regret trying to help them. We would have run out eventually anyway. At least we escaped.

Where are those kids now? I push away the thought.

I do all of the machete chopping; if Dad's wound were to reopen, tropical microbes could spell his doom. I shouldn't, but I pick at my itchy forehead. I have no idea how far we've come, and I've all but forgotten why we felt we needed to slog through the rain forest instead of sticking to the road, when we arrive at a river crossing and stumble upon the bloated and naked body of a woman floating in a rocky pool. Facedown, she twists in lazy circles, her skull brushing the edges of rocks as she turns. The long shaft of an arrow protrudes from her neck.

"Oh, no." I drop to my knees. We're looking down at the body from a five-foot-high ledge above the pool. Water rushes along the center of the river, but here, near the bank, it trickles, filling dozens of babbling pools along its meandering course. The woman's back and legs are puffy and purple, cracked open in places. Flies feast in busy clouds. I turn away.

Dad runs a hand through his hair. Words fail him.

"They just shot her and left her? They couldn't even collect the body?"

"She probably fell into the water and was carried away. Come on."

"Shouldn't we . . . bury her, or something?" I whisper.

Dad's voice is soft. "I wish we could. But no. Come on." Dad looks about nervously, and I feel unseen eyes spying on me from every tree trunk and fern.

We walk upstream to cross the river and fill up on water, clambering up a steep rock face above a short waterfall. We're going to have to get wet to cross this time; the water here is deep and swift. A taller waterfall gushes farther upstream.

We take a moment to guzzle from our water bottles and refill them, always glancing around. I know we're upstream from the body, but it must have passed by here at some point, and the thought of drinking from this river at all turns my stomach. Still, I know that with all of our sweating, we can't afford to pass up any water.

I wade across the river, submerged up to my chest. We rest the packs on our heads to keep them dry as we cross and quickly strap them back on once we're safe on the far side. Ahead of us the foliage is thick, brambly, steeply sloped. I unsheathe my machete.

"Let's get out of here," Dad says. I begin hacking away at the thorny plants choking our way forward.

I hear the growl of a dog. Close.

We freeze. The dog barks. A brown blur materializes out of the trembling underbrush and I fall, a searing, white-hot pain ripping into my thigh. I'm screaming. Dad is screaming. A pile of hell-bent muscle writhes on top of me, razor-sharp teeth clamped into my leg. I bring the machete up and around as hard as I can. The dog yelps and recoils. My blade slices farther through its shoulder, and it whimpers and slinks into the underbrush.

"Lei!"

Another dog attacks Dad from the other side. I swing around and swipe with my machete. Adrenaline and rage guide my weapon down on top of the dog's back. Blade meets bone. Vertebrae snap. The dog crumples, its back legs limp, and convulses in agony, yelping wildly.

Someone above us curses.

More barking dogs fan out in a great arc around us. A *whoosh* near my head. Another. An arrow sings to a halt in my backpack.

I'm stunned. Is that me laughing?

"Sheriff's Department! You're surrounded. Surrender."

"The river!" Dad seizes my hand and whips me forward.

A warm pain throbs along my thigh, but I race beside Dad, hunted like a wild pig.

"Stop *now*!"

We hurtle blindly back along the path I've cut, the dogs growing nearer. We come upon the rocky bank of the river and leap, packs and all, and then swim with the current toward the short waterfall. A single gunshot rings out above. The current draws us to the edge of the waterfall.

My hands reach for something to grab, dropping the machete, but my pack is too bulky and the water too strong—I tumble over. Nothing I can do but brace to be dashed against the shallow boulders below.

The pool directly beneath the waterfall has been gouged deep by thousands of years of water. I disappear under the water with flailing arms. A great weight crashes down on top of me, sending me farther down. Dad has fallen on me.

My lungs burning for breath, I push for the surface, dragging my pack with me, and finally arise, gasping.

"Lei!" Dad yelps. I clear my eyes and follow his voice. We're pushed farther downstream by the current. Suddenly my feet are brushing against the boulders of the bottom. Behind Dad I see a dog scrambling down the steep slope of the embankment, growling and barking, delighted by the hunt. Dad and I swim frantically downstream.

Two other dogs join the first. All three of them stop before the body of the woman turning aimlessly in the water. The dogs are torn—inspect their earlier prey or pursue us? One jumps into the river and paddles toward us with patient desire, eyes on us as it concentrates on its difficult task. It could almost be returning a tennis ball to me. But it wants to retrieve me for its master.

Dad plants his feet into the pebbly floor as if applying brakes. He grips me by the shaft of the arrow protruding from my pack and steadies me. The dog overshoots us and begins to paddle against the current in vain. The current will carry it away any second.

Now there's shouting above the waterfall. Dad shakes my shoulder. He snaps the arrow loose and discards it. "Play dead."

I go limp, letting the swift current drag me into another

accelerating funnel. I see four men rise into view, silhouetted against the ledge of the waterfall. The second man holds a compound bow. He points at us and shouts orders. The fourth man lifts a handgun and fires at us. I don't move. There's nothing I can do.

We tumble over another waterfall. This one is a longer drop, the water below shallower, but we both land on our backs, packs cushioning us from the rocks beneath the water.

Dad coughs and grunts. I take a deep breath. My eyes are everywhere at once, focused and keen. No dogs. No hunters.

"Up the far bank." Dad pulls me along. We trudge through the water as if running in a nightmare, going more slowly the harder we try. The dog that swam after us surfaces before me and I stifle a cry. But the dog is dead. One of us may have landed on top of it. I push the limp carcass away.

I see a space behind a patch of hanging brambles. "Dad, in here. Quick!"

His eyes light up as he spies the hole. It's our best bet; we can't outrun the dogs, and I don't know how many waterfalls we can survive.

Dad snatches the red collar of the dead dog and drags it behind him. We press through the narrow opening between a boulder and a ledge and duck beneath the vine. We're suddenly huddled in a tiny alcove carved into the rock: me, Dad, a couple of backpacks, and Fido. In water up to our chests. One big happy family.

I eye Dad. He whispers, "If they find the dog, they'll expect to find us. If none of us are around, they may continue downstream, or figure we were sucked into a rock tube."

I bite my lip. My lungs are burning, my thigh is on fire, and my bruised arms feel as if I've used them to shatter bricks. The horror settles in, and I hold Dad tightly. *This is insane. They attacked us!*

"Shhh. Stay quiet. They'll miss us. We just need to wait it out."

"Are you hit? Are you hurt?" I whisper.

"No. Are you?"

"Bad dog bite on my leg, I think."

"Jesus," Dad mutters.

"What the hell, Dad? Why are they doing this?"

"Shhh, honey."

It makes no sense. I can only close my eyes and clench my jaw.

"Lei, your bag's open! You're losing stuff!"

I turn to secure my pack, and my stomach sinks. A shirt and a blister pack of iodide tablets rush away from our hiding spot on the strong current. "No!"

"Stay here." Dad pulls me back. "Too late."

"I know, but . . . if they find it, they'll know what we have."

Dad shakes his head. "Too late. Shhh."

The voices approach and then drift away. We are as silent and still as the rocks for several minutes. Then the voices sound nearer. Dad and I shrink against the back wall of our hollow.

A gunshot.

Barking.

The voices grow agitated—and more distant.

Machine-gun fire. Screams.

What's happening?

Far away, a car horn honks. A motor fires up; then the sound is lost below the rushing water.

"Dad, should we go?"

"No. Could be a trick. Just wait. It'll be dark soon."

We wait. And we wait. Tiny fish nibble occasionally on my thigh, and I cage the wound with cupped fingers to keep them away. The mosquitoes don't have any trouble finding us, and my face soon feels like a pizza. We wait until nightfall before we wade across the river, shivering and starving, stumbling once again into the jungle, this time without even a blade to clear our way. The pain in my leg is exquisite, but more than that, I am tortured by every twig snap, terrorized by the thought that it will trigger another onslaught of dogs and murderous foes. But we must take that step. And the next. One after another into the endless swarms of bloodsuckers, through the night and beyond the dawn.

It is our only way home.

CHAPTER 24

The zombie apocalypse is upon us. Dad and I trudge all day through the dark underbrush like the undead, me dragging a hurting thigh and plucking stitches from my forehead, Dad hunched over with exhaustion. We're covered from head to toe in mosquito bites. We'd make a great outdoor-outfitter ad: sporting our baggy, tattered, dripping-wet quick-dry shorts and button-up shirts, smeared with soils of every color and matted with fern fur. A snapped arrow shaft juts out from my ragged pack.

In the afternoon we stumble into a clearing in the jungle. A dirt road with a wide shoulder on a steep slope cleaves the forest into halves. We have a grand, uninterrupted view of the Pacific Ocean to the north or northeast.

We see a long train of naval ships. Dozens upon dozens of craft—from smaller red-and-white Coast Guard boats all the way up to battleships—are clustered in a great flock ten miles off the shore, traveling away from Maui at a slight angle.

Dad says, "That's the entire Hawaiian fleet out there."

"Wow," I mutter. "Maybe . . . they're deploying some defense."

"What if we're at war?" Dad thinks aloud. But he concludes, "No. They wouldn't be taking Coast Guard tugboats into battle. This doesn't make any sense."

I remember what Aukina said to me at the Marine Corps Base the afternoon before we escaped: *"We're out of gas. Unnecessary flights have already stopped. We need what's left for something big. Our orders are to . . ."*

But he had trailed off. And finished by saying, *"I'd take you and your dad with us if I could."*

I'd take you with us. . . . Something big . . . "Dad," I say. "These are the orders Aukina was hinting at. They've been ordered to leave. They're just . . . leaving."

Is Aukina on one of those ships? Did he take his family with him? I hope he's safe.

"Lei, the U.S. military's not going to *leave* Hawai'i. The generals wouldn't ditch this state. The reason these islands were occupied to begin with is their strategic significance in the Pacific. They're going to clamp down on supply lines and farmlands and snuff out all the bickering. People don't abdicate power for no reason."

"Dad. That was all before. Everything's changed."

We sit down and watch in silence as the distant battleships grow smaller.

As I see all that power and might drift away on the open

264

sea, I'm reminded, absurdly, of how I felt the first time my parents left me alone to babysit Kai. I watched their car pull out of the driveway feeling scared and excited. I was on my own.

There's no excitement now. The United States has ditched us. The barbarians who hunted us yesterday might cheer. But what if an enemy shows up on these shores?

"We're no longer part of America," I whisper.

Dad's eyes widen.

I cough. Tiny droplets of blood spatter my fist. I wipe the evidence away. "Where are they going? San Diego? What are they going to find?"

"Klingons."

"I'm serious, Dad."

"We may never know." Dad scratches his beard. "We may never find out what the hell has happened to the world. Who's going to flee *to* Hawai`i?"

I shrug. "The Chinese?"

Dad soaks up my comment for a moment. "Can you imagine?"

"Hysteresis," I say.

Dad gives me an approving wink. "You're right."

Hysteresis is another ecology word I've heard at home. It describes when things are harder to fix than they were to break in the first place. Like a rubber band: they stretch a lot, but when you pull too hard, they snap, and there's no going back to the way it used to be.

No doubt now: Hawai`i has snapped.

* * *

We can only march forward. Dad and I press on.

We break through the trees as dusk begins to fall and find ourselves standing along the edge of a one-acre clearing planted with *pakalōlō*. Rows upon rows of marijuana plants. Dad tosses his bag to the ground, falls to his knees, and declares, "We are done for the day."

"We can't stop here! This belongs to someone. What if they come along and find us?"

"Then we'll all get baked together." He grins. He's serious. "Lei, we have to stop. I can't keep going. We have to clean out your dog bite. We both need medical attention. I can't think of a finer apothecary on all the islands."

"Medical attention?"

This is the stupidest idea I've ever heard. I've never smoked pot, though plenty of kids at school regularly do. I don't have an opinion about it, but this strikes me as insane.

"We all have our limits, Lei. I was going to stop anyway. This just makes it all the more worthwhile. Why don't you pitch our tent somewhere nearby? I'll be over to help in a few."

"You can't smoke freshly picked *pakalōlō*. Even I know that."

"It's the end of the world, Lei. And we're both exhausted and in pain and homesick and hunted and hungry and chafing and swarmed by mosquitoes and thirsty and infected and angry and half-crazed. We're in the middle of the jungle. The big boys just jumped ship. Savages carry the badge now. Body snatchers control the president. We can do whatever we want."

I wander away and set up camp. I know when I'm beat. Truth be told, I was ready to ask that we do stop. If Dad wants to get a bad high off damp weed, what do I care?

Later in the evening we're crouched low in our small tent. The stars shimmer through a dusty atmosphere and the persistent glow of the Emerald Orchid. I've just cleaned my dog bite again with alcohol wipes when Dad presents me with a bong made out of an emptied tuna can. Dad found plenty of long-dried flower buds and plant tips to fill his invention. "I insist," he says.

Will wonders ever cease? I hold it up awkwardly. "What about my epilepsy?"

"Is this really your first time?"

"Are you lōlō? I'm a good girl, Dad. And epileptic! My meds worked. I wasn't going to jeopardize that."

"Yeah. But pot won't interfere with your meds. Some people think it actually helps."

I stare at him.

"I looked into it once. In case, you know, you ever did smoke."

"Are you trying to talk me in to being a pothead?"

Dad laughs. "No. Forget I said that."

He shows me what to do, and I do it. I finally get the hang of plugging and releasing the choke as I draw in my breath. For a long time I feel nothing but the urge to cough. Then it hits me. My aches and pains and fears are soon forgotten, and I'm riding an emerald wave of another sort through the stars.

"Maybe this would help my social life."

Dad doesn't say anything. He probably doesn't know how to respond. "Awkward!" I sing, and then I laugh.

"I knew you were having a tough time. I never knew it was that tough."

"It's okay. It's not your fault. You asked, and I always lied. Aside from Tami . . . Hilo's impossible. People aren't mean; they're just too tight already to bother putting in the effort. It's hard to fit in with light skin. And fits . . ." I add with a giggle. "It's too hard to fit in with fits."

"I'm glad you didn't have any issues with that yesterday," Dad says. "I was worried."

"Yeah, can you imagine?" I try to picture losing it like a washing machine, in that cramped alcove with the dead dog, while bad guys searched for us. I grow panicky just thinking about it.

"But," I say, "I can't wait to get back there. Hilo's home. And it can't be harder than here! Or O`ahu!"

"Amen to that."

"You know what else? Pele taught me something. You can't just wait around for others to accept you. You have to go out and get it. Defend your turf."

"Pele taught you that?"

"Yeah. She did."

"K'den. Amen," Dad says.

Now I feel the electricity in my brain, stored there like a humming, thrumming power plant. I'm at the center of a ball of lightning, ready to roll down the slope of a giant hill in my fiery zorb. I crackle and I sizzle and I spark. Blue arcs spit off my fingertips and out through my stitches and my hair is standing on end like I'm the Bride of Frankenstein. I *am* Pele: goddess of fire and volcanoes and lightning and all things that "rock." I *am* the Emerald Orchid. Leilani. The Flower of Heaven. I sewed the green lightning and cast it over the night sky, and I rest upon the mantle of the Earth, a queen in a fine, green silk gown, looking out upon the destruction that I've wrought. But I am greater still than Pele. For I know the day, the hour, the moment of the end. I am the goddess of the cosmos. I come when it suits me. I do as I please. My stormy brain obliterates satellites and circuit boards. I take it all away. Now you're back to warring and smiting and pillaging.

Smiting. I laugh. *Hilarious word.*

That *Lord of the Flies* Jackie-Jack sheriff yesterday loved to use his fancy compound bow, yeah? Smiter extraordinaire. I know what it's like to be hunted, the fear of the prey. But Jackie-Jack doesn't know what it's like to hunt me. I'm no Piggy. No stupid boar. I'm just as smart as you are. I hacked a two-headed beast in half with a sword, and I kept my cool. I was tested by fire, and I kept my cool. That's because I am the goddess of fire, the rainmaker of hellfire, I can hear the gods—even if I have no idea what they're saying—and I surf the Emerald Orchid.

I take another hit from the tuna can and pass it to Dad. I cough into my fist, then wipe the blood spatter on my shorts. I never want to touch this stuff again—but right now, it seems like a great idea.

"Is the iodide getting to you?" Dad asks me after a few minutes—or hours—of silence.

"Yeah."

"I wish I knew what to do. Everything we know is second- or thirdhand. I don't even know if it's worth it. Man, what's happening out there?" Dad says. "What's happening in Greece?"

"Greece?" I giggle.

"Yeah. Greece. What's happening in France? Kansas? Iran? How are the Mongolians dealing with this? Who's out there wondering about Hawai`i?"

I crack up. "Aloha, Hawai`i. Howzit? Please send more macadamia nuts." OMG. Bad joke. But I can't stop laughing.

Dad heroically rediscovers his train of thought. "Are tourists stuck in Peru ever going to find their way home? How long do you suppose the food lasted in Manhattan?"

"I just care about Mom and Kai. That's what drives me crazy. I want to know what *they're* doing."

Dad leans forward and seems to sober up a bit. "Lei, they're all right. I promise."

"It's been five weeks now, Dad. Thirty-five days." I wipe tears away before they can pour down my cheeks. "But who's counting?"

He squeezes my shoulder. "Hey. They're with Grandpa. They're better off than we are. The Big Island is now the land of milk and honey. Plenty of food. Wild pigs. Folks could eat coqui frogs. The island has one of the biggest ranches in America. People will adapt. We've been eating less . . . and surviving. Everyone will be getting by on less. There hasn't been enough time for *everything* to unravel."

We're silent, and my thoughts shift to that pyre smoke we saw behind the Maui airport. *Tell that to the first round of losers.*

"The point is we can handle it," Dad continues. "And you know Mom. She has those chickens and that garden. And our neighbors. The Millers would take a bullet for her. She's got a good family name, too. Grandpa's kahuna. Lots of friends in those parts."

"They're probably running the island, for all we know."

"Ha! Wouldn't surprise me. See? They're *fine*. Kai pops eggs each morning, coqui frogs for dinner, and a nice salad for lunch. They probably have luaus every couple of days with the pigs your grandpa hunts."

I laugh again. "Remember that time Mom went spearfishing with that marine-science guy and stabbed his shoe when she tripped over the lava?"

"She'll never live that down."

We cackle with laughter for what might be hours.

I'm feeling better about them. Still, Mom has to be worried about us. We've been hunted, attacked, shipwrecked, shot, held prisoner. I've leapt from a burning building, and I'm coughing blood and high on pot. She could hardly have feared any worse. I just want her to know that we're still here, and that we'll hold each other in our arms soon.

"Hana in the next day or two. We'll find some way to get across the gap, and we'll be there, just like that."

"I really hope you're right. I can't take much more of this."

"Oh, but you can. And you'll have to. We both will: this is only the beginning, Lei. Hunters and gatherers. Tribal serfdoms. Survival of the fittest. We're not going to be at the top of the food chain. We don't have what it takes to be powerful. Mean. It's groups like that sheriff's posse that will be in charge. Shoot first, questions never. Fighting for what's ours is the new norm, hon."

I can feel panic returning. What happened yesterday was so *wrong*. I can scarcely grasp it.

I clasp on to images of Mom and Kai. "As long as we're all together."

"Amen."

The old life isn't *all* gone. Our bonds haven't *completely* disintegrated. The weave is in our DNA, isn't it? We'll always start again. "Moloka`i was working. Starting fresh. What if all this technology and braininess got in the way, and now we can finally be back in touch with reality? What if it's an *opportunity*? If Uncle Akoni's right, and the Emerald Orchid's actually absorbing radiation, what if it's all for the best?"

Dad is silent. "I've heard that crisis and opportunity are the same word in Chinese."

"Hey, yeah."

"A global catharsis. A do-over. Yeah. Remind me to get stoned with you more often." Dad suddenly belts out in song. *"We've got to get our-se-elves back to the Gaaaaarden . . . !"*

Some seventies thing. I laugh.

Dad lies down. "I can't believe it happened this way. I always thought it would be some Malthusian catastrophe: water wars, soil collapse, disease, swine flu, heat waves, ice ages. You name it. But no. It's a Georgia O'Keeffe painting. Some . . . giant . . . fertility goddess from outer space finally did us all in."

"Dad!"

"Well, am I wrong? Look at it! Am I wrong?"

I stare at the Emerald Orchid. I may never unsee what he just put in my head. Leave it to a *guy* to get all anatomical. It's just a cloud. Definitely not a UFO. It's a glowing cloud of gas or plasma or whatever. Like puffy summer clouds, you can see anything you want to in its shape.

This thing hasn't changed shape much, though; it's more rigid than a cloud. More substantial. But it's different now. Out of focus. There's something that wasn't there on the first night I saw it.

"Dad, you see that other thing? Like a separate flower. Inside it, maybe? Behind it? I can't tell."

Dad sits up. "Yeah, I do. I saw that a couple of nights ago. It's moved since then."

It reminds me of the jellyfish at the Monterey Bay Aquarium. I recall an image of those beautiful orange globules and their neon tentacles, serenely suspended within their aquarium against a dark blue backdrop. The baby jellyfish and the adult jellyfish, all see-through and seemingly tangled, would align behind the glass the way this Emerald Orchid and its . . .

It is a good thing. It is done and my purpose is done.

Suckle. Gather your strength.

I gasp.

A whirlwind of memories assails me, each building on the next. Those dark seizurescapes, the snatches of imagery, the voice, the echoes of thought flowing through with my own consciousness like ropy folds of bloodshot pahoehoe flowing over rocky `a`a.

I do not want to remember any of my seizures. Or what follows. But I can't bury what I now see. It's all coming back, like a furious swarm of hornets rattled from a hive, and the truth stings white-hot:

The Emerald Orchid is no cloud.

CHAPTER 25

I have dreamt of these shores. I was born here, but I slipped away. Now I have reached the shallows, at long last, guided across the endless waters by ancient stars. These islands and their sacred tides call me forth.

"Dad!"

"What?"

"It's alive. The Orchid's alive!"

There is new heat within my belly, and I yearn to spill the urge . . .

Dad is playful. "Whoa. I like it: some ancient, alien creature stirred from the cosmos itself. That's . . . stellar."

"No! I'm serious!" I want off this high. It's no fun anymore. My mind is afire, racing to assemble the last pieces of a puzzle. I can't believe it; it's all so obvious now.

I belong here, and I am well. It is almost ready to come out.

"Dad. It's come here to calve! It's given birth. It . . . It's . . ." The words can't keep up with the flood of imagery, the snippets of consciousness. *I can hear its thoughts!*

"The EKG is broken. I'm trying to make sense of your chart from yesterday. I compared it to your records from Hilo—the pattern is totally different—gibberish."

"Have you heard them?"

"You a good listener, Leilani?"

The EKG could detect it. And Uncle Akoni could. He was *half* right: the Orchid surges through our minds as well as our motherboards! I wasn't hearing transmissions, though; just thoughts. The signals churned unnoticed through my wandering thoughts as familiar imagery, forgotten once the black shroud of my fits had lifted.

I see the sacred honu *. . . heaved ashore, bridging sea and surf, pushing back the sand to lay its eggs . . .*

276

"A cosmic sea turtle." I test the words.

"Yeah." Dad is still having fun. "A heavenly *honu*, drifting through space, coming to shore."

"Dad, *stop*. Listen to me. That thing is alive. Uncle Akoni was almost right. We can hear its thoughts."

He's looking at me now. I say, "I only put it together just now! But it *is* a . . . cosmic sea turtle! It was born here. It's just returned to lay its eggs, or spawn, or whatever it does. It's feeding on the atmosphere. That's how it works!"

Dad stiffens. "Damn. Could this thing be a *creature*? Does it come *cyclically*?"

"I'm not crazy," I say. "I'm not. It's really true: I heard it. I didn't realize. Maybe epileptics can hear it. Like our neural . . . weirdness . . . allows us to tune in to the signal."

"Lei, calm down. I'm following you, okay?"

"Fo' real?"

Dad stares up at the Orchids. I watch him closely and lose track of time. I can't tell what he's thinking, but his mind is in overdrive. Finally, he says, "Maybe you're right. What if you are? This could be the answer to the riddle! Depends on how often it comes to . . . to calve. But this could be the reason for each mass extinction. Could it be iridium based? Could iridium interfere with electronics and stuff? Maybe in combination with some other ionization? Does it drop meteors and muck up the atmosphere each time it comes?"

I'm trying to follow. "Wait. You've got to be kidding—the dinosaurs?"

"I'm serious. I think you're on to something. We've been seeing lots of meteor-like activity. What if this . . . species . . .

came and . . . shed materials, striking land and sea—the haze in the sky, the tsunamis. Last time it killed off the dinosaurs. And before that: the Permian-Triassic extinction that wiped out all trilobites; and—"

"Dad! No one cares about that."

The sudden silence is startling. Dad looks over as if I've just slapped him. "I believe you," he says. "All this talk about aliens. I was debating it in my head more than you know. It primed the pump. But this . . . this feels like it actually fits, somehow."

I squeeze his hand. "You believe me, though? Really?"

He nods. "I mean, this very well could be a natural phenomenon, repeated again and again over millions of years. The Earth absorbs the blow, resets. This just happens to be the first time we've been around to witness it. Unless the Mayans knew something, eh? But the impact on our technology would be purely side effect. I can't even begin to imagine the anatomy and physiology of some creature that lives out its life cycle in the vacuum of space, but, damn, I guess it's *possible*. It's so crazy, you really do have to be stoned to entertain the idea."

We both lie down and stare up at the Emerald Orchid— and its baby.

My own mind is tying itself in knots.

Others have been here all along! They roam the spaces between stars. I catch a glimpse of my father's wonder: if our terrestrial turtles will cross oceans, unaware of the drifting continents, then how much grander are these creatures, who voyage between worlds?

This is right. . . . This one has not warmed before.
I will linger, then, as I have done on other shores. . . .

Other shores? Have *other* civilizations suffered? The universe has shifted under my feet, and I fall back, spinning.

My home is an island, cut off, adrift. And so is my world.

I stare through the mesh of our tent at a real alien creature blossoming across the night sky, and I surf the waves beyond the stars.

What else do you have to say?

I glance over at Dad. He's asleep. Imagine that. His exhausted body vanquished his excited mind. My muscles cry out for me to follow his lead, and I leave the mysteries and the majesty of the cosmos behind.

* * *

It's morning. I'm lying awake inside the cramped tent. My head feels fine, and my thoughts are clear. Focused. Last night my mind was all over the map. It was like I was in one of those carnival booths with a million dollars cash and a wind machine blowing at hurricane strength, but I couldn't reach out and snag even a single bill.

This morning there's only one thing on my mind:

I'm an alien psychic.

I laugh.

"Wuh?"

I nudge Dad. "Wake up. Let's get going."

He props himself up on his elbows and presses his palms into his eyeball sockets.

"Do you . . . do you remember what we figured out last night?" I ask.

"Oh, yes."

"And you still believe me?"

"Hon, I'll believe anything."

"Even the part about being able to hear it?"

He hesitates, but pats me on the shoulder. "I'm open to it. It might explain why your blackouts have been so unnaturally long. You'll have to explain it again."

"Okay."

"On the trail, though. Let's go," he says. "We've been in one place for too long."

I take a pill. Now I have two left. *Two left.*

We break camp and continue our slog.

My thigh feels a little better; I think it's going to heal. The mosquitoes, though, are unrelenting. If we stop for even forty-five seconds to adjust a belt strap, we become a feast.

I tell Dad about my dreams and the visions during my recent fits. I explain how I confused the consciousness of the Orchid with the familiar *mo'olelo* of my Hawai'i. I pictured islands, not planets; tides instead of gravity; volcanoes, not radiation.

And this one spits fire. It oozes the heat. . . .
I will linger, then, as I have done on other shores,
and we both shall have our fill.

Her consciousness has come to me in other ways. Snippets of thought directed at her baby.

280

You are Leilani. I am Leilani.

And what does it matter, anyway? So what if my mind can randomly tune in to and translate the signals? I feel like Cassandra from Greek mythology: I have knowledge, but I'm powerless to act. What can I do?

Dad listens. He doesn't say much. But he knows that I believe what I'm saying.

And one *other* person shares the truth with me. How did Uncle Akoni figure it out? He got the details wrong, but he was keen enough to notice *something* was happening. Would I have stood by these crazy notions if Uncle Akoni hadn't paved the way? Or would I have thought that I was going insane?

His statements run through my head:

"Nānā i ke kumu. *Look to the source.*"

"Go up on the mountain. Stand at the mouth of the cave. And when you hear the whisper, see if you can't answer back."

"Everyone wants them to leave. God forbid they do."

It's clear that Uncle Akoni wants me to try *something*. But can I succeed where he hasn't? If I can hear its thoughts, can it hear mine? It's one thing for me to be aware of a being hovering over the world unmindful of its own destructive force. It's another thing entirely for *it* to notice *me*. Have I ever singled

281

out the interests of one frazzled ant scurrying atop a flattened anthill? And even if it could hear me, would it realize it? I mean, it took *me* five weeks to put this connection together. Would it understand me?

And even if all those obstacles were surmountable, what would I say to it? Then I remember Uncle Akoni:

> *"I love the Big Island. Wish Moloka`i had mountains like that. Mauna Kea's, what, fourteen thousand feet high?"*

Does Uncle Akoni think that our connection will be stronger the nearer we can get to it? Maybe fourteen thousand feet will make a difference. Once I'm home—once our family is whole again—I *will* go up on Mauna Kea. I will make the pilgrimage of my ancestral *ali`i*, pay my respects to the most sacred of places in Hawai`i, and talk to the gods.

But we have to get there first.

The interminable gorges continue. Every hour, like clockwork, we must descend steep ravines, cross waterways of varying size, and scale back up the opposite slope. The rain comes and goes, sometimes heavily. I have no idea how far away Hana is. There seems to be no reward for our progress— we're incessantly death-marching through a gorgeous hell.

"They call this paradise?" I joke.

Dad grins. "Yeah. We were the ones raptured. Welcome back to the Garden."

CHAPTER 26

We step out of the trees and onto the four-wheel-drive path, sheets of rain stinging us, and the long shaft of an arrow sinks into Dad's backpack. If I hadn't been behind him and seen it appear, it's possible that neither of us would even have known. Like magic, it's just there.

The fletchings of the arrow tilt upslope. I wipe my eyes, turn to look—and my throat goes dry.

An archer with a sheriff's badge stands in the middle of the path, about fifty yards away. Farther back, two deputies jog into view, holding back a leaping mass of growling dogs. "Come on. Hand it over," the archer shouts over the rain. "I could've hit you."

"No," Dad whispers. "Don't do this. Dammit. No."

"You got more pills?"

Dad and I share an uncertain glance. Our hesitation

triggers a response. The pack of hunting dogs barrels down upon us.

"No! Stop it!" Dad shouts.

Instinct takes over. Dad and I run blindly, splashing over rocky potholes and lumps of worn lava. I've never run so fast or so hard in all my life. Still the dogs gain, barking with wild excitement, gliding over the rough terrain.

We race along a slight bend in the road and come upon two trucks parked on the path, facing downhill. We dash over to the first of the four-by-four vehicles and scramble into the bed over the top of a network of dog cages. It takes effort to pull ourselves up onto the slippery-wet tailgate and over the cages, especially with our bulky packs. Dad winces as he lifts himself up. The bed offers immediate sanctuary; the pack of dogs swarms around us, unable to leap aboard.

Panting, I look for a weapon. Only bungee cords, arrow packaging, dog food, and pliers. Wrenches. I grab a big one, feeling less naked. Dad peeks into the cab. The dogs are barking madly, circling like frenzied sharks. Dad points forward and says, "Get to the other one."

We climb onto the roof of the first truck and jump down onto the hood. The lead truck is parked near enough for us to jump between them. It's a long jump, and the dogs snarl, but we manage.

The dogs leap and scratch at the bed of the truck, baring vicious teeth. Dad sheds his backpack, and I drop my pack with its precious iodine tablets into the bed of the truck.

"Give me that," Dad says, wiping water off his face, and I

hand him the wrench. He uses it to smash the back window of the cab, reaches inside, unlatches the sliding window, then shoves the shattered and jagged window frame to the side. "Can you fit?"

"Sure."

I hear shouts over the pelting rain as our hunters appear around the bend. Dad motions me into the cab and I squeeze through the opening.

"What's going to happen?" I feel panic closing in.

"Any guns in there?"

I crawl into the front seat and open the center console. CDs. A deputy badge. The glove box houses a pistol. I stare at it, then snatch it up and pass it to Dad.

He seizes the gun, whips away, turns, and fires four shots. I yelp at the sudden, piercing cracks. In the rearview mirror, I see two men fall back behind the storm-gray ridgeline.

"Go, honey!"

"What!"

Drive? I look around for keys. This truck has a stick shift. He might as well ask me to fly us out of here.

He ducks down and peeks in the back window. "Key's in the ignition. Just remember what Grandpa taught you. Release the brake and hold down the clutch all the way. Then give it a turn."

Yeah, but Grandpa showed me how to drive a clutch in a parking lot. "You do it, Dad!"

"Go! They're coming."

The dogs won't allow Dad to jump in the truck using a

door. I see one of the men poke his head up over the hill again. Dad fires another round, and a tendril of blood explodes from the side of the man's face. Dad groans. I scream. The shouting reaches fever pitch.

"GO!"

I spring the brake release and punch the clutch all the way to the floor. The truck begins to roll even before I crank the ignition.

Oh, my God, we just shot that guy in the face.

The truck roars to life as I try the key. Dad shouts, "Good, hon. Just keep holding the clutch down. Don't try anything yet."

The steering is incredibly stiff, but I pull on the wheel enough to guide the truck along the dual tire tracks in the rocky path. I can't see anything; the windshield wipers won't turn on. Behind me, Dad fires. I think I hear a tire blow on the truck behind us.

"Okay, try releasing the clutch slowly while giving it gas. Just a little bit, though!" I do as I'm told, and the truck lurches to a halt, falls silent. The dogs are still with us, barking and growling. I turn to see our hunters appear over the hill, shouting. Gunfire. The man with the bow pulls back another arrow.

I'm shaking. "Dad."

Dad drops below the level of the sides of the bed. "Hold the clutch down again. Keep it down this time," he shouts. "We need some distance before we try again."

I push the clutch all the way in and urge the truck forward with gentle rocking in my seat. We begin to coast downhill and leave the dogs behind. I turn on the engine after we're rolling. Another back window shatters. Something pokes into my back. I scream and twist around. An arrow point protrudes through the back of my seat.

"Leilani!"

"I'm okay."

"Don't stop!"

We're going too fast, and I'm coming up on a sharp curve in the path that I can scarcely make out through the distorted windshield. In a panic I try the brake, and we jerk to a halt. Dad tumbles forward with a thud. "Dad, I can't do this!"

"Doing great. Be gentle on the brake. Once you're going again, let the clutch out halfway. The gears will slow you—but don't slow down too much. We're still in their line of sight."

I get us moving again and then release some pressure on the clutch. We slow, and I push the clutch back in, pull hard on the wheel, and we take the turn. But the road becomes too bumpy at this speed. We're bouncing and rocking as if we're tumbling down a cliff. My left front tire slams into a hole. Dad's gun fires. I regain control of the steering wheel and guide us down the road.

"Dad! You okay?"

"I'm fine. Good job."

They're going to kill us.

"Is that man okay?"

"I don't know. Go."

The engine is revving like crazy.

"Shift, hon!"

"What?"

"Lei, hold the clutch in again, use the other foot to brake. I'll trade you now. But don't release the clutch!"

I drift to a halt, following his instructions. He leaps to the ground and opens the driver door. He places his own left foot on the clutch and scoots into the driver's seat while I sidle over.

"Watch the tip of that arrow."

Dad settles into position with his back arched.

I laugh, sick to my stomach. Dad effortlessly commands the truck into motion.

Gunfire cracks behind us. I turn.

Our enemy is following. One of their wheels is flat, but they barrel over the uneven terrain steadily. The dogs trot beside the truck in drunken ecstasy. A stout figure stands in the back of the truck, pistol raised high. He fires a shot.

We accelerate. I bounce so hard that my head hits the roof and I land on my side. I latch on to the handlebar above the passenger door. A house materializes to our left; we pass one on our right. I'm beginning to hope that we'll drive straight into Hana when we slam into something and burst a tire.

Another bullet hits the truck. Both trucks are now crawling over the lava road. A ramshackle house drifts by.

"Is there ammo in the glove box?" Dad asks as we rattle slowly forward.

I pull out a heavy box. Two hundred rounds. "Hand it over," Dad says.

I give him the ammo and he slams on the brakes. "Okay. Run."

"What?"

"If the road improves, they'll gain on us. We block their truck this way."

I eject myself back into the pouring rain. Dad winces as he whips on the pack with all the iodide. We ditch the other pack and bolt down the path. After a minute of sheer sprinting, I stutter to a halt, coughing blood. Dad pauses and reloads his handgun, spilling rounds to the ground. He fires at the dogs chasing us, felling at least three.

We race forward, and the road improves around the next bend. Dad fires once more. A dog yelps. Return fire fills me with icy terror, and I don't turn. Side roads branch off rows of houses in every direction. The hunters whistle, calling back their dogs. We're in some run-down neighborhood overlooking a slope that spills to the sea. A town sprawls below us, pummeled by curtains of rain. *Hana?*

Window slats shut abruptly as we run by. We've wandered into a tropical Western shoot-out.

Dad turns down a side street, runs through a yard, and bolts up to the front door. He wipes his brow and raps on the door. "Help! Please help us!"

No response. He tries the knob, but it's locked. A voice calls, "Go away."

"We're being chased. We—"

"You're on your own. Get outta here. They'll find you here. Go!"

Dad dashes off the porch. We race to the next house. This time a thirty-something Hawaiian woman props open her door. She ushers us inside.

"Thank you. Thank you so much—"

"Quiet, now." We're rushed downstairs into the kitchen. She points to a little door under the stairs, and we duck into a small storage area. Dad removes his pack and shoves it into the low space below the bottom steps. The woman holds the door open and studies us. "You better hope they don't come to the house. If they come to the house—"

"Please," I say, panting. "They're trying to kill us. Thank you."

Our protector smiles grimly. She leaves the door open and sits down at the kitchen table, watching us, uncertain. "We'll do what we can. Quiet, now."

Dad kisses the back of my head and hugs me from behind. "It's going to be okay. Hang in there."

I wipe rainwater and tears from my eyes as the woman and I stare at each other. The terrifying sound of dogs returns. They're excited; they know we're near. I close my eyes and hold my breath.

I hate dogs.

A voice calls from the street in Hawaiian. I catch a few words—"enemy," "duty"—as the woman's eyes narrow in fear. A voice translates into English, competing with the rain on the aluminum roofing. "Don't even *think* of harboring these murderers. Give them up now and no trouble comes to you."

Murderers? Did Dad kill that man?

The woman and I lock eyes. Her expression is tortured, terrified. "Please," I whisper.

She rises and paces between the counter and the table.

The dogs are nearer. One growls in the stairway above. Others yelp and bark. With a trembling touch, the woman turns on an old record player connected to a car battery. She carefully sets the needle down on a spinning record and raises both of her shaking hands to her temples to steady them.

The ukulele music haunts me with the promise of comfort.

Hawaiian words, then English, ring out from the street. "If we find him hiding in your house, Kana`ina will banish you. Do it right. Serve your Hawai`i!"

The woman looks at us. "I'm sorry. I really am."

"No!" I whisper. "Please. You're all we have."

"Ma'am, please." Dad's voice is shaky.

The voices grow stronger. "He killed seven dogs! He shot a deputy in the face! Don't you dare help him!"

I close my eyes as warm tears stream down my cheeks. I pray to God. I invoke the aid of my ancestors. I beg Pele, and all the gods of Hawai`i above her. I scream out with my mind to the Emerald Orchid to do something—anything. *Please. Let us get out of here.*

"There's nothing I can do. The dogs know. There's nothing." The woman is still holding her fingers to her temples, slowly shaking her head.

Dad pleads. "We don't want anything from you. Just a chance. Tell them we stopped here and then went up the road. We'll run back to the forest. A chance."

The woman listens. She's considering it. I hold my breath. *Please.*

A dog appears at the sliding door to the back lanai and barks in triumph. The woman cries out in surprise, then: "They're down here! They have a gun. Down here."

Dad nudges me forward. "Run!"

As I spill out of the closet, a Hawaiian man appears in the doorway. We lock eyes, lethal victory in his cold gaze. I gasp and back up into the hole, pushing Dad in. I swing the door shut. We're lost in darkness. "Dad, oh, God. I . . . wa . . ." I can't breathe. He squeezes me tight.

"Cover your ears." I hear the hammer of his pistol cock, and I shrink into a ball. We're going to shoot our way out of here. *Okay. Okay. We have to.*

Then the deep voice speaks a foot away. "Push your gun out. I'm pointing one right at you. You fire, I fire. I kill you *and* your daughter."

A groan escapes Dad. He pushes open the door and tosses his gun.

"No, Dad!"

The stout man strides over, tucking a pistol into his pants with a vicious grin. He snags Dad's gun and reaches a hand into the closet, grabs me by my hair, and drags me into the kitchen. I scream and slap at his clenched fists.

"No! Stop!" Dad rushes my captor, eyes afire, but the man whips him in the face with the side of the gun. Dad spills over a chair. The woman whimpers, eyes shut tight.

"Dad!" I cry. "Dad!"

He stirs, dazed. Two more men push into the kitchen. One in a police uniform. A gold star over his heart. Pure muscle.

"Stop this!" I shout. "What're you DOING?"

The sheriff looks me over.

The stout man laughs. "Shut up, *hapa*."

"Please!" Dad says. "Her mother is the first daughter of a kahuna. Lani Hawika. Spare her."

The sheriff stiffens. "*Lani Hawika?* Was a cop over here?"

Dad nods.

"Kahuna? Kahuna my ass."

My captor spits on Dad and yanks on my hair. I scream.

The sheriff looks at me. "Lani Hawika's granddaughter?"

"Yes," Dad says.

"Malia's kid?"

"Yes!"

The sheriff looks at the ground. "Goddammit. Put her over there."

I'm dragged to the far side of the dining table.

The sheriff eyes Dad, pulling his gun from his holster. Realization dawns.

He's only going to spare me.

Dad's eyes are closed; he knows that this is the end.

"Stop!" I say to the sheriff. "Please. Your men tried to kill us. The dogs attacked. We hadn't done anything. We didn't mean to hurt *anyone*."

The sheriff points at me. "You should've surrendered. We only wanted your stuff. No one comes through here without payment. No one sneaks *iodide*. I decide who gets medicine. Sure as hell no one shoots my men in the face."

The Hawaiian grabs Dad by the shirt, drags him into the middle of the kitchen, and tosses him down.

293

"What are you doing?" I scream, jump up to go to Dad. Someone grabs my arm.

The sheriff points his gun at Dad's head.

"Stop! STOP!" I scream. "NO NO NO!"

"I love you, Lei." Dad looks at me with eyes that are calm and fearful. "I'm so proud of you."

The woman crouches in a corner, hands over her face.

"No! NO!" I shriek, struggling to free myself. "This is your new Hawai`i? This is your gods and your people?"

My vision flickers. The sheriff lowers the gun. My head begins to buzz. Knocks echo in distant parts. *Not now, goddammit! Go away!* I stare at the sheriff.

He studies me. Raises the pistol to Dad's head. Cocks the hammer. Dad looks at me with eyes that have already moved on.

"NO! STOP!"

A thunderous crack. Darkness. Lightning flashes across the void, and I fall backward. Magma boils my skin and melts it away. I'm engulfed, swallowed by *Po*. The shaking stops. The lightning dies. There is only darkness and a gentle breeze.

In the silence, I listen.

CHAPTER 27

I am Leilani. You are Leilani.
The pulling tide. The yellow fire. I am worn.

Can you hear me? Do you know I'm here?

The giving has purpose, but I am weary. I crave the depths, the comfort of no tides. I will show the peace of the depths to the new one that I gave.

Please. Hear me.

The islands that ooze the heat are good. But I have had my fill. This island hotness will linger—it will ooze for a while now.

The giving was good but very hard. I have had my fill. I will leave the rest for my return.

No. Stay. You cannot go.

Oh, God, Daddy's gone. He's gone.

The sheriff of Hana sits over me. He's looking out a window. I'm on a bed in a small room, dimly lit by the evening light (or is it morning?) passing between the gently rustling curtains. I study his profile. He is weary and preoccupied.

He executed my father on the floor of a kitchen. I heard the thunder. And for what?

"Where's my dad? Let me see him. What have you done with him?" But I'm not sure it came out that way. The sheriff looks down, realizing that I'm awake. He watches me. He must see my eyes filling with hatred, but his only narrow.

I can feel it coming again, like the blade of a fan slowly getting faster. An angry mob stampeding down the next street, torches raised. They're coming for my body and my mind.

The void. The Orchid wants to drift, too. It wants the void. It wants to leave. Its calving and its fight with our sun's gravity have exhausted it. But it will return—it always does.

The Orchid's thoughts—they're not really thoughts, just . . . urges, instincts. I can grasp them now, even though I'm awake. The meaning danced on the tip of my tongue before.

The Orchid gives birth in the surf—our outer atmosphere. It grazes on radiation, like a sea turtle on algae. It feeds on the stars, but now finds our fallout to be sweet. The planets that ooze like this are a special treat. The planets that have toyed with atoms—rich in both atmosphere and radiation—are like bowls of milk to a cat. But it has had its fill. It is ready to leave these shores and return to the ocean of space.

It's saving the milk for another visit. After all, the radiation will continue spilling around the globe for ages.

The sheriff brushes hair from my forehead. The touch is gentle. I gather the strength to spit on his face, but the bed quakes. I'm falling

Are you ready, little one? Shall we go? You see the smudge? That is where we go. Remember. You will come back when you are ready to give.

We will swim slowly until we are beyond this nearest tide, then go fast. Then we will be away from the pulling fires. We will do the long fastness to the other pool. We will be long in the ocean between the pools of fire.

But we like the depths. We are many, there.

Dad's face. Brilliant white light floods outward from behind him. Clouds. My body rocks gently. I'm floating through the sky.

"Dad." I swoon. To see his face . . .

"Hush, darling."

"Am I . . . ?"

"Go back to sleep. Everything is okay. I'm always watching over you."

"No, Dad. I don't want to leave you."

"Hush. Rest."

More clouds. The sky is still yellow, though. It's hell. Dad is gone, and the Devil himself stands over me. I awaken to find the sheriff guarding me. *Am I one of his belongings now?* He's looking away toward the horizon, unaware of my white-hot eyes.

We're on a boat. A giant double canoe with two upside-down triangle sails. He glances down at me, looks away. "She woke up."

I sit up with a grimace. So thirsty. Sore and stiff. But my thigh is bandaged and feels fine. My thousand mosquito bites have faded. A pit of nausea within me—anguish. I'm not ready. I will never be ready. Let oblivion wash over me so I can dream of Dad. I don't want to grieve. I sense the pain emerging. The agony of true loss blooms.

There he is.

Dad.

Crossing the plank from the other hull. Rushing over to me. *Alive?* I struggle to breathe, stare at him with wonder. Tears pour down my cheeks.

"Leilani!" He embraces me. "Just in time." He points. "Look!"

Tall cliffs loom to our right. We are about half a mile from shore. An immense valley opens up before us, breathtaking. A black, sandy beach stretches across the gap. Far behind it, barely visible at this angle, a waterfall a thousand feet tall pours serenely and silently from its distant heights. I gasp. "Waipi`o?"

Dad offers a warm smile in confirmation.

My heart soars. *The Big Island? This is the Big Island?* We're almost home. Hilo's only forty miles down the coast. Maybe this isn't real, after all. It's a delusion. Shielding my tattered mind from true fate.

"Are we going home?" I whisper.

"Yes," Dad says. "We'll be home in a few hours."

I sit up carefully and embrace my father.

The majestic waterfall of Waipi`o Valley, narrowly visible back in its canyon, drifts out of sight as we rush south over the waters. Finally, Dad and I unlock our arms.

"Oh, Dad." I'm sobbing. "How? Why? How long have I been out?"

"Two days. On and off."

"What happened? I thought . . . I thought . . ."

"No, no." He embraces me.

"But . . . what happened?"

Dad squeezes my shoulder. "You had a bad grand mal," he whispers. "One hell of a show."

"I don't get it."

Dad shrugs. *I don't know what to tell you.* "You took . . . all the air out of the room. They stopped."

"I—I . . ."

"Quiet, hon," he says in a low voice. "We're not out of the woods yet. This guy's reputation is very important to him."

The sheriff watches us. I watch him back. His expression is guarded.

"Thank you," I say.

He furrows his brow and looks toward the shore.

"What's your name?" I ask him.

"Hon." Dad's eyes are sharp.

The sheriff glances at me again. "Kalaimanokaho`owaha. Call me Kana`ina."

I stifle a dry laugh. He goes by the name of the chief who slew Captain Cook in 1779.

I look around the boat. The canoes are filled with provisions and artillery and ammo. Almost twenty faces are watching me, mostly men. I see the men who chased and shot at us. The stout one who pulled my hair and hurt Dad. Several are heavily armed. They return to their tasks as my eyes meet each of them.

"Dad," I whisper. "I still . . ."

Dad shakes his head, looks up at the sails, and then meets my eyes. "Relax a bit. We'll be home soon. Just focus on that."

The quarter hours pass as one waterfall after another gushes from the cliff face of the Hamakua Coast between Waipi`o Valley and Hilo Bay. I occasionally see old vehicles driving the lonely highway. One world may have ended, but people will always come and go. I've traveled the coastal road often, zooming across the soaring bridges, never knowing the breadth of the beauty that hid over the edge of the road. I study each ravine and gorge from this new vantage point, remembering—not only with my mind, but with my aching body—the horrors of this same terrain on Maui.

From time to time the cliffs dip to the sea, and the naked peak of Mauna Kea can be seen touching the bluest part of the sky. The observatories crown the sacred summit. Such a joy to see this familiar sight. *I really am home.* We made it. In spite of everything.

The sheriff shouts orders to anchor in the bay up ahead.

And then I recognize where we are. I've never seen it from the water, but it's Onomea Bay, the refuge of the Hawaiian Botanical Gardens. Our house is several miles up, directly above.

We're going to walk home.

"Close enough," the sheriff commands.

The mainsheet is released and several of the crew dip paddles into the water. We hover within several hundred yards of the wave-wracked inlet. An old dining-room hutch bobs in the surf to my right. Tsunami debris.

"Jump?" Dad asks.

The sheriff nods.

I look between them. I can't help it. "Why . . . why are you doing this?"

Kana`ina stares at me. He doesn't answer.

The hair-pulling thug sidles over and leans in close. I

shrink back, try not to show my disgust. *Just a few seconds more. Don't make them change their minds.*

He says, "He owed your Grandpa one big debt."

The sheriff overhears. He glances down at his polished boot, silent.

"Oh," I say.

The hair puller grabs my upper arm and pulls me to my feet. "Remember: we only do what it takes to rebuild Hawai`i."

I stare at him. They think they're, what, part of ancient Hawai`i's noble warrior class? A shiver goes down my spine.

Kana`ina turns to Dad. "You tell Lani Hawika to stay out of this. My price. His debt. Don't make me regret it, yeah?"

"I'll tell him," Dad agrees.

"You *make* him."

"I know."

"Go."

"Dad," I whisper. "Our stuff? The iodide?"

He shakes his head. "Get ready to jump."

"Leilani," the sheriff says. I turn.

He tosses something at me. I catch it, barely. My Hawaiiana book. In a ziplock freezer bag. I look up at the sheriff. He turns away.

I leap into the water, half expecting to be shot in the back. Dad is right behind me.

HAWAI`I

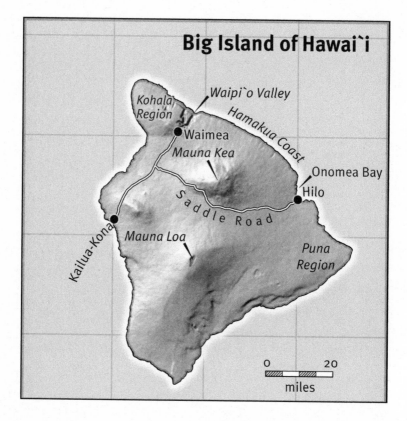

Big Island of Hawai`i

Kohala
Region

Waipi`o Valley

Hamakua Coast

Waimea

Mauna Kea

Onomea Bay

Hilo

Saddle Road

Kailua-Kona

Mauna Loa

Puna
Region

0   20
miles

CHAPTER 28

THURSDAY, JUNE 4

W e scramble up the boulder-covered shore and race into the trees, come upon a narrow path with a bench, and sit down. We're in the botanical gardens, surrounded by overgrown tropical plants. A bright red sign stands erect next to the bench, broadcasting one of the great dangers of an ancient past:

WARNING

DO NOT STAND HERE

FALLING MANGOES

I point the sign out to Dad; we burst into laughter. Then we're crying, holding each other, exhausted. "We're on the Big Island," I say. "We're home."

"I never allowed myself to believe that he would make good on that," Dad says.

I inspect the freezer bag with my book. Looks dry. I won't open it until we get home. I'm grateful, but the sheriff's gift doesn't fool me. "That is a bad, bad man. A *moke's moke*. I hope I never see him again."

"There's going to be more where he came from. A lot more."

"I know," I sigh. "What was he doing? What are they going to do with all those guns? Arrows?"

"He wants to rule the islands."

"He said that?"

"Not in so many words. But yeah. He already controls the channel between Maui and the Big Island, most of east Maui, some of the Big Island's Kohala region. With the military gone, he's thinking big. Off to pick a fight with several families in Puna right now."

"He's gonna ambush *Puna?*" That's the large area on the Big Island south of Hilo. Hawai`i's Wild West. Some antigovernment types, people who live off the grid and like to be left alone. "That'll be epic."

"Strike hard. Put his own man in place there, control the orchards, run all the firepower that's piled up there."

"Wow. Every man, woman, and child in Puna probably owns a gun or two."

"I know. They don't call them *Punatics* for nothing."

"What was all that about Grandpa?"

"He and your grandpa were once partners on the police force."

"*What?*"

308

"Yeah. Back on Maui. In Kahului. That sheriff is why Grandpa retired."

"What? Why?"

"I don't know. I'm just connecting the dots the best I can."

That's crazy. But I see the truth in it. Grandpa has complained to me about his time on Maui more than once; too many hotheads on the force, corruption. Racism in all directions. I never thought to ask him all about it. Now I can feel his guiding spirit, protecting us even from the past. Something he did decades ago saved our lives this week. More evidence that he's a time traveler. I smile. "Small world," I say ironically; it's something people say all the time on these islands.

"And getting smaller every day."

"What about the man you shot?"

"He's alive. Grazed. The sheriff seems more interested in settling an old debt with Grandpa than in taking vengeance for a bumbling soldier.

"Let's move. I can't shake the thought that he'll decide to come back."

We march up a steep garden trail, hiking side by side from the shore to the road. We're high up on the bluff now, with a breathtaking view of Onomea Bay. The sheriff and his posse are nowhere to be seen. They've probably reached Hilo Bay by now.

I can think about only one thing.

Home.

I've waited so long for this moment. Letting go of the

anticipation and bracing for the reality of what's to come is almost painful. I reach for a naupaka plant, rip off a branch covered in white half-flowers. I whisper, "I want to see them so badly."

"They'll be there." He squeezes my shoulder with a shaky hand. "We're almost home."

We continue to march mauka, straight uphill, my naupaka branch clutched in my hand. I'm surprised at how steep and long this road is. It takes us a good hour just to cross the highway that goes into Hilo.

As we cross I recognize a girl from school walking toward us from town. One of the local *titas* that was giving me the stink-eye at Honoli`i Beach. I tug on Dad's shirt and pick up my pace.

"Leilani!" she calls. I stop. I had no idea she even knew my name. She trots up to us, a bright smile on her face.

I look down. *No. Look up.* I meet her eyes. "Hey, Aleka, howzit?"

"Haven't seen you around. All good with you? You . . ." She glances at Dad. "You look . . . all banged up."

"Uh, long story," I say. "But, yeah, doin' good, I guess. You?"

"Surf's been touch and go. Only been out twice since . . . you know."

"Oh, yeah? How's the water? Lotta rubbish?"

"It's getting better. See you out there soon, yeah?"

"Yeah, I hope so. Where you headed?"

"Waiting for a ride out to Laupahoehoe. My cuz is due any minute. You?"

"I'm walking home."

"K'den." She gives me a hug. At first I'm stiff, but then I return it. "So many people are missing," she says, her voice cracking. "I'm glad you're safe."

"Me too. I'm glad you're safe, too, I mean."

She finally lets go, clears her throat, and continues on her way.

Dad and I resume our hike. "We've been here, what? An hour?" he says. "And you've already got friends bugging you to surf?"

I thought she hated my guts. But I smile.

When we step into our long driveway, my heart pounds like a drum. My legs grow weak. I'm squeezing the naupaka branch in my fist so tight that the stem has grown mushy. I can't wait for Mom to know that we're safe, to see her relief. I can't wait to tell her what we've been through, and to see her eyes widen. I can't wait for her to embrace Dad and never let him go. I can't wait to have Kai run up and jump into my arms.

I can't wait to tell Grandpa about the Orchid and my weird connection to it.

We reach the upper driveway. *Why am I so nervous?* Our old, beat-up Civic and the hybrid and Grandpa's Tempo are parked in their spots. My legs grow weaker.

They must be here. I can scarcely believe that this moment is finally here.

"Dad, they're really . . . ?"

He nods, but his eyes are filled with hesitation.

We go up the lanai steps. My palms are clammy. Dad tries the doorknob. It turns. We step inside.

No one in the living room. Without a word, Dad goes upstairs; I drop my Hawaiiana book and the naupaka on the coffee table and head for the dining room. No one. *The garden? I'll approach softly. They'll turn, and we'll rush each other.*

I enter the kitchen, and a strange man peeking into a cupboard barks in surprise. I bark back. He draws a handgun and fires a shot above my head. I scream and dive under the table.

"Get out!" the man shouts. "I was here first!"

Dad bolts down the stairs and into the kitchen and recoils as another shot goes wild. Dad bounds across the kitchen, tackles the trespasser, and pins him to the ground. The gun spins over to the dishwasher. "Where are they?" Dad spits.

"*What?* Who? I don't know! Please!"

Dad shakes his captive. "Where are my wife and son?"

"Dad!" I crawl out and grab the gun.

He looks up as if in a daze. His eyes seem to clear. He shifts his position and puts one of his knees on the man's chest.

I'm just realizing that Mom and Kai and Grandpa aren't here. The house has been empty long enough for a squatter to show up.

My worst fears from the past month are stirring awake.

They're gone. You'll never see them again.

Dad's voice is strained. "How long have you been in my house?"

"Your . . . ? I'm . . . I'm sorry. No one was here. I was just—"

"HOW LONG?"

"Just today. Today."

"What do you mean, no one was here?"

"Nothing. Just . . . it was empty when I showed up."

"And all three cars were in the driveway?"

"I guess so. Yeah." He doesn't know anything. He doesn't know jack. We're going to have to piece it together some other way. They were supposed to stay here, wait for us.

"What have you touched?" I hover over him. "What have you taken? Did you find any notes?"

The man shakes his head. God, does he smell. *Do I smell that bad, too?* "Nothing. I swear. Just some fresh eggs. In the fridge. Power's out. Some tomatoes. I'm sorry. I'm just hungry. I'm from New Jersey. I'm just trying to—"

"Shut up." Dad takes his knee off his chest and rises, takes the gun from me. Mr. New Jersey sits up and scoots against the cabinets.

"They're around. They have to be," I say to Dad.

"They haven't been gone long. Fresh eggs in the dead fridge. And they would have taken some chickens or left a note if they were planning to go far."

Did they flee for some reason? Did they leave with someone? Are they at a neighbor's up the road? Out hunting pigs with Grandpa? Mom would have left a note—unless . . . unless . . .

Stop it, Lei. Don't go there.

"Get out," Dad says to Mr. New Jersey. He scrambles to his feet and runs out the back door.

Dad holds the pistol tightly. "Look for a note—anything that might suggest where they went."

We both search. No note. But Mom's and Kai's hiking boots and rain jackets are missing from their rooms. I relax a little.

"They're hunting with Grandpa," Dad says, running a hand through his hair. "I'd bet the farm on it. Probably nearby. They wouldn't leave the house unguarded for very long. Maybe we should try to look for them."

"No," I say. "Our turn to stay put. No leapfrog."

Dad clenches his jaw. "Okay. You're right. Now we wait."

"How about a bath? Some clean clothes? And some food—I'm so hungry I'll eat raw eggs like a lizard."

"Yeah. Go get cleaned up. I'll put something together."

The water comes out of the faucets just fine. Gotta love our private tank upslope. Dad's right: maybe life hasn't been as bad around here as on the other islands.

Even if that's true, it'll get worse. After all, if it took *us* this long to get to the Big Island from O'ahu, then it'll take others even longer. But the hordes are still coming, I bet.

It gets me thinking: What if the sheriff has been keeping the flood of arrivals to a trickle? What if that blockade has kept this house, this area, safer?

"Remember: we only do what it takes . . ."

I shake the thought away as I stand beneath my cold shower. *Don't dare be grateful. Not even secretly. Remember the woman floating facedown in the river. He would have murdered Dad.*

I haven't had any medicine since the morning of the chase, and I left my pills on Maui. I rummage through my sink drawer and find two more bottles, each containing a dozen or so.

I'll run out in a few weeks. So that's it? Wear a helmet for the rest of my life? I swallow one and then head downstairs.

Dad and I chomp on fresh lettuce and tomatoes and scrape fresh, fried eggs off our plates.

"How much propane is left? Do you know?" I scoop up another bite of hot egg.

"About half. It's down from when we left. More evidence that they've been around until recently."

Another hour goes by. The worry gnaws at me. Dad's doing what he can to keep busy.

"Should we try the Millers?" I ask.

"Maybe tomorrow. Their gate's locked. I just want to stay here in case they come home. I don't have the energy to trudge up to the house. If I see one of the Millers coming, I'll flag them down."

"Okay." Our nearest neighbors live more than two miles up a private drive.

Evening comes. The coqui frogs start:

Coqui? Coqui?

We sit on the lanai through the evening, willing head-lights, flashlights—anything!—to come winding up the driveway. I use a candle to page through my book until my eyes grow strained. Aside from my clothes, this is my only possession that made it home. It feels too valuable to read anymore. I'll put it away somewhere safe—a trophy.

If we live through this, I'll read it once a year, gently. Add my own story to it. Then I'll pass it on when I'm old and gray, full of *mo`olelo* for a new generation.

Dad guards his new pistol in his hands and constantly scans the perimeter of the property. Nothing. It grows dark as we wait.

The stars are brilliant, brighter than they've been since the hotel in Waikīkī. It only takes me a second to figure out why: the Emerald Orchids look just a little bit smaller in their corner of the sky, casting less of a green glow through the haze of the atmosphere. The haze itself has improved steadily over the days. The Orchids are still aligned in a way that would fool most eyes: one of them is directly in front of the other, so that you might think they were a single object.

"Well, isn't that something?" Dad marvels. "A cloudless night in Hilo. Great view. They're even smaller tonight. That's the third night in a row."

"Wait. What?"

"I wonder if they're actually going away now. Could you imagine?"

"No," I say, standing up. Once again memories from my blackout come flooding back. "They can't!"

"What is it?"

"They can't go away! They can't!"

"Sure they can. Why not?" Dad places his gun on the railing and rises to meet me. "I'm not—"

"Dad! I heard the Orchid again. The mother. I heard it when I was out. Twice. I tried to talk to it, but it was useless."

"Sweetheart—"

"No! Don't sweetheart me! They *are* going away. It said they were going to. Beyond the dark. Another . . . another *galaxy*."

Dad sits down.

"Dad! That sheriff took our stuff. He kept the iodide."

Dad nods slowly.

"The Orchid and the newborn are feeding on the radiation. If they go, won't our atmosphere be filled with it?"

"Hon," Dad begins softly. I bristle. His tone suggests that I need to be gently reasoned with. "Akoni was wrong about his alien-invasion theory. Why should we take his 'radiation mop' talk to heart?"

"Please. The meltdowns are everywhere. They're still happening, right? One after another for months, yeah? But these creatures are somehow sponging up the radiation. This isn't a *theory*. It's true."

"But how can you know that?"

"BECAUSE I CAN HEAR THE ORCHID'S THOUGHTS!"

Dad leans forward on his porch chair, rubbing his forehead. "Okay. Just . . . just give me a second." He holds his head in his hands. Finally, he looks back up at me in the soft, green darkness. "So you're telling me those things really were preventing nuclear fallout? All over the globe?"

"I—I really think so."

"What if . . . I mean, how can you be sure how much fall-out there is?"

"Enough that it's taken notice. It likes it. It'll come back for it. But not for a long time."

We will do the long fastness to the other pool. We will be long in the ocean between the pools of fire.

"Dad . . . It's taking its baby to another galaxy. The Orchids aren't coming back in our lifetime."

"Another *galaxy*?"

"Far, far away." And then it hits me. My thoughts tumble away. Dad had talked about how some turtle species that once crossed straits were fooled, over centuries, into crossing oceans. But these Orchids . . . *They've been fooled, over eons, into crossing between drifting galaxies.*

Dad's voice pulls me back. He shakes his head. "I'd convinced myself that the iodide wasn't a big deal, that we weren't really going to need it after all. Either way, what good is cancer prevention if food stops growing?"

I shake my head. "If they leave now, we're all dead. Other parts of the world might already be in trouble. We're isolated. Maybe we're safe for now, but . . . didn't Akoni mention there were enough meltdowns to eventually sterilize a lot of the planet? The aircraft carriers around here, the submarines—would they eventually melt down? What if that's why the military bolted?"

"Akoni and his 'calculations,'" Dad says.

"Well, let's see your numbers. What does *your* global network of ham radio operators think? You said this could be a problem before we even met Uncle Akoni. And . . . don't you remember? The night all this began, you were making popcorn in the microwave. But it wouldn't pop."

Dad falls silent for a moment. "Because . . . there was no radiation in the microwave."

He's starting to understand.

"But . . . if you're right . . . what do you want me to do? If radiation levels are rising again, now that the Orchids are leaving, how would *we* ever measure it?"

My legs grow weak. The iodide is gone. *It's over, isn't it? It's all over. Unless . . .*

"What if I called them back? Got them to stay?"

I shiver. *Why would I even think such a thing?* They've done us so much harm. Turned us wild. Into killers. Erased a century of technology in the blink of an eye. If they were to go, maybe we could get that back—not all of it, but most of it. It's not too late to pick up the pieces.

But if the threat of global radiation *is* real . . . it would all be over anyway, wouldn't it? We'd turn on our toys just in time to be buried with them. That wouldn't make any sense at all, would it? Maybe crews could contain the fallout once the power comes back on. Maybe the Orchids could stay just for a few months. Just long enough for us to get the word out and make sure all nuclear materials are stored somewhere safe.

"How would you call them?" Dad asks.

I shrug, but even as I do, the answer comes to me:

319

"The second you reach Hilo, you go up on the mountain. Stand at the mouth of the cave. And when you hear the whisper, see if you can't answer back. You promise?"

"We have to go up to Mauna Kea," I say. "We should try."

Dad is silent; then: "When?"

I shrug again. "Now? They're leaving. We don't have much time."

"Tonight? Lei, what about our family?"

Where *are* they? Why can't they just *be* here? When will this nightmare end?

This is ridiculous. What am I proposing? "I don't know. I don't know what we'd do, anyway."

Dad changes his tone. "The scientist in me needs more proof, Lei. But I'm going to take that hat off, okay? The Dad in me has faith in you."

"Really?"

"We'll go in the morning. We'll find a way. But we'll go at first light, okay? It's insane, but . . . I'd rather try and *know* than watch you all get sick, wondering."

"Thank you," I say.

CHAPTER 29

I awaken from a sound sleep just after dawn. Strangely, I was dreaming of Aukina. We were holding hands on the beach. I shake the image away. *Aukina's on his way to the mainland right now. Forget about him.*

Dad is already up, working on various projects. Mom and Kai and Grandpa have not magically appeared, and I steel myself against a growing sense of panic. The sunrise is beautiful through our broad living-room windows, casting a pink ribbon across the distant ocean horizon, but I have no room for joy.

They're okay. They're not far. Don't worry.

I see the T-shirt Dad's wearing and bark with laughter. He grins. It's the exact same grin Kai gets after he makes me laugh.

"You're sick, you know that?"

The shirt is printed with a windy, jungle-covered road. Bright green letters say I SURVIVED THE ROAD TO HANA.

We eat fast, leave a note, and pile into the hybrid. I'm wearing fresh clothes. They feel glorious, even though the shirt hangs on me and I need a belt to keep my pants up. A warm jacket sits bundled on my lap; the cold on top of Mauna Kea is a force of its own. I frown absently. The note we left might as well have read:

Hi, Mom! We're back. Everything's okay, but we had to run off for a bit. I can talk to the Emerald Orchid. Turns out it's an alien, and it thrives on cosmic radiation. It has a soft spot for our atmosphere and for thermal nuclear meltdowns—which are happening all over the globe, btw. We're heading up to the summit to try to convince it to stick around for several hundred million years—or at least long enough for people to fix nuclear power plants around the world. You know, save all life on Earth and all that. Wish me luck! Brb.

Dad presses the start button on the hybrid. Nothing. "I can't even turn it on to check the charge?"

I crack up. "'Go green. Save the planet.' So much for *that*."

"It won't even turn on."

"Let's forget it, then. Okay? It's a stupid idea anyway." I already know that he thinks this errand of ours is just as foolish as I do. But even as I say the words, I know that we must try.

"No, hon. We'll do it. We'll figure it out."

The Civic is nearly empty, which was why Dad thought to take the hybrid, but we switch over to it when he finds half a gallon of gas in the old lawn mower at the back of the garage. The car turns on after the fourth crank of the ignition.

We reluctantly pull away from the house. I can't believe we're leaving so soon. It feels like we're abandoning a dream, acknowledging that there was no happy ending. As we wind down to the highway, I keep reminding myself we're coming right back. We're not ditching Mom and Kai, or giving up on their return.

We pull onto the highway and scan the lay of the land. A truck drives toward us from the direction of town, so we press forward, cautiously optimistic that the highway leading into Hilo is passable. Every couple hundred yards we pass heaps of cars. Mostly rentals. I'm guessing they were abandoned during the chaos surrounding the tsunami.

As promising as the roadways near Hilo prove to be, neither of our cars would have a prayer on the steep dirt switchbacks of the summit's final ascent. We try firing up several abandoned rental Jeeps, but there are no keys hiding above visors, no way to start engines.

This is nuts. What are we doing? We're in denial, that's what. The Orchid is long gone. Nuclear winter is around the corner—even for Hawai`i. "Thanks for doing this, Dad," I sigh.

I think he's going to suggest we turn around, but he doesn't. "Let's keep trying. We can do a little more."

In Wainaku, just a stone's throw from Honoli`i Beach, I spot a rusty old four-by-four with a Baptist church sticker, facing downhill. Dad parks the Civic off a side road to make it look like it's been abandoned, and we scurry over to the van. The driver's-side door pops open. We jump in.

"Father, forgive me, for I'm about to sin," Dad mutters.

He searches briefly for keys. Nothing. He sticks his Civic key in the ignition, and I'm shocked that it turns. "Just like my old Ford," he says. "Three decades of sea-salt damage. I bet a quarter of the cars in Hilo will start with any key." The ignition won't turn over, though. He presses the clutch to the floor and we begin to roll. When he pops the clutch, the vehicle springs to life and the needle shows that it's three-quarters full. "Bet you a million bucks we're not the first people to steal this piece of junk."

The van backfires loudly. "Don't be so sure," I say. "There may be a good reason why this rust bucket was dumped here."

Out of habit I try the radio as we slowly advance into Hilo. The old thing works, but we get only static.

As we turn up Waianuenue Avenue, we pause. I feel light-headed and shaky as I see the destruction. The Hilo that I knew is gone. The old downtown is burnt to the ground, a rotten cavity along the bay front. The highway and parks in the low-lying areas are buried beneath debris. Hilo Bay is a giant stew of rubbish. The water laps against the shore like a heaving, swollen landfill.

"So many lives," Dad says. "So many. If we hadn't been away, that could have been us."

The chilling thought sends waves along my back. "What if Mom and Kai were here, Dad?"

"They weren't. We already know they've been around home, as recently as a few days ago."

I close my eyes and take a deep breath.

As soon as we can talk to the Emerald Orchid and find

Mom and Kai and Grandpa, I know what I need to do next: find Tami and her mom. Their house is on the corner of a street across town that is marked with a LEAVING TSUNAMI EVACUATION AREA sign. Around here it doesn't look like the damage has reached as far as the warning signs, but it's impossible to tell for sure.

We continue up the mountain. Above the tsunami zone, Hilo breathes—but just barely. Cars seem deliberately parked, rather than discarded, but the rubbish heaps are everywhere. Many lawns seem tidy, but roadsides are overgrown with grasses and weeds. Pedestrians are skittish. Lots of cyclists. An open market bustles in the ball field near Rainbow Falls. It's probably the farmer's market that used to happen on the bay. It's a relief to see people carrying on some of our old ways.

The upper edge of town provides our first serious challenge. There are abandoned cars all over, and we have to break through several tight squeezes between vehicles. Our van is definitely on its last journey. We listen with dread as it struggles up the steep saddle between the world's biggest mountain—Mauna Loa—and the world's tallest when measured from the sea floor—Mauna Kea. We might find ourselves stranded twenty miles away from anything. The Saddle Road is a ghost highway.

It takes us well over ninety minutes to reach the top of the road, a trip that used to take about half an hour. But we've made it this far. Dad's sigh of relief is barely audible over the groaning of the motor. "Well, we'll make it one direction, at least. Feel anything yet?"

I shake my head. *No.*

What are we doing?

From here it's another ten minutes to the observatories' visitors' center, perched at ten thousand feet. We turn onto the summit road and slog forward. Just before the visitors' center, we pass a large sign, often shrouded in mist but real. Like the falling-mango warning, another artifact of a strange age.

BEWARE OF INVISIBLE COWS

It means that roadside cattle are hard to see in the fog. "Try not to hit one, okay?" I say.

Our old joke. Dad glances around. "I don't see any. Do you?"

The visitors' center is a necessary stop: you have to acclimate to the high elevation before scaling the final four thousand feet to the summit. Dad turns the van around and faces it downhill so that we can easily pop the clutch again. There's only one other car in the lot. I'm used to seeing herds of tourists here, filing into and out of buses. This place feels very lonely—which is somehow fitting.

As I jump out of the van, soaking up the silence and the stunning view, for the first time I feel that something has been *corrected* by the disasters. These high slopes were always overrun with tourists, but they *should* be lonesome. I stare across the silent expanse toward the distant bulge of Mauna Loa. The largest shield volcano in the world (and the third largest in the *solar system*), Mauna Loa is nearly as tall as Mauna Kea, but its slopes fade into the sea, as if it prefers to be mistaken for a pitcher's mound. Mauna Loa presses in on the ocean floor sixteen thousand feet deep, like a thumb indenting the surface of a balloon.

These are sacred places. Who could ascend these slopes and absorb their stillness—broken only by the volcanoes' occasional trembling—and not feel that they are trespassing upon the home of a power far greater than any human? My heart stills, as if it has finally achieved its true homecoming.

If ever there were a place to speak to the gods . . . to the creatures of the stars . . . this would be it.

Dad and I stand beside each other at the overlook, staring at the distant sea. "Thank you for doing this," I say.

"I'm glad we came."

"Me too. Dad, what if this doesn't work? What if it's already too far away, or it doesn't come back?"

"Lei. This isn't your burden. It never was. This was . . . never going to work."

We sit on the stone ledge overlooking the world for about twenty minutes. No traffic interrupts the silence. Nobody comes or goes, searching for the exit. It seems that we have all of creation to ourselves.

"Are you ready?" I finally ask Dad.

He lifts a can of diet cola. Full of aspartame; it should trigger a seizure. "I guess so."

"Don't shake it, *lōlō*."

"Oh, yeah."

As we walk toward the van, I'm surprised to see the front door of the visitors' center standing open.

Uncle Akoni's voice echoes across the windswept stillness:

> "Go up on the mountain. Stand at the mouth of the cave. And when you hear the whisper, see if you can't answer back."

I enter.

CHAPTER 30

The interior is dimly lit by skylights. Inside, flashy curiosities of science are on display, trinkets for sale. There is a small movie theater with thirty or so chairs facing a blank canvas. Framed posters on the walls. Large telescopes on rolling tripods crowd the foyer.

At the counter stands an older man with a bushy but trimmed brown beard. He's wearing a plaid-flannel longsleeved shirt with red suspenders. He grins at me over the cash register as I step inside, as if he's been expecting me.

"Oh, hi," I say.

"Good morning."

"Are you . . . are you *open?*"

He smiles gently and motions toward the open doors to say, *I believe so.*

"Why?" I approach the counter.

He shrugs. "People still show up. Not so much in the mornings, though. There's not much else for me to do during the day, to tell the truth."

"Who are you?"

The man waves to Dad, who enters behind me. "I go by Buzz. I'm an astronomer."

"Like Buzz Aldrin?" I ask.

"No. Comes from Buzz Lightyear, I'm afraid. And a bad haircut a few years back." As he talks, he spins a gyroscope on his pointer finger. "I was in charge of a very big telescope. Now . . . I'm back to looking through actual lenses. But there's still a lot to learn—if you know how to look."

"If you know how to listen."

He nods. He leans across the counter and transfers the gyroscope from the tip of his own finger to mine. Childish delight dances in his eyes. "And why are *you* here? Who are *you*?"

"I'm Leilani. This is my dad, Mike."

"Flower of Heaven."

"Actually, we . . ." I pause.

"What is it?" he asks.

"Nothing. Forget it."

Dad says, "Lei, tell him."

"I . . . can't," I whisper to Dad. But Buzz has captured me with his patient gaze. Tractor beam. I look up from the toy balanced on my fingertip and take the plunge. "Did you know it's alive? That it's a creature?"

He startles. "We . . . but . . ." He falls silent. His expression

330

grows grim, focused. "Richard. He put you up to this, didn't he? Richard!" He calls out the front door.

"There's no one out there," I say. I lower my finger to the countertop and help the spinning gyroscope hop to its surface. "She's leaving, isn't she?"

"*She?*" Buzz's eyes flick between us.

He knows, I think. *He won't admit it.* "The Orchids," I say. "There are two of them. A mother and a baby."

"Orchids?" he asks. "I haven't heard that. We call them Star Flowers."

"The O'ahu newspaper called it the Emerald Orchid. Name stuck," Dad explains.

"So . . . ," I say, "you're admitting there are two?"

Buzz stiffens. "What in the world makes you think . . . ?"

"Lei can hear the mother's thoughts," Dad says. "During her seizures. She's epileptic. Some . . . electrical thing. We came to see if we could . . . if Lei could talk to it. We can't let it leave."

Buzz studies us. "Uh. Seizures. Well, this isn't your average visit, is it?" He snatches up the gyroscope, freezing its momentum. "You talk to it? You interpret its signals?"

I shake my head. Buzz's eyes drill into me. "No. I can't talk to it. That's why we came here. I want to try. I can only hear it. I don't know why, or how. I'm not the only one, though. There're epileptics on Moloka'i who put it together first."

"Wait, so . . . can all epileptics hear it?"

I don't answer immediately. The way he said that bothers

me. Then it hits me: I don't like the idea of sharing the Orchid. "I have no idea."

Buzz stares at me.

"I know how it sounds, believe me."

Buzz clears his throat. He circles around the displays to stand in front of us. "Epilepsy." It's not a question, just a word, as if he's thrown it up on a chalkboard to study it.

We wait.

Buzz takes a deep breath. "That Star Flower's signature has been off the charts every which way. We were studying it like mad even before it blossomed onto the visible spectrum. Then it surged, of course, destroying most of our equipment. But we recognized that the transmissions were from a sentient being from the moment it entered the solar system."

"Hold on. You knew about this thing before it . . . blew up in everyone's faces?" Dad asks. The weight of his question punches me. Everything we've been through . . . If we all could have had more warning . . .

"Slow down." Buzz raises his palms defensively. "No one's ever dealt with a first-contact scenario before. We had no idea it would pop all of a sudden."

"The president knew." Dad raises his voice. "The prime minister of Japan knew! We were thirty miles away from the observatory! Why did *they* get all the warning?"

"The Subaru scope up here—it's funded and operated by Japan. You'll have to ask those folks what they relayed to their government. We're on the same mountain, but we don't necessarily coordinate. As for us, we contacted the Defense

Department, in accordance with protocol. They called the shots. There's a mandatory cooling-off period built into the protocols. No leaks."

"A *cooling-off* period?"

"Dad."

Buzz drops his head. He runs his hand through his hair while he looks at his shoes. "Look, if I had to do it over again, we would have gone public immediately. Hindsight is . . . We had no way of knowing."

Dad relaxes. "Yeah. I guess so. But the president still—"

"The White House has its own protocol in the event of first contact. We never gave them anything actionable. They had their reaction all lined up sixty years ago. Earth-visitation scenarios always assumed a far superior technology or intellect than our own. A defensive posture was the only logical one. Anyway, the president changed his mind. He was trying to tell the whole world it was arriving when it blossomed and fried our satellites."

We're quiet, watching Dad toy with the eyepiece of one of the big telescopes near the foyer.

"It's not intelligent," I say. "I mean, not like us. It's more like a . . . a sea turtle."

"A sea turtle." Buzz loses himself in thought. "Okay. A giant . . . space turtle. Just doing its thing. Coming ashore to lay eggs. Wow."

Dad pats Buzz on the shoulder. "Sorry, Buzz. You have no idea what we've been through. We would have stayed on the Big Island if we'd known—"

"You guys were off-island when the blackout began?"

"O'ahu," I say. "We just made it back. Yesterday."

Buzz stares at me, agape. He shakes himself out of his trance. "We effed up, big time. I honestly don't think it would have changed anything, but we should have done more. Learned more. I don't know. Maybe it's not too late. It's finally leaving—which is *not* a blessing, believe me. But maybe those of us left can make do. Go underground. Rebuild. Repair all that integrated circuitry. No more tungsten, obviously. I've noticed that some analog circuits can still function. Basic batteries, resistors, transistors, and diodes *can* work. Edison would still be in business. We just have to go back to the level of technology that was around when he—"

"Buzz . . . what about all the meltdowns?" I ask.

He stammers. "You—you know about that, too?"

I nod. "The Orchids—they're radiation mops. If they leave, nuclear winter falls."

"How did you figure that out?"

"A priest on Moloka'i started us thinking. He'd figured it out. There have been meltdowns, but no radiation."

Buzz laughs. He gathers his wits and says, "At least thirty plants have gone supernova, last we could count. As failsafes buckle I bet we'll average a couple a week from here on out. Right—the crazy irony is that these Star Flowers seem to render the radiation inert. Like I said, it's *not* good that they're leaving. We *need* them now."

"What if we can bring them back?" Dad says.

Buzz turns to me. "You came up here because you've found a way to talk to it?"

I shift my feet. "Not really. I tried to get its attention once, but it didn't work. But I thought that if I were just a little bit closer to it, maybe it could hear me."

"Because you're higher up?"

Dad and I nod.

Buzz's expression is kind. "Okay. There's a lot going on here. First thing: you haven't gotten closer to anything. The Star Flowers are drifting away at about *fifteen thousand* feet per *minute*. Since we started this conversation, they've already moved about four times as far as this mountain is tall."

"Oh." I steal a glance at Dad. I don't think I've ever felt so stupid in my entire life.

"The other thing is that we're turning. Relative to Hawai`i, it's on the other side of the globe right now. It won't rise until about four p.m. So, technically, as far as distance is concerned, at this particular moment you'd actually be closer to it if you were at sea level."

"The Orchids rise at four?" Dad asks.

"They come over the horizon at four. We don't see them until dark, but we'll be in line with them by then. That doesn't really seem to impact *their* effect on *us*. But if *you* want to get *their* attention, it's best to wait."

"Oh." I cast Dad a questioning glance. He shrugs.

"What did you have in mind?" asks Buzz. "How can I help?" I see the hope in his eyes.

I was going to drink a diet soda. That's it. That's all.

Mom and Kai and Grandpa could be at the house right now, reading our note. We could be together. Are we wasting time up here—time that we can never get back? For Uncle

Akoni's romantic notions of caves and mountains. All the things he could do with those telescopes and . . . and . . . ?

> "I love the Big Island. Wish Moloka`i had
> mountains like that. Mauna Kea's what, fourteen
> thousand feet high?"
>   "Yeah. Think so."
>   "All those telescopes and radio dishes."

"Radio dishes," I say. I turn to the astronomer. "Radio dishes."

"Of course! The array!"

Dad looks between us. "Radio dishes? Sending a message by radio telescope?"

Buzz's eyes are aglow. "We don't have one big dish, but a bunch of smaller ones. We can link them and blast something out to the Star Flowers. We tried it once, but we didn't have any idea what to say, or how. Pummeled the poor thing with prime numbers for two days. Lot of good that did. Can you imagine: a scuba diver shoving an abacus in a sea turtle's face? But . . . but if Leilani can somehow manifest its thoughts, maybe her brain can formulate something that it will be able to interpret."

"The dishes weren't damaged?" asks Dad.

"Well, the computers—all the integrated circuitry—are fried. But I've still got my slide rule. I can physically align all the dishes. I know exactly where to point them. And aside from some gas generators to give them some juice, we won't need any power. Leilani's going to provide the signal herself. I really think we can do this."

"Lei," says Dad. "What do you think?"

I offer a hesitant nod. "What do we do now?"

Buzz reaches over the counter and grabs his jacket. He's already on his way out the door as he replies, "If Mike can help me arrange things up there, I think we can be ready to go by Flower-rise. Leilani, you've got the hardest job of all."

"What's that?"

"You need to figure out what you're going to say."

CHAPTER 31

I walk alone over a Martian landscape high above marshmallow clouds, chanting a familiar prayer.

Ai, Ai, Ai.
Ho`opuka e-ka-la ma ka hikina e
Kahua ka`i hele no tumutahi
Ha`a mai na`i wa me Hi`iaka
Tapo Laka ika ulu wehiwehi
Nee mai na`i wa ma ku`u alo
Ho`i no`o e te tapu me na`ali`i e

Rise up, rise up, rise up.
Make a hole in the sun and find the light hidden inside.
May the light of the gods dawn on me like the rising sun.
Come to me through your breath and take me by force.

Come, drift upon me, and spread.
Bring me the means of life.
Come to me like the creeping of lava,
and may this sacred ceremony of the *ali`i*
bring me meditation and release.

The wind ruffles my hair. The air is frigid, and I wrap my arms around myself to keep warm. Mighty white domes of telescopes look down upon me from their high thrones. Relics, shrines to a fading era, guarding great secrets, yet silent as the mountain beneath them.

Ahead lies another temple.

Lake Waiau is little more than a pond that sits in a gentle bowl at the top of Mauna Kea. It was once thought to be bottomless. For many Hawaiians it remains a threshold between worlds. It has an emerald glow, caused by nutrients in the form of human umbilical cords, which have been fed into it for centuries. Hawaiian chiefs would come here and offer the *piko* of their firstborn sons, securing their chiefly status in this life and the one to come. My grandfather's umbilical cord was placed in this lake. And now I will make an offering.

Along the ridge overlooking the lake, I sing and chant an ancient Hawaiian *oli kāhea*. I ask permission of the land and the akua to enter their sacred dwelling place.

Ke ka-nae-nae a ka mea hele,
He leo, e-e,
A he leo wale no, e-e.

Eia ka pu`u nui owaho nei la,
He ua, he ino, he anu, he ko`e-ko`e.
Maloko aku au.

In the stillness, I feel them stir. They grant me permission.

I proceed down the slope slowly. The shore of the small green lake is just before me now. I pause, listening to the silence. My heart beats slowly but with great purpose. I remember how Aleka gave me that warm, welcoming hug. She was glad to see me. She was glad I was home.

I belong.

We're all in the same boat now. We belong here. We belong to each other.

This is my home, and no one can ever take that from me.

I yank the medical bracelet with its corkscrew serpents off my wrist. I keep it in my hand along with my last pills and squeeze.

Pele fought her sisters here. She won her right to remain on the Big Island. Dad and I fought our way home, and we won our place here, too. But now we must win another battle.

And how shall I win it? The Orchids arrived as pale green angels of death. Now they would flee. But if we are to survive, they must stay—even if just for a short while. It means a future filled with hardship and suffering. But at least it means a future.

E iho ana o luna
E pi`i ana o lalo

E hui ana na moku
E ku an aka paia

Chants and ancient whispers dance through my mind, loudest among them all the prophecy of the arrival of King Kamehameha. So many forces have led me to be here: Uncle Akoni; the sheriff and Grandpa, once partners; finding a van with gasoline; a mountaintop guru who can wield a slide rule and a radio-telescope array. The timing of my trip to Oʻahu to change up my meds is itself an amazing thing. I don't know whether it is fate or chance or God or gods. But I feel the mystery in the air.

That which is above will come down
That which is below will rise up
The islands shall unite
The walls shall stand firm.

There is no fear or doubt. No shame. No denial or regret. No choice. There is only acceptance—and a sense of honor.

I will never again run from who I am, or from where I belong.

I throw my medical bracelet and my remaining pills into the green waters to meld with the life-delivering flesh of my Hawaiian ancestors, and I prepare to fight for my family, for my islands, and for my world.

* * *

We stand among the radio telescopes, very near the highest peak of Mauna Kea. The sun is low on the horizon, bathing the mountaintop and the puffy clouds below in a fiery orange befitting the end of the world. Soon the heavens will be given over to the night, in its velvety gown, dazzling with sequins and pearls and emerald-green flower brooches. I can feel the cold seeping into my bones. But soon I will reach out and touch the stars.

* * *

"Are we really going to do this?" Dad asks. He and I are sitting on the tailgate of Buzz's old truck, parked at the center of the array. "Have these things here for the rest of our lives? No more computers? Internet? Phones?"

"We'll grow old together," I say.

"I'd give *everything* for that."

"It's not for life, though. Years? I mean, we need enough time for people to box up the world's nuclear material. Stuff it all underground, in that Yucca Mountain place in Nevada or something. Then I can send the Orchids away."

"Piece of cake," Dad says. "We'll just send instructions to every nuclear nation by carrier pigeon."

"We'll think of a way."

Buzz yells. "Looks like we're ready." He dashes between a tight-knit grid of garage-sized satellite dishes as if he were a Hawaiian honeycreeper pollinating giant flowers. The roar of several gas generators penetrates the stillness.

Buzz huffs and puffs into view. He studies me kindly, attaches makeshift electrodes to my head. "We have about twenty minutes before your dad and I have to adjust all the dishes. I imagine we'll be adjusting the orientation all night, though. Don't worry if it takes a while."

"You all set, Lei? I'm right here." Dad holds my hand.

I smile and pop open my can of diet soda.

"I'm right here to keep you safe."

I kiss him on the forehead. "I know."

I turn east, opposite the sunset, and cross my legs. The sky above the carpet of clouds is pink and orange and red. No hint of green. But I trust Buzz, and I trust my father, and I trust myself. Dad braces me. I close my eyes and drink.

Leilani. I am Leilani. I am with you.

I go toward the depths. It is time for the long fastness now.

Return to the shores. Rest here. Remain with me. Stay with the sweetness until it has finished flowing.

The hotness is sweet. I like the hotness. But I need the long fastness. I need to leave.

No. You don't. Stay.

Stay.

I yearn for the depths and the long fastness to the other shores.

No. You don't. You only want to do that because it's what you've always done. What the one who gave you always did. Stay. There is purpose in staying. We need you to take up all the hotness until it is gone.

I do what is always done. Yes. It is good.

You like the shores. You want the sweetness. It is best for the young one. It is better here than in the deep. Best for the young one. To feed. To feed. Feed the young one.

The depths are good. The long fastness must begin. Yes, I like the shores. The other shores. I am almost free enough of the current to begin.

No. We need you. Stay.

Hello? Leilani? Where did you go? Please.

It is time to begin.

There you are.

I can feel the fastness building. Soon we will rush.

I am Leilani. I will return to the shore that I just left. The one I gave needs the hotness. I want the depths, but I want to do the good thing more. The good thing is to stay.

I need to go. The long fastness is best.

I need to stay. It is best for the one I gave. I am safe here. I will stay. Here the young one grows strong. Strongest young one of them all. We will stay. It is just a moment. Just a moment until the sweetness is used up. Then we will go. The depths are not good. Not without the strength. The others will take the one I have given. I must protect the one from harm. We are safe here for now. We will stay. The others will come and steal this sweetness. I must protect the sweetness. I must use it. The sweetness is good and it will keep me safe it will keep the one I gave safe it is the good thing to do yes I want to go but I want to stay too I want to stay more than I want to go it is just a short time I will stay for a short time more and then go for the other shore and enjoy the fastness later.

I want to stay. It is safer to stay and grow strong and protect the one that I gave and do the fastness later.

Yes. To stay is good. I want to stay and make myself and the one that I gave stronger. That way the long fastness will be even more pleasant and the one that I gave will have an

345

advantage over all the other new ones and the sweetness is too sweet to let go especially now when I am weak from the giving and the one I gave is still weak and I want to stay not long just until all the oozing is spent and then I can go I want to stay for now and enjoy the sweetness which is hard to find I like these shores the surf the seafoam rocks me the one that I gave will be with me and we will be together for longer and it is good it is good to stay it is what I want to do it is what I yearn to do it is good and the sweetness is good and I am very satisfied.

I yearn for the seafoam of the shores where I gave the new one. I yearn for the hotness sweetness and we will stay here until we are strong and safe and all the sweetness is gone.

I am Leilani. We are Leilani. We will stay. It is our purpose now. We are one. We are *ali`i nui*. We are the guardians of the shores and the surf and the islands and all the mysteries that dwell within. We hunger for the rumbling of rock, the creeping swirl of orange light. We have dreamt of these shores. We were born here, but we slipped away. Now we have reached the shallows, at long last, guided across the endless waters by ancient stars. These islands and their sacred tides call us forth.

We are home.

We are Leilani. Spellbound, we blossom.

We are Leilani. Spellbound, we blossom.

CHAPTER 32

Hilo has always been dark at night—dimly lit to assist the observatories in their endless safaris through the skies—but it was never *this* dark. Squares of candlelight seeping through kitchen windows hint that the town remains home to tens of thousands of people, but the streets seem deserted on this green, moonless night.

We drive by Tami's. I see candles in their windows! The house is fine. In the van, I blink back tears. I'll find her tomorrow. But we can't stop.

Home first.

We retrieve the Civic as we retrace our path. Dad is so relieved to have his car back, as if that's the thing that has been pressing on his mind most. I stifle a laugh.

I glance out the window to admire the two Star Flowers. They are fully separate now; everyone will know there are two. They blossom much larger and nearer than they ever have. I may be able to hear the mother's guileless mind even now. A switch has been flipped in my brain; some door, once seamless in the walls of my mind, remains propped open. Yes, I do believe I can hear . . . something.

Can she still hear me?

I think she can. We are Leilani, after all. We are somehow one.

I did it. I brought them back. And I can *feel* the mother, somehow. It's like beginning to wiggle a foot that has fallen asleep. She's a part of me now. So odd. So marvelous. I can sense her drawing up radiation from the Earth's surface, neutralizing it. The sensation reminds me of a bone-dry sponge in my hand, growing soft and moist as I press it against a countertop spill.

We were right to do this. We saved the world. Everyone. *Everyone.* Our race may still have a future.

My eyes study the silhouetted slopes of Mauna Loa. Pele's home, where she stopped running and took a stand. Her throne does not rise as high toward the sky as Mauna Kea, but she exerts a greater force upon the world. She simmers within, biding her time, shaping her paths with infinite confidence and patience.

The bearer of the future, she rises, and at the pace of her choosing.

* * *

An old Jeep is in the driveway as we pull up.

A freshly skinned pig hangs from a hook in the carport, and Grandpa's hunting knife lies on the cement below it.

My heart soars.

And now, in the headlights, I spot Kai jumping up and down on the porch. He turns and yells into the house. I am melting. I am finally coming undone.

"Oh, my God," Dad manages.

I jump out of the car before it comes to a complete halt. My rubbery legs carry me up the steps, and Kai and I slam into each other with formless cries of joy. Mom is at the window beside the porch door. Grandpa stands behind her. Her eyes are frantic and ravenous and wild with hope.

And then she sees me.

The door whips open, and all five of us seize each other. We are finally together. Once more, underneath the watchful, starry eyes of majestic and mysterious forces, we are whole.

CHAPTER 33

Kai has fallen asleep with his arms wrapped tightly around me. I'm half sitting, half lying on the couch, my brother draped like a warm blanket over my tucked legs. I run my fingers through his dark hair. My hands tremble. I can't help it.

We just had a luau's worth of food. Stuffed ourselves like . . . it was the end of the world. I'm savoring every silky stroke of his hair, but still I'm nervous that this isn't real, that I'll awaken from a dream at any second and all this will be gone.

A row of ten kukui nuts is aligned on the coffee table. Grandpa places a lighter above each one until they're all consumed in flame. The ancient Hawaiians used these oily nuts as candles. I feel our family entering the past as the darkness softly lifts. For once, we're going backward in a good way.

Grandpa knows the path between the past and the present better than anyone.

Beyond the kukui light, on the opposite couch, my parents hold each other.

Grandpa breaks off a stem of the naupaka branch I brought home and chews on it. He was delighted that I had it, because it helps to heal cuts and scrapes and rashes. Grandpa transfers the mashed-up stem into a koa-wood bowl and begins to sing the prayer of enlightenment and healing he once taught me:

> *Ai, Ai, Ai.*
> *Ho`opuka e-ka-la ma ka hikina e*
> *Kahua ka`i hele no tumutahi*
> *Ha`a mai na`i wa me Hi`iaka*
> *Tapo Laka ika ulu wehiwehi*
> *Nee mai na`i wa ma ku`u alo*
> *Ho`i no`o e te tapu me na`ali`i e*

His voice is so beautiful. Tears sting my eyes.

He nears me as he sings, motions for me to sit up. I rest Kai's head on my lap. Grandpa rubs the naupaka into the scar on my forehead with his thumb. He applies it to the bite marks on my leg, and to the mosquito bites and scrapes along my arms, legs, and neck.

In the flickering orange kukui light, he starts a new chant to treat Dad.

> *E ola mau ka honua,*
> *E ola nau ke ao lewa,*
> *Ho `ola hou ke kanaka*

Long life to the earth
Long life to the heavens
Restore life to the person

After a moment of silence following Grandpa's chant, Mom explains, "We prayed for your safety every morning and every evening. The three of us never missed a prayer. Your brother has developed a beautiful voice over the past month."

I smile, look down at him. My hands still tremble as I absently stroke his hair.

"I had . . . moments of doubt," Mom says. "But I found hope. Always. It was a battle of patience; I knew you'd get here as soon as you could."

"Did you get any of my letters?"

"Just one. Right before the military left. It did more to upset me than calm me down, to be honest. To know that you were still on O'ahu nearly two weeks after the blackout . . ."

"I'm sorry for that." I think of Aukina, who promised the letters would get to Hilo. I wonder how long he'll linger in my dreams.

"Oh, Lei, you were right to try."

"Your mother was very strong," Grandpa says. "One of us went into town at least every other day. We developed a checklist of places to search, where others had been arriving. We also heard plenny horror stories. But we tuned them out."

"Doesn't matter," Mom says. I can see the toll those trips into town took on her. "We're all here now. We're all safe."

"Hilo doesn't look very good," Dad says. "I wouldn't exactly say we're 'safe.'"

We all stare at him. "Sorry, but we have to be realistic. Someone was in our house when we got here. He had a gun. He was nothing, but . . . We need a plan for when that happens again."

"I've been talking story with Hank," Grandpa says. Mr. Miller from up the road. He and his wife used to keep to themselves. "He's been saying the same thing. We'll go see him tomorrow, eh? He'll be thrilled."

"Good," Dad says. "Hank Miller—I wouldn't be surprised if he has a basement full of heavy artillery."

We all laugh, but it dies off in a somber note.

"And what about this sheriff, Lani?" Dad asks Grandpa. "He nearly executed me. He knows who we are. He'll come calling for favors at some point down the road—"

"Mike." Mom cuts him off.

Grandpa's features are stern. "You don't owe him anything. We're even now."

"Why?" Dad asks. "What'd you . . . ?"

"We'll deal with that *moke*," Grandpa answers. His eyes broadcast: *Not tonight.*

We're silent, waiting on Dad.

"Fine," he answers. "Meanwhile . . ." He hesitates and glances at me. "There's more to our story."

I look down at Kai, make sure he's sleeping. I bite my lip, studying Mom and Grandpa closely. Then I dive in. I tell them about the Orchids—the Star Flowers. I tell them everything.

Explain why we disappeared up Mauna Kea, why it couldn't wait. What we did when we got there.

They listen patiently. Mom looks worried—like she's trying to decide whether or not I'm crazy. She keeps looking at Dad, but he nods reassurances every time; he's got my back.

Grandpa, on the other hand—Grandpa has a twinkle in his eye.

"You've always had a special door open in your mind, Lei," he says when I'm finished. "A *puka* in your head. I'm not surprised by a single word."

Mom smiles at me kindly.

"Malia," Dad says, "I struggled with it, too. I followed her lead on faith. But the scientist in me now has proof. Those Star Flowers were leaving. They came rushing back. They're here *because of* Lei."

Mom maintains her smile, thinking hard. She'll come around. I don't blame her for her reaction. It still sounds completely *lōlō* to me.

We are Leilani.

"So, what are we going to do with this?" Grandpa asks. He's almost giddy. I can tell he won't sleep a wink tonight.

"It's late," Mom says. "We're not going to do anything about it now. Bedtime. Lei's out of meds. That's *my* biggest concern. She . . . needs her rest. Come on." She rises, stern and motherly. But I can tell she's overwhelmed and trying to hide it. "Upstairs. Everyone."

I lower my gaze to Kai. Sound asleep in my lap. A little angel. "I'm just going to crash here with Kai, okay, Mom?"

She hesitates, smiles. "Fine with me. Dad, lock the doors before you go up."

Grandpa sets to his task. Mom and Dad give us gentle kisses. Mom whispers into my ear, "My beautiful angel. My powerful woman. I'm so thankful to have you back." Her tears drop onto my cheek.

She and Dad disappear into the upstairs darkness hand in hand.

Grandpa squeezes my shoulder and turns toward the stairs.

"Tūtū," I say.

"Yes, Mo'opuna?"

"Hand me that naupaka branch, would you?"

Grandpa lifts the remains of the plant from the coffee table and gives them to me. He squeezes my shoulder again and disappears, the creaking of the stairs quickly replaced by the chorus of coqui frogs.

I'm left alone with Kai in the soft light of the four kukui nuts that still burn. I pluck two half-flowers off the branch.

I place them together, complete at last, into Kai's palm. I press his hand into a fist, never letting go, and drift off to sleep.

Leilani's story will continue in
BOOK TWO

ACKNOWLEDGMENTS

This novel, and my long years of development as a writer, would never have been possible without the wisdom and patience of my amazing wife. Thank you, Clare, for making my life a dream, and for helping me to make the dream of publishing this book come true.

I owe a debt of gratitude to my top-shelf team of no-holds-barred test readers (oh, what a long road it's been!): Liz Chamberlin and Sam Veloz, Jennifer and Jeremy Ridgeway, and Alex Bennett (who also took the photo of me that appears on the back flap). I give thanks also to journalist Lauren King, whose editorial ear helped me make my newspaper clippings sound authentic.

Thank you, Julie Just, my agent, for loving this book so deeply and for fighting for it every step of the way. And a special shout-out goes to Shoshana Shoenfeld for making sure Julie saw my query.

Wendy Lamb, my publisher and editor, I am especially indebted to you. Thank you for everything, for believing in me, for being patient, for sharing your unparalleled gifts, for loving Hawai`i, and for having a sweet tooth for crazy plot twists. I am grateful to your talented team members, as well, including Dana Carey; Alison Impey, whose cover design is amazing; Trish Parcell, for her attention and care to the interior design; and copy editors Ellie Robins, Colleen Fellingham, and Alison Kolani, who expertly navigated not only the intricacies of English, but the Hawaiian language as well!

I'd like to acknowledge the Bishop Museum in Honolulu, and especially the ʻImiloa Astronomy Center in Hilo, for inspiring a tale, and for letting me walk endlessly through their halls, absorbing the amazing stories and wonder of Hawaiʻi. I am also grateful to countless sources who have made Hawaiian culture and mythology publicly accessible via the Web. Alan Weisman, you may recognize a concept or two burrowed into these pages from your awesome book *The World Without Us*. Thank you for your thoughtful research and inspiration.

Any errors, typos, or failures in the book are mine alone.

Finally, I'd like to tip my hat to the life and great works of my father-in-law, Jerry, a teacher and a writer, whose final words of encouragement to me were "I know you'll get published one day, Austin."

ABOUT THE AUTHOR

AUSTIN ASLAN was inspired to write his debut novel, *The Islands at the End of the World*, while living with his wife and two children on the Big Island of Hawai`i. He earned a master's degree in tropical conservation biology at the University of Hawai`i at Hilo. A National Science Foundation Graduate Research Fellow, he is pursuing a PhD in geography at the University of Arizona. Austin loves traveling, backpacking, and photography. He continues to write fiction and looks forward to the publication of this novel's sequel. Follow him on Twitter at @Laustinspace.

CONTINUE THE ADVENTURES

It's a few months after the end of *The Islands at the End of the World*. Hilo is dangerous, and warring groups known as Tribes patrol the coast. There's not enough food on the island. Lei and her friends Tami and Keali`i go night diving for "slippah" lobsters in Hilo Bay and are shot at by members of the Hanaman tribe. Lei, Tami, and Keali`i swim under a breakwater to escape.

And then . . .

Excerpt copyright © 2014 by Austin Aslan. Published by Wendy Lamb Books, an imprint of Random House Children's Books, a division of Random House LLC, a Penguin Random House Company, New York.

My friends pop up to the dark surface of the water.

"Lei, Tami got cut," Keali`i says. "It's pretty bad."

"Where?"

"My thigh," she says. "Right below my shorty. Coming through one of those turns in the wall. Scraped an exposed piece of rebar."

"Are you okay?"

She adjusts her mask and tries to hold on to the floating marquee, which bobs away from her. "I don't know. It hurts. Feels gross, deep. Pretty sure I need stitches."

A stab of fear. *Blood in the water.*

She doesn't answer. I look at Keali`i; he'll know if we're in trouble. *Sharks?*

He shrugs. "Look, they're here. Hammerheads and tigers are common. Seen one take the `okole right off a surfer by Richardson's. They *do* come in. Black tips, white tips, reef sharks, big noses . . . barracudas, too."

"Oh, God," Tami moans. "Get me out of the water. *Now*." Her voice rises. If she panics, the Hanaman might hear us even at this distance.

I look at the breakwater. "I don't like it, but we have to go back."

"I can handle him," Keali`i says. "It's three on one. We sneak up behind him, I'll clock him with my weight belt. End of story."

"What if he starts shooting?"

"He'll never know what hit him."

I don't like it—it's never that simple. "What a nightmare," I mutter.

"Guys, come on. I'm bleeding a lot." Tami's voice wavers, betraying the effort she's putting into staying calm.

I turn to Keali`i. "Don't kill him. Promise me."

"They were trying to kill us."

"I know. I don't care. We're better than them. Just . . . promise."

"Fine. I won't do anything on purpose. Just pound 'im good and knock 'im out."

The dark below me now feels like one giant mouth, closing in on our legs. "Okay, let's go. Back to the breakwater."

Tami attempts a smile. Keali`i draws in a deep breath. As I'm dog-paddling, I brush his leg with my fin.

He yelps and launches half out of the water. Tami and I bark. We scatter. It takes me a second to realize—and then to trust—that we're jumping at shadows.

"Guys, that was just my fin," I whisper. "Calm down. It was me."

Too late. The Hanaman rises along the breakwater. "Hey!" he shouts. "Got you!"

"We're done. It's over," Keali`i breathes.

"Kea, I'm so sorry. I—"

"*Whatevah.* It almost worked. But this is nuts. Tami needs help."

"No." Tami shakes her head. "I'm not going to be the reason this falls apart."

I can't help thinking: *But she could be the reason we get eaten.*

"Hey!" the Hanaman shouts. "Come here! Now!"

Keali`i slaps the surface of the water. "Idiot thinks we're going to swim over there just because he tells us to. *God!*"

I know the rest of his thought, unsaid: *And we're going to do exactly that, make it easy for him.*

Tami's eyes narrow. "No. We're not going to him. You're right."

"Tami," I say. "We can't stay in the water."

"Your turn to follow me," she says. "Stay back a bit. Just in case."

Tami jettisons her weight belt and swims away. Keali`i and I share a look of confusion. Visible on the water against the Orchid's brilliance, a sailboat turns into view around the far end of the breakwater. It's moving slowly—there's very little breeze.

Leaving a trail of blood behind her, Tami disappears.

She's going to intercept the sailboat.

"Tami! Wait!" I shout. She doesn't hear, or she's too determined. She's a fast swimmer.

"Why's she doing that?" Keali`i asks, mouth agape.

I whip around. "Because you'd never have let her hear the end of it if she didn't try something."

Keali`i releases an exasperated sigh. "Ah, man," he says. "Let's go get her. She's completely *lōlō*."

Distantly, the Hanaman continues with his empty threats. "This is my last warning! Get over here, now!" He fires a round from a pistol. Keali`i and I flinch.

I unstrap my weight belt in a flash and hold it out to Keali`i.

"Drop it," he says.

I let it go and turn to swim away. Keali`i grabs my leg and pulls me back. I yelp again and then gather control. Sharks—barracudas—could be swarming us. Or they could be miles away. "Don't grab me like that!" I spit.

"Lei," Keali`i says. "Don't follow her directly."

My eyes widen. Tami, out there all alone, churning up the water in noisy fits, her blood pluming out behind her.

If a feeding frenzy starts, we're all goners.

"Give me your lobsters," Keali`i says. He has the other full bag of slippahs around an elbow, the dive light in his hand. "Catch her. I'll follow. Reach the boat before it overshoots us."

The Hanaman lets off three more rounds. I hear one of them enter the water to my right.

The mainsail of the sailboat flutters. The boat is turning away from the breakwater. Whoever's piloting it must think the shots are being fired at them.

"Go!" Keali`i shouts.

I fly over the water, my fins like rockets. I push the fear away, focus on my breathing. If something comes from below, there's nothing I can do about it.

Just go.

I hear Tami shouting. "Wait! Stop! Help!"

I swim hard. We're in trouble if we can't catch it, if we can't get on board. Coconut Island is far to my left, connected to shore by a footbridge. We could reach it after a long swim, if the sharks don't find us first, but the Tribe will be in that very area.

We're putting a lot of faith in whoever's on this yacht. Could be *anybody*. I haven't seen a new sailboat come into the bay in weeks. Those that come get commandeered by the Tribes and fitted with tribal flags. The crews are tossed overboard or killed.

"Stop! Please!" Tami yells, desperate.

I feel myself slowing. My side cramps with pain; my lungs and my throat are burning. When I raise my head to catch a glimpse of the boat, it seems impossibly far away. Whoever's on board may not even know we're in the water. I slow, overcome by a sense of defeat.

I stop and catch my breath. Tami's still swimming, just ahead. Keali`i chugs along behind me. I watch the sailboat. It's a sixteen-footer. Nothing too big. What are they doing here? Folks from Kaua`i, migrating to the Big Island like everyone else? I see the flag catch a bit of breeze on the mast. I can't tell the colors, but the shapes are familiar. The bottom half is one solid color. Along the top half, stripes radiate from a five-pointed star set in the center. I know that flag from visiting Dad's childhood haunts in the Southwest.

Arizona.

A sailboat from Arizona?

Doesn't make any sense. But then it hits me: This boat's from the *mainland*.

Adrenaline charges through me. I feel like I'm Popeye with a can of spinach. *I need to talk to the people on that boat.*

I bring my fingers to my lips and force a piercing whistle. I whistle again, and then I scream, "STOP! HELP US!"

I turn to Keali`i. "Shine your light at them! Flash them!"

I charge forward in the water, reach Tami. She pauses and watches me swim past. My friends shout pleas; Keali`i's dive light illuminates the boat in jostled circles. In the distance, the Hanaman is silent. Either he's given up or he's racing back along the breakwater to his gang. I'm sure he knows that if we reach the boat, we get away.

A figure along the port side of the sailboat. They know we're in the water. The mainsail swings to the side; the boat turns to port. They're stopping! I barrel toward them.

"Please, help!" I shout as I reach the hull.

"Who are you?" A woman.

"I'm"—I cough—"just a girl. My two friends . . . chased. For fishing without permission. They're gonna get you, too. You can't dock here."

Silence.

The woman says, "Wait there."

"My friend is bleeding badly. Please, we need to get out of the water."

"Wait there." She disappears. Another figure is at the tiller, frozen, as if trying to remain unnoticed.

Tami swims beside me. "What are we waiting for?" She's panicky. "Let's go!"

"Shark!" Keali`i screams. "SHARK!"

"Oh, God." Tami claws at the prow of the boat, pulling herself up.

Electricity surges along my spine. I scan the waves. Every shadowy crest looks like a dorsal fin. I slap the side of the boat. "Get us out of here NOW!"

The woman returns, pointing a gun. I want to scream, but it comes out as more of a whimper. *It never ends.*

"Hurry! What are you *doing?*" Tami cries. "I'm cut, bad. PLEASE GET ME OUT OF THE WATER!"

"Pull her out," the woman with the gun says to her companion. "Slowly. Make sure she's not hiding anything."

Tami starts crying but chokes her sobs back. The other figure, a man—mostly bald, with a ring of white hair—lowers a metal ladder off the stern. Tami and I paddle to it.

"No quick movements. You hear? From either of you." The woman with the gun is nervous. She reminds me of Dad back on O`ahu when we stole the fishing boat at gunpoint.

Tami removes her fins and hands them to the bald man. She pulls herself up and tenderly swings her legs into the boat with a grunt and a moan. She outran the sharks. Bravest thing she's ever done, swimming away from dry land with a gushing leg.

Keali`i is yelling. I only hear one word.

"Fin."

I jump out of my skin. The gunwoman's "slow and steady" command is the last thing on my mind. I leap for the ladder and pull myself up, use my knees on the rungs and awkwardly flip into the boat with my fins.

Keali`i!

I look at the bald guy hovering over me. "We need to get him up here!"

Fin. He saw a shark.

The bald man nods, turns, throws the boom of the mainsail wide to the side. He pushes the tiller in the opposite direction. The sail and the jib fill with air and we cut left. The woman lowers the gun, her eyes everywhere at once—on us, on her shipmate, on the water.

I rip off my fins and spring to my feet. Keali`i is easy to spot with his dive light bobbing on the surface. He's still and silent, drawing the boat toward him with a tractor beam gaze.

He's white as a haole. He definitely saw something.

We glide beside him to port. The woman puts her pistol on the deck and leans over the rails, arm outstretched. We slow with a jerk. Keali`i reaches up and clasps the waiting hand of his rescuer. I scramble, hopping over Tami, and help the woman pull Keali`i, his dive light, and two big bags of slippah lobsters into the boat.

"Hoo!" Keali`i sighs. "Shark fo' sure."

My heart pounds. "Keep going," I tell the bald man. "Don't slow down."

"Hold on a sec," he says. "You're—"

"Listen," I interrupt, "you've been spotted by some very

bad people. They plan to take your boat. If they have a motor-boat waiting back in one of those inlets, they could still catch you. They're armed."

"And they're good at what they do," Tami adds.

"Ha," says Keali`i. "Not as good as us. You did it, Tami! Those Hanamen gonna be so pissed!"

"Go," the woman says, waving a hand to the man. She leans forward and retrieves her gun. Her grip around the handle is white-knuckled.

"Rachel . . . ," the bald guy starts.

"Just go," she says. "We'll figure it out."

She turns back to the three of us and points the gun right at Keali`i. "Okay, talk. You better start making sense. You drawing us into a trap?"